The Fine Line Between Love & Hate

A *Mistik Ridge* Novel

ASHLEY ERIN

Great things *never* came from *comfort zones*

-Unknown

The Rental
November

Evie

PARKING MY CAR, I smile when I see the cute house before me. It's perfect. Despite the snow blanketing the grass and shrubs, I take immediate notice as to how immaculately the yard and exterior of the house has been kept. The siding looks brand new, the porch freshly stained. Even the driveway is crack free, unlike every other driveway in the neighborhood. I sure hope the lady—Lorraine, I think her name was—likes me, because now that I've seen this place in person, I want it. Everything is falling into place, and this would tie it all up into a neat bow.

A car pulls into the driveway, the woman who steps out can only be described as elegant. Her hair is in some neat twisty knot, showing off the fine features of her face. Her makeup is subtle, but impeccable. When I see the A-line skirt and silky blouse she is wearing, I second-guess my casual appearance.

Oh well, this is me. Skinny jeans, with my cozy winter boots. The sweater I'm wearing is loose and comfortable, falling off one shoulder to show off my ink. It's currently covered by my worn leather jacket. It's freezing outside and I'm completely unprepared for the cold weather.

Locking my car, I walk up to her with a warm smile.

"Hi, I'm Evie." Holding my hand out, I try to exude confidence. I'm not typically intimidated by people, I'm confident in who I am, but this woman looks like she belongs on the red carpet, not in some small town with less than six thousand people.

Mistik Ridge is idyllic. An hour's drive from the nearest big city, it sits on a cliff overlooking the Mistik River. It's not a huge tourist spot, despite the vast number of attractions close by. I like that it's an undiscovered gem, and I admit to imagining living here being similar to an episode of *Gilmore Girls*.

"Lorraine Greene. It's very nice to meet you, Evie. Let's get out of this cold, and I will show you the house." She leads me up the walk, unlocking the door.

I can't help the sigh of relief at how warm the house feels.

"I think I mentioned moving here from the West Coast, I'm not used to the blistering cold or the snow. Good lord, is there always so much snow?" Shrugging out of my coat, I hang it in the closet.

"It's been pretty frigid this year. More so than usual." Her smile is friendly, and I begin to relax as she shows me through the house.

The bungalow is split into two halves. The first half is the kitchen and living room, open to each other, but separated by a railing. The kitchen is to die for, with new stainless-steel appliances, dark granite countertops, and mahogany cupboards. It looks like it's been recently renovated.

"My son owns the house. He's out of town, so he asked me to help find a tenant for him. He just finished renovating the entire house this past summer. As mentioned in the ad, it's fully furnished so everything in here is yours to use as you wish." Continuing the tour, she shows me the bedrooms, there are two. The master has an amazing bathroom attached to it.

I love the entire house, the only thing I would change is the color of the walls. They are all beige and that's so boring.

Once the tour is through, she goes through the rental agreement. I will have a three-month grace period to ensure it's a good fit, and she smiles widely when I say I want to sign a two-year lease.

Her eyes sparkle as we chat, my usual quirkiness shining through.

"Evie, I think you will be the perfect tenant for my son."

By the time I leave, I've signed the paperwork and I have a key. Finally, I can move out of the damn hotel I've been staying in while trying to find a place in this small town.

The Tenant

Charlie

OPENING THE DOOR to my hotel room, I check to make sure everything is exactly how I left it. I forgot to put the "Do Not Disturb" sign on my door, and the thought of housekeeping messing up the order in which I laid out everything has been bothering me all day.

Typically I love professional development days. However, this one has been stressful. I hate staying in hotels, and I'm relying on my mother to show a potential tenant the rental house.

Glancing at the clock, I pick up my phone and dial her number. She should be finished by now.

"Hi, darling. I was just about to call you. I should've known you would beat me to it." Dropping into the generic hotel chair by the generic hotel table, I lean on my elbows and grin. Mom is one of the rare people who can tease me about my, as she calls it, "anal retentiveness." I just call it being precise and organized.

"How did it go?" Straight to the point. She may be able to make me smile, but I won't be distracted.

"We signed the agreement."

Sitting up, I frown. "That quickly? I know I said I trust your judgment, but…"

"But nothing. She's a nice girl. A librarian. Trust me on this, she will be a good tenant for you." I hear her car door shut, the beep of the horn as she locks it.

A librarian. I imagine a quiet, subdued woman. Someone studious and serious. The anxiety that was building all day fades away completely. "Okay. If you say she's a good fit, I believe you."

It Begins
May

Charlie

M Y EYES AUTOMATICALLY look over at my little rental house as I drive by. It's my afternoon ritual. In the morning I don't drive by, since my gym is not on this route, but in the afternoon I always check to make sure everything looks as it should.

A flash of color catches my eye. Braking, I park the car and gape at the brightly colored flowers now filling the flower beds. The flower beds I meticulously planned out and planted.

No. It specifically says in the rental agreement that the flower beds are to be maintained as they are. Grabbing a pen and paper, I jot a quick note for my tenant, before slipping it into an envelope.

Exiting the car, I tape it to the door before going down the steps and taking a closer look at what she's done to my hard work.

Begrudgingly, I admit she did a nice job. It's obvious she tried to complement what I had done, and she's put a lot of effort into it. Shaking my head, I dig a box out of the trunk of my car, kneel down and gently begin to dig them out.

They may look nice, but I specifically stated that I didn't want any changes made to these beds. Everything planted was specifically chosen to fill in the empty spaces over the next few years.

Washing my hands with the garden hose, I bring the box of flowers to the back and set them in the shade. She's more than welcome to plant them in pots.

Before I leave, I take one last look around the outside of the house, only getting back into my car when I'm satisfied that everything else is as it should be.

First Notice

Evie

POURING MY COFFEE into a to-go mug, I race out the door with one last look at the clock. God damn it, Everett wins the pool this week. Again.

Heels clacking on the pavement, I race down the walkway to where my car sits in the driveway. It takes me less than five minutes to get to work. As I open the doors to the Mistik Ridge Public Library, I spot Everett strutting around the desk waiting for me.

"I win. You would think after the past six months you would know better than to bet against me." He rolls the overflowing cart of books that need to be shelved over to me, his smile triumphant. Normally we tackle the task together, but I foolishly bet him I could make it to work on time three days this week. I haven't made it on time once since we made the bet last Wednesday.

"Gloating is not a good look for you." Slipping my sweater on, I look around the empty library. "Where's Lola?"

"Every look is good on me." He points to the closed office door. Right, Monday, which means Lola is enduring the weekly conference call with the board of directors. She's going to need a strong pot of coffee once that's done.

Grimacing at Everett, I roll the cart to the stacks, eager to get this over with.

"Enjoy, darling."

Glancing around the empty library, I flip him the bird.

By the time Heather and Sophie come in to relieve Everett and me, my entire day has been spent shelving books. Everett followed me around all day, mocking and teasing as he watched me work.

"I forgot to mention, what with watching you do such a great job today and all, that I'm having a party on Friday. You and Natasha should come." Everett opens my car door for me, leaning against the frame.

"You just want to see Natasha." I met Natasha one day when she came into the library. She owns the inn fifteen minutes out of town, and I helped her research gardening for some new thing she wanted to try. Shaking my head, I promise to invite her before starting my car and driving the short distance home.

Parking, I grab my purse and the stack of books I brought to read over the next couple of weeks, I'm halfway up the driveway when the flower beds catch my eye. All the flowers I had planted amongst the boring shrubs are gone. The splash of color the yard is sorely missing disappeared.

What the hell?

That's when I notice an envelope taped to the front door. Stalking up the steps, I don't even have a chance to enjoy the cute little porch, the feature that sold me on the house, because I'm tearing open the envelope. The neat cursive taunts me as I begin reading.

Ms. Jackson,

    I was driving by this afternoon, on my way home from work, when I noticed the flowers in the garden. I don't know if you recall the part in the Rental Agreement about the yard, but it specifically states not to change the existing flower beds. I have placed the flowers in a box in the backyard. If you wish, you can always plant them in pots. Please refer to the Rental Agreement if you wish to make any changes around the house.

    Thank you,

    C. Greene

By the time I'm done reading, I'm seething. I have yet to meet my landlord, and we've never clashed before, but apparently he's come out of hiding.

I can't believe he dug up my flowers. Who does that? They looked nice, they were colorful and pretty, and I had worked damn hard on ensuring every plant would work together and fill in the empty spaces between the shrubs.

Crumpling the notice in my hand, I storm into the house. Part of me wants to plant them again, just to spite him, but I don't want to get evicted.

Me: I'm fuming.

Natasha: Why?

Me: My landlord dug up my flowers. At least he didn't throw them away, but apparently I can't plant them in the flowerbed.

Digging out the agreement I had stuffed in a drawer, I scan through it. Sure enough, there is a clause about changes that are *acceptable* to make to the yard.

Who the fuck is this guy?

Natasha: He's been so quiet up until this point.

Me: Yeah, I guess now that the weather is nice he's come out of the hole he's been hiding in.

Natasha: I guess you better just do what he says. You have another year and a half on the lease.

Me: I know. And I love this house, but wow.

Grumbling, I pace throughout the house. I can't afford to buy my way out of the lease. Besides, I love this house. I can play by his rules. It pains me, but I will curb my temper and do exactly what he says.

Order vs. Disorder

Charlie

SHUTTING DOWN MY computer, I stack the papers on my desk into a neat pile before moving about my classroom straightening everything before I head out for the day. I hate having a messy classroom, actually, I just hate messes in general.

Life is much simpler when it's orderly. You know what to expect when everything is done in a precise manner. My students learn early on, if they follow my rules and do their best, the year is easy. If not, it's unpleasant for them and for me.

Locking up, I check my bag to make sure the papers that need grading are in there. Of course they are, but it's a good habit to be sure.

The parking lot is full, it usually is this time of year as my colleagues are trying to catch up with curriculum and preparing for the end of the year. Shaking my head, I wish they would listen when I try to point out different ways they can structure their time to be more efficient. It never goes over very well, but it's their decision. When everyone else is running around stressed, I'm winding down and finally breathing easy.

Walking around my car, I check the tires and make sure

everything is as it was this morning. I do the same inside. I check the rearview mirror, the side mirrors, and adjust my seat slightly when it feels off.

At the intersection, I turn towards my little rental house as per my usual afternoon ritual. I never miss a day, but I feel it necessary to make sure my tenant got the notice I left her yesterday afternoon. I worked damn hard on those flower beds, measuring the correct distances, and researching the types of plants that do best with the shrubs in there.

I was explicit in the rental agreement, but when I called Mom to ask if she went over the entire agreement with Evie, she just laughed and said it's easy to forget those details.

I disagree.

My eyes scan the yard as I pass by the house. Blinking rapidly, I slam on the brakes before backing up and gawking at the sight before me.

The yard is full of brightly colored, gaudy flowerpots. She must have bought more flowers, because I know I didn't dig out enough flowers to fill those pots.

Counting them, I see seven. Each pot is a different color.

Upon closer examination, they're the colors of the rainbow. It looks so… so… unorganized. There is no rhyme or reason to the way she's put them throughout the yard. I notice she was also careful to put them on the stones throughout, so I can't even ask her to move them.

Or can I? I mean, maybe I can cite complaints from the neighbors. Seeing Mrs. Jesperson toiling about her yard, I roll down my window.

"Hi, Mrs. Jesperson!"

She walks over with a huge smile on her face. She was my teacher in the eighth grade, and I recall her being an orderly person.

"Hi, dear, how are you?"

"I'm well, thank you. I just wanted to check and make sure my tenant's flower display isn't bothering you. Those planters are quite large, and…"

"Oh no, dear. I adore Evie and the color she brings to the neighborhood. All the neighbors adore her. She's so spunky, it's nice and refreshing for us old folks."

Crap.

"Great! I just wanted to check. Take care of yourself."

When she's back on the sidewalk, I pull away from the house.

Okay, I can deal with the awful planters. They're not harming anyone, and maybe now things can go back to normal. Evie has proven to be a quiet and responsible renter until this point, I'm sure this is a one-off.

Once I'm home, I check the chicken fajitas I prepared this morning and put in the slow cooker. It's ready, and my stomach grumbles at the delicious scent. Before I serve myself, I grab Sebastian's food from his cupboard, measure out the exact amount directed by the label for his age and weight, and settle his stainless steel dish onto his mat.

Calling him, I smile when he comes slinking down the stairs, his black fur shining as he rubs against my leg, purring, before going to eat.

I set my place at the kitchen table, before filling a serving dish with the steaming fajitas. Placing the serving spoon inside, I set it on the table and sit down. Spreading a napkin on my lap, I dish up and eat in the peace and quiet of my home.

Once I'm done, I clean up. Everything washed, dried, and put in its place.

Glancing at the clock, I pick up the cordless phone and call my mom.

"Hi, darling."

"Hi, Mom. How was your day?" Walking into the living room, I straighten a pillow and settle onto the couch for my weekly check-in.

"It was fine. Your father was having a good day, so I spent the entire morning with him. He asked about you, you should make time to go see him." She sounds happy, something I haven't heard in her voice in a while.

"I can probably fit it in this weekend." Visiting my father is something I dread. He had a stroke in January, and it completely changed the man I grew up with. Every time I go see him, I never know what to expect and I hate the unknown.

"Did you sort things out with Evie?"

Filling her in on the flowerpots that are now spread out over the front yard, I'm shocked when I hear Mom laugh. "It's not funny. It's awful, and there is nothing I can do about it. I think I should book an inspection with her, make sure she hasn't gone too crazy inside."

"Charlie, she's a nice girl. Some colorful pots are nothing compared to what you could be dealing with." She tries to placate me, but I'm already planning on sending her a notice of inspection.

First *Meeting*

Evie

Mr. Jackson,

    I would like to schedule a six-month inspection for this coming weekend. Sunday, at two in the afternoon. I have included my card. Please email to confirm this date and time at your earliest convenience.

    Sincerely,

    C. Greene

Tossing the notice in the drawer, along with the first one and the rental agreement, I send my landlord a quick text stating that Sunday works. I will finally meet the man whose neat handwriting with uptight wording has been taunting me all week.

I'm not surprised that he left another notice wanting to check out the inside of the house. If the flower incident is any indication, the guy has a stick shoved so far up his ass, it's all the way in his throat.

Thankfully, I don't think he will find fault with the changes I've made inside the house. I painted a feature wall in each room, but ensured they matched the color schemes in the house. Which means, darker neutral tones. I added color throughout the house with throws, photos, and more flowers.

After receiving the first notice, I read through my rental agreement cover to cover. This guy obviously has control issues, and I want to make sure he can't find fault with my behavior. That doesn't mean I can't find ways to have fun within the limitations of the agreement, especially if he continues to ride my ass. I hate being restricted into the confines of a contract, however, I don't have enough money to buy a house yet. It's part of my two-year plan, the only plan I ever live by.

> **Landlord:** *Hello, Ms. Jackson. I appreciate the quick response; however, I specifically requested an email response, as I require the documentation for my records. Thank you.*

Rolling my eyes, I open my laptop and send him a quick email. This is ridiculous.

It's Friday night, he's given me forty-eight hours' notice. That gives me tomorrow and Sunday morning to walk through the house and make sure it's presentable. Tonight is about getting out and forgetting everything but having a good time.

A knock at the door distracts me. Shutting the drawer, I walk to the front door. As expected, it's Natasha.

"The party has been moved to a pub. Everett decided it would be simpler than dealing with everyone at his place." Stopping in front of the full-length mirror I hung in the foyer, I adjust the short black dress. It's backless, which means I can't wear a bra, but damn it makes me feel sexy. It's also sleeveless, so it shows off my ink.

"That's fine."

She looks gorgeous in dark jeans and a strapless top that shows off her chest. She's voluptuous and curvy, absolutely stunning. But that means nothing when I see the frown on her face.

"What's wrong?"

Grabbing my keys from the hook behind the door, I lock up and wait for her to spill.

"It's nothing I want to think about. For tonight, I want to remember I'm young and carefree." I can hear the air quotes she puts around the word carefree, but if she doesn't want to talk about it, I'm not going to push.

The music is loud as we shove our way through the crowd towards the bar.

"I'm going to go to the bathroom," Natasha yells in my ear. Nodding, I try to maneuver my way through the crowd.

Someone shoves me, knocking me into someone else. Strong arms wrap around me, the only thing preventing me from falling. Turning, my words of gratitude fail when I lock eyes with one of the most gorgeous men I've ever seen.

He towers over me, everything about him is big and muscular. As I look up, my head tilting back until I finally meet his gaze, my heart stutters. Holy shit. His hazel eyes are stormy, he has the moody look down to an art. His hair is short on the sides, and long on top. Everything about him screams "put together."

I can feel the air thicken, my pulse reacting to the hold his gaze has me locked in. My nerves crackle where his skin touches mine, his large hands splayed on my bare back.

19

I want to press into him, feel those arms close around me even tighter. I've never felt so safe. It's a bizarre feeling, my history with men is mediocre at best and my trust is not given easily. Something in my gut tells me this man is steadfast and reliable.

Clearing my throat, I finally speak, "Thank you."

He holds me a moment longer before tilting his head in a nod as he drops his arms and turns, disappearing into the crowd. My heart thunders, reacting to the loss of his presence. Wow.

I stare into the sea of people, no longer seeing the mystery man, but unable to tear my eyes away from the crowd that swelled around him.

"Evie." Jumping at the voice in my ear, I turn to a grinning Everett, giving him a quick hug.

"Hey! I need a drink." Following him to the bar, I glance behind me one last time, knowing I won't see him but unable to resist the urge to try.

The rest of the night, I find myself looking for him. I catch glimpses, he's with a couple of other guys, all good-looking men, but my gaze is pulled back to him.

"Who are you looking at?" Natasha leans in when she catches me checking out the room for probably the tenth time.

"No one. For a small town, I'm surprised I don't recognize more faces." Mistik Ridge has less than six thousand people. The town is so isolated, it's like its own eco-system. People rarely move here, almost everyone has been raised here. Yet, despite its isolation, it thrives and the people who live here embrace the close-knit community.

"You haven't been here that long. Soon you will wish you knew less people." Natasha laughs, but I know she loves this town. That's why she's never moved away. I wouldn't even have known it exists if it wasn't for getting a job at the library.

Looking back over the crowd, I frown when he's disappeared from view again. My vision is blocked by some guy in a Star Wars t-shirt. Grumbling, I try to peer around him.

"Hey. I'm Darcy. I haven't seen you around here before." The voice is deep and filled with humor.

Looking up, I grin when I see it's one of mystery man's friends. "Hi, I'm Evie. And I haven't been here before."

He moves next to me, leaning against the bar and clearing my view to search for his friend.

"My friends just left for the night, but I didn't want to leave without saying hello." He looks me up and down. Smirking, I plant a hand on my hip. I'm not into one-night stands and I can tell that's what he's looking for.

"Darcy." Natasha moves in next to me. Her eyes narrowed.

"Tash." The warmth in his eyes fades away. He leaves without another word.

"Ugh. Sorry, he's just such a jerk." Natasha turns to me, the coldness bleeding from her eyes. Suddenly, she looks contrite. "Wait, I hope he wasn't the one you kept looking at."

"No." Sipping my drink, I watch her for a moment. "No love lost there?"

"No, he's a couple years older and friends with my brother, Guy. I'm surprised I didn't see him here. Anyways, he's always been kind of a jerk to me. Not to everyone, just me. But he treats women like they're disposable and I didn't want you to deal with that," she rambles on, unaware that her eyes haven't moved away from the direction he walked.

First *Impressions*

Charlie

PICKING UP THE file folder from the front seat of my car, I glance at the car I've parked next to. It's a small sedan, conservative looking. Fitting for the quiet librarian living in my house. After the flower incident earlier this week, things have settled down.

I'm feeling more confident about meeting her after her calm reaction to my request for an inspection. Making my way up the sidewalk, I begrudgingly admit that while the planters she chose don't really fit with what I tried to create here, at least they are well-maintained and tidy. In fact, the entire yard has been well-maintained.

Knocking on the door, I inspect the front porch, satisfied that nothing has been altered or damaged. When the front door opens, I turn to greet Evie Jackson.

The air is sucked from my lungs as a familiar blue gaze looks up at me in shock. The woman from Friday night. The one whose simple touch and genuine smile seared into my soul. My muscles jump at the memory of her slight body in my arms, my hands burn with the memory of her skin against my palms.

Her tattoos stand out vibrantly against the white of her tank top. She is wearing black leggings that show off her toned legs. As I look back at her face, I see the recognition written all over it.

"You must be Evie." Holding out my hand, I pretend I hadn't held her in my arms the other night. There is no simple way to categorize the fact the woman I've been fantasizing about since that night is no other than my tenant. I need time to process the information, and then resist the fantasy. I don't do complicated, and any dalliance with someone living in my house is complicated. "I'm Charlie."

"Hello." She takes my hand briefly, my skin jolting at the contact. Her gaze is still locked on mine as she drops it and opens the door for me to step in. Her voice isn't the soft tone from the other night. It's strong, but feminine. Without even speaking, I can already sense that she isn't the quiet, mousey librarian my mother led me to believe she was.

Closing the door, I narrow my eyes as I take in the house. The first thing I notice is that she's painted some of the walls. At least they match the color I had painstakingly selected. The second thing I notice is that there is no order to the way she has moved the furniture or organized her things.

Books are piled on the coffee table, a blanket tossed on the couch, and this morning's coffee cup is sitting on the wood of the table, rather than one of the coasters sitting less than a foot away.

My eye twitches.

Grunting, I make note that everything in the living room and kitchen appears to be well-cared for and intact. Despite the clutter, the house is clean.

"What are you writing?" She lifts onto her toes, trying to see my notepad. Clutching it to my chest, I ignore her and continue to check out the living room and kitchen.

When I'm satisfied things are as they should be, aside from the disorder, I make my way to the bedrooms. Evie follows me, her arms crossed as I check out the guest room. She's turned it into a library. It's the most organized space in the entire house.

Bookshelves lining the walls, a leather chair sitting underneath the window. Shutting the door, I turn and enter her bedroom. My skin crackles at her proximity behind me.

The bed is unmade, but again there is no fault in the care she puts in maintaining the house. My heart thuds in my chest a little harder as I step further into the room to check the bathroom. Images of her gazing up at me at the bar flash through my mind as she leans against the wall, watching me carefully. I peer into the bathroom, swallowing hard when I see lacy lingerie hanging from the shower door.

Turning on my heel, I brush past her and head back to the living room. She is silent as she follows me, but despite this I can feel the defiance radiating off her.

"Everything looks satisfactory."

She snorts, her face less than impressed. "Thanks, I guess."

"I wanted to discuss the flowerpots. I appreciate that you put your flowers in pots, but don't you think it would've been better to select something more in keeping with the tone of the house? They're a little—bright. I believe I have some in the shed that you could use."

"No. I like them."

Stunned, I stare at her before nodding grimly. "Fine."

Despite the defensive look on her face, I'm struck again with how beautiful she is. Even her tattoos, which normally I hate, fit her. Something about her makes me anxious. She doesn't fit into the organization of my life, and yet here she is. Renting my house.

Tucking my thumbs into the pockets of my jeans, the sudden urge to pull her into my arms is startling. Usually, the realization of who she was would eliminate any allure she holds, but there is something about her that calls to me. It's unexpected and uncomfortable.

"If that's all…" She trails off, looking at me expectantly.

"Oh, yes. I would appreciate if you could look through the

rental agreement, just to ensure we don't clash in the future."
Looking around the living room, I realize that we already do clash,
but hopefully we won't have another flower incident.

"I read through it this week. Don't worry, I know what I'm
not allowed to do." She smirks then, filling me with unease.

I excuse myself to check out the backyard.

Before I leave, I notice that the front door is scuffed, probably
from her purse. Peering into the house, my stomach flips when I
see she's lying on the couch, with her feet resting where her head
is supposed to go. "Ahem."

She looks over at me, not righting herself on the couch.

"I notice there are some scuffs on the door. I would appreciate
it if you could eliminate them and be a bit more careful with your
purse coming in and out of the house."

She stares at me stunned. "You want me to get rid of the scuffs
on the door?"

Nodding, I swallow when she narrows her eyes. Instead of arguing,
she just smiles, her eyes glinting in a way that makes me nervous.

"Okay. I will fix the door."

Thanking her, I shut the door as I leave with a sense of dread.

Evie Jackson is nothing like I expected.

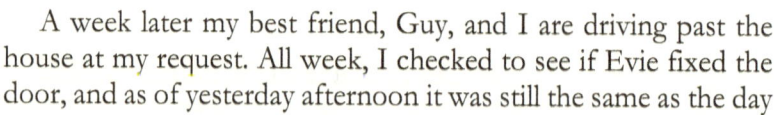

A week later my best friend, Guy, and I are driving past the
house at my request. All week, I checked to see if Evie fixed the
door, and as of yesterday afternoon it was still the same as the day
of the inspection.

"I know you like things done a certain way, but I can't believe
you asked her to unscuff the door." He chuckles. He's listened to
me go on random rants all week about the disarray in the house.
He thinks it's hilarious, I do not. But that's how Guy is, he's
disarray, while I'm orderly. I don't know how our friendship
works, but it does. Probably because I don't have to live with him
or deal with the chaos that is his life.

"The stain was worn right down to the wood." That's a slight exaggeration, but I'm tired of him judging me. There is nothing wrong with expecting excellence. She gets a newly renovated house at a more than reasonable rate, I expect it to stay in pristine condition.

Guy looks out the window, blocking my view of the door, and bursts into laughter. "Oh shit, man, I don't know what your mom was thinking."

Leaning around him, I growl when I see the door.

It's purple. Fucking. Purple. And there is nothing I can do about it.

"What the hell?"

"Dude, there is no way she's met you and still thinks that you would be okay with that."

Grinding my teeth, I'm about to pull away when Mrs. Jesperson waves at me, walking over. Rolling down my window, I paste on a smile.

"Good afternoon, Mrs. Jesperson," Guy and I greet her at the same time.

"Hello, boys. Charlie, I love what Evie did with the door. It's so sweet of you to let her add her own character to the house. Why don't you come over for dinner on Wednesday? Keep an old woman company." Her eyes crinkle as she smiles and there is no way I can say no.

"That would be nice, thank you."

"Wonderful. Dinner is at six."

Shutting my window, I glare at Guy as he cracks up.

"Oh shit, that's hilarious."

"No, it's not. I hate her. She did that on purpose, just to bother me. I have to look at this every day on my way home from work. It's going to be fucking torture."

Guy just laughs even harder.

Gripping the steering wheel, I seethe as I try to think of what I can do. Obviously she just wants to make my life hell because Guy is right, there is no way she could be disillusioned into thinking I'm okay with the front door being purple. I need to make an amendment in the agreement.

The Clash

Evie

EVERY TIME I leave my house, I can't help but gloat when I look at my door. I painted it Saturday evening, it's now Wednesday morning and I haven't heard a peep from him.

I've met Type A people before, but Charlie makes them look like tree-hugging hippies. The man needs to learn how to relax, be a little more flexible. I mean, the flowerbed issue was ridiculous enough, but worrying about a few minor scratches on a front door?

Shit, I am still trying to wrap my head around that one.

I don't think I've ever met someone so rigid, the complete opposite to me, and yet, despite my irritation with him, he still has been the shining star of my dreams. My body doesn't seem to understand that I could never tolerate being with someone as uptight as he is.

After his walk-through of the house a week and a half ago, I took the time and memorized the rental agreement. I know what I'm allowed to do, and what I can't. That doesn't mean I will play fair. I've never been the type of person that stays in the confines of a neat little box. I'm spontaneous, colorful, and quirky. At twenty-seven, I doubt that's ever going to change.

I walk into work right on time, much to Everett's surprise.

"Good morning." Greeting him and Lola, I tuck my bag in the cupboard.

"Hi." Everett pouts.

"What's wrong with you?" I shove the sleeves of my sweater up my arms.

Lola grins over at Everett. "We have some high school students coming in this morning at nine. Everett is pouting that he might actually have to work before the usual rush at eleven."

She fills me in on the English class coming to find novels for a novel study. The library at the high school is decent, but they often collaborate with us when it comes to fiction.

I have yet to interact with any of the classes, though, so unlike Everett, I'm excited to chat with the students about books.

"Why don't I pull some novels that would make great study material?" I love looking through books, finding themes and different genres to tempt even the most dubious reader.

"Great idea. Everett, since Evie's obviously more interested, she can deal with the students while you man the desk. I have to go do some paperwork." Lola leaves us, Everett's mood lifting at the prospect of staying away from the crowd.

I wander through the stacks, the hour passing quickly until I've filled a table with some of my favorites. I'm arranging the books when I hear the students chatting and Everett directing them over to me.

Turning with a smile on my face, I'm shocked when I see Charlie standing amidst a group of approximately thirty chatting students who range from looking eager to be here to bored out of their minds. My mouth dries at the sight of him. The skin on my back tingles where his hands have left their invisible imprint.

Seriously, what is wrong with me? I've never had this type of reaction to a man before, and his personality could not be any more opposite to mine.

The look on his face when he sees me isn't friendly. It doesn't take a genius to figure out he dislikes me, but the feeling is mutual. He's so—beige. Boring, structured, and likes things to be his way all the time. Regardless, I nod at him and turn to the kids who are quickly losing focus.

"Listen up, guys." Charlie's eyes don't leave mine as he calls attention to his students. They settle right away, and I grudgingly admit to myself that I'm impressed. Looking away from him, I try to ignore the heat I feel, knowing he is watching my every move.

"Hey everyone! I'm Evie, and I got a bit of a head start selecting some novels I thought might appeal to a different variety of tastes. I have sci-fi, paranormal, romance, fantasy, historical, and horror." I lift examples of each genre for the students to see. "I'm sure Mr. Greene has already explained what you want to look for, the books on this table all have the qualities he will expect for a novel study."

I encourage them to search on their own and ask for help if they need. Charlie stands back and watches as his students look through the books I've selected, often asking me about ones that pique their interest. He seems impressed when I can talk about each book. I don't work in a library because I've never picked up a novel. And I like a little bit of each genre, mixing it up so I don't get bored.

"Evie?" The young man who stands at my side is on the scrawny side. He also looks like he's about to jump out of his skin at any moment he's so nervous. "Mr. Greene gave me permission to study an adult novel. I was hoping you could help me find something a little different."

"Do you know what you want?"

He shakes his head. Chewing on my lip, I look at the ceiling as I scan through different options in my mind. Smiling at him, I gesture for him to follow me.

I wander through the stacks until I see the book I'm looking for. I notice that Charlie has followed us but avoid looking directly at him.

"This is called *The Book of Lost Things.* It's a fascinating read, and I think you will enjoy it." Pulling the book off the shelf, I hand it to him. He flips it over to read the back, nodding to himself as his eyes move over the words.

With a muttered, "Thank you," he scurries out of the stacks.

"Good choice." Charlie stands in front of me, blocking my way. "While they're busy, I want to discuss the newly painted door situation."

"What about it?" Crossing my arms, I smirk.

I don't think I've ever seen Charlie smile, not that I've spent any substantial amount of time with him, and today is no exception. His expression is serious, bordering on a scowl. "It's purple. I'm pretty sure you didn't need to paint the entire door to get the scratches out."

I can't help the gleeful grin that forms. "I read the rental agreement. It doesn't state anything about the doors, so I took the opportunity to add a splash of color. It fixed the problem you saw, and I get a purple door. Win-win."

He sighs in exasperation. "How is this win-win?"

"For the reasons I just said." Brushing past him, I ignore the way my heart jolts at the contact.

His hand wraps around my forearm, sending tingles shooting up my arm. He holds me in place, his grip firm but not enough to bruise. "We're not done discussing the door."

"I think we are. You asked me to fix the scratches, they're fixed." Tugging my arm out of his grasp, I brace myself for the argument I can sense brewing.

"You painted the door purple!" Charlie's voice rises. Catching himself, he lowers the timbre so his next words practically caress my skin. "Evie, why are you trying to be difficult?"

"Look, did I assume you wouldn't be happy about the color of the door, yes. Did I think you would corner me at work, because apparently you can't handle even the slightest bit of color in your life, no. So I'll tell you what, when my two-year lease is up, everything will go back to the beige world you like to live in, you won't even be able to tell I was there. Is that satisfactory?" I don't give him a chance to respond, I push past him once again and walk back to where his students are milling around without looking at him.

"Tash, he cornered me at work today. I have never met anyone so rigid in my entire life." Holding the phone between my shoulder and ear, I tug my jeans down my legs leaving them in a pile on the floor.

"What's this guy's name again?" Tash's voice is filled with humor.

"Charlie Greene." I yank the black dress over my shoulders, fixing it in place and zipping it up, only pausing when Natasha starts laughing like a hyena over the phone. "What's so funny?"

She snorts. Literally snorts.

"Oh, Evie. I've known Charlie my entire life. I don't know how the two of you are going to survive you renting his house. You couldn't be more opposite. No wonder he hates you, you don't fit neatly inside his world." Her laughter fades, but I can imagine the grin on her face.

"What happened to make him like that? There must be some reason for a person to be that—unyielding." Fluffing my hair, I check myself in the mirror.

Mrs. Jesperson caught me as I arrived home this afternoon and invited me over for dinner. The woman is hilarious and almost as quirky as me, so I couldn't say no.

"There is no reason. He's just like that; always has been, always will be."

Hmmm. I guess it does take all kinds to make the world go round, I just can't imagine living my life that way. I love chaos and spontaneity. I love having a whim and running with it.

Moments later Tash and I hang up, it's time to head over to Mrs. Jesperson's. She told me to arrive at six, it's now ten after. I gave up being on time for anything a decade ago.

Slipping my feet into a gorgeous pair of stilettos, I make my way across the street to her door. Knocking, I straighten the hem of my dress while I wait for her to answer the door.

The door opens—to a scowling Charlie.

"What are you doing here?" he asks gruffly, not moving to invite me in.

"I'm here for dinner." Ducking under his arm, I ignore the conflicting emotions that arise being near him. The physical reaction of my body is instantaneous, while my brain automatically wants to push his buttons.

I don't let him see that I'm surprised he was also invited to dinner, turning my back on him and following the sounds of Mrs. Jesperson moving about her kitchen, I finally find the door and enter with a smile.

"Can I help you with anything?" Wrapping an arm over the woman's shoulders, I worry about how frail she feels. The bones of her shoulders poke me in the arm.

Making a mental note to stop by more frequently, I sit down when she denies my request to help. Charlie is already seated at the table, so I sit opposite him. It means I need to look directly at him, but it saves me from feeling the heat that seems to form between us.

Obviously my body hasn't gotten the memo that we're incompatible, despite the fact it's blatantly obvious.

Incompatible.

The word might as well be in bright lights blinking over our heads every time we're in the same room.

"So, Evie, I'm guessing spring is much more to your liking than winter was." Mrs. Jesperson sets a casserole in the center of the table, handing Charlie the serving spoon.

Smiling, I angle my body towards her as Charlie fills her plate. "Much. I like that it's a dry warmth compared to the humid heat of Vancouver."

Charlie holds his hand out for my plate. Surprised, I hand it to him with what I hope is a genuine smile. He may be uptight, but at least he has manners.

"Does your family miss having you close?"

"No. I grew up in the foster care system. I emancipated myself when I was sixteen." I can feel Charlie's gaze burning into me as I shrug, twirling my fork into the steaming casserole on my plate.

I'm not ashamed of growing up in the system. Despite being moved around a lot, I didn't have horrific experiences with my foster parents. Some weren't as good as others, but they all treated me well enough.

She looks at me with empathy, not pity, which I appreciate. "What about friends?"

Lifting my shoulder again, I swallow the bite of food I've been chewing and look down at my plate. "I haven't really had anyone worth keeping in my life until now. I finished high school, got a bunch of scholarships and went straight to university. I didn't want to stop with an undergrad degree, so I went right into my master's and doctorate."

Lifting my eyes, I meet the incredulous stare of Charlie. My lips lift in a smirk. It's funny, he's categorized me into whatever type of person he sees. My drive shocks many people, especially since I can't be on time to save my life and I don't care for order.

"Impressive. You're what, twenty-seven years old?" Mrs. Jesperson draws my attention from Charlie. My grin widens when I see the wicked glint in her eye. Sneaky woman. This is a matchmaking attempt. I don't know where her head is at, but I'm amused nonetheless.

"Yes, ma'am."

I bite back a grin when she turns her attention to Charlie.

"How's your father feeling?"

I watch him out of the corner of my eye, his discomfort palpable.

"He has good days and bad days. The stroke impacted his speech quite a bit, but he's regained some ability as the weeks pass. We still haven't seen much improvement in his mobility." Charlie's voice is wooden, the speech he's reciting no doubt one that he's probably said a thousand times.

Tilting my head, I watch him carefully. Behind the guise of nonchalance, I can see how much the changes in his father has impacted him. My heart aches for him. I can't even imagine how difficult it is for him to deal with that. His need for order probably makes the chaos in the aftermath of a stroke impossible to deal with.

"Day by day, my boy. Day by day." She reaches out and squeezes his hand.

I help Mrs. Jesperson with the dishes, despite her protests, and then excuse myself for the evening.

"I better head home. I am in charge of the weekly recommended readings and I have a stack of ten books I need to read this week in order to make my selection. Thank you for dinner." Hugging Mrs. Jesperson, I slip into my shoes and rest my hand on the doorknob, turning towards Charlie to say goodnight.

"Charlie, please walk Evie home." He's pushed in my direction looking about as thrilled by the suggestion as I am.

Swallowing a groan, I open the door and leave with one last wave. Charlie's body heat beats against my back, my skin thrumming from his close proximity.

Once the door is shut, I finally look at him. "You don't need to walk me home. I'm positive I can make it across the street in one piece."

It amuses me when he doesn't even crack a hint of a smile.

He just points to the flutter of the curtains in the window, before resting his hand on the small of my back as we walk down the driveway.

The spot where his hand rests feels like it is on fire. Stepping away, I watch his hand fall to his side. He doesn't say anything, but when I glance up at him, he is watching me with a mix of annoyance and disappointment.

I'm sure the disappointment is in the fact I'm nothing like he anticipated. I'm not someone who fits into the order of his world and I definitely push his boundaries in a way he's not comfortable with.

We don't say anything else as we reach my door. I have the urge to draw this out, but I dig my key out of my purse and unlock my door.

"Have a goodnight, Charlie." Closing the door behind me, I lean back against it in bewilderment.

I don't fit into his world, and he certainly doesn't fit into mine, but I can't deny that the few times we've been near each other there has been this draw.

So, I want to irritate him because I can't stand how rigid he is, but I'm attracted to him? How does that even make any sense?

I guess he's physically everything I would look for in a man, sans tattoos obviously. There is no denying that Charlie is gorgeous with those dark hazel eyes, that artfully messy hair—the only messy thing about him—and there is no denying that I find his largeness in comparison to me appealing. Everything about him is big. His height. His muscles. I'd be willing to bet he's not lacking in size in other areas as well.

At the end of the day, the appeal of someone's physical appearance fades if they're not compatible personality wise. I learned that at a young age. People have been drawn to me because of my petite size. I overheard one of my foster parents tell one of their friends that they were drawn to me because of my physical appearance. They went on to say they had no idea the devil could be disguised as an angel.

I wanted to school them on the fact that the devil is an angel, but in a rare show of self-restraint, I held my tongue. A feat for me at fifteen. That woman just disliked me because I would call her out on her hypocrisy. I was there for thirty-four days.

I've always been outspoken, spontaneous, and a little wild.

The wildness has quieted over time, but the quick temper is still there when I'm pushed too far. I like to push boundaries, make people push their limits. I also like to be challenged, within reason.

Maybe that's part of the draw I feel towards Charlie. He has so many limits, watching them break away would be immensely satisfying.

Distraction

Charlie

THE BELL RINGS, signifying the start of class. Most of my twelfth graders are already in their seats, with one exception, Stacy.

My classroom policy is "if you can't make it on time, don't come at all." However, I've bent the rules for her because I think out of every teacher I'm the only one she has even an ounce of respect for. Apparently, my class is the only class she shows up for consistently at all.

Sure enough, ten minutes into my lecture on analyzing style and content in novels she is rushing into the room with an apologetic look before taking her seat next to Elliott.

I don't miss a beat, handing her the worksheets and continuing on with my lecture.

"You will want to use these techniques as you finish the analysis on the novels you've selected for your novel study. I will be staying after school for the remainder of this week until five o'clock if anyone needs extra help." Wrapping up the lecture, I walk over to Stacy.

I notice she has a new tattoo on the side of her neck. One remarkably similar to the tattoos on Evie's arm.

"How's your novel study coming along, Stacy?"

She's fumbling through her binder, a mess of papers that makes me cringe. Every other student in my class has their binder organized in the way I outline at the start of class, everyone except Stacy.

Her chaos would normally give me hives, but she is smarter than most of the other teachers give her credit for, and her home life is less than perfect. She's one of the rare students I have a soft spot for because I can see her potential. I can see the honest effort she puts into the work and to being present in class.

"I'm almost done, Mr. Greene." She finally looks up at me, fidgeting with the ring in her lip. Her eyes dart out to look at Elliott. Those two have been best friends since the eighth grade, they're now a month away from graduating. Despite their differing personalities, they've maintained their close friendship which is rare for their age. Then again, Elliott is more mature than any other seventeen-year-old I know, even running his own business. And Stacy had to grow up quickly since her parents are both fairly useless.

Raising my brows, I have to focus on schooling my features to appear less surprised. When I glance at Elliott, he's also gaping at her in shock. "Yeah?"

"I liked the book that Evie helped me pick out."

Recalling that day in the library, after my confrontation with Evie, I remember seeing Stacy sitting at a table alone until Evie went up to her and sat down.

"I'm glad. I didn't notice which book you selected." I didn't give the students much to go off of, I wanted them to choose what they would find interesting.

She reaches into her bag and pulls out *The Crystal Drop* by Monica Hughes.

I'm unfamiliar with the book, so I hold out my hand to read the back.

"I know it's directed towards younger audiences, but Evie was asking me questions and she said based off my answers this book would be a good fit. I don't really understand why, but I definitely enjoyed it and feel the analysis on it is well done." Stacy's voice fills with excitement.

I'm curious what kind of questions Evie asked her, but I don't want to pry, especially since this is the first assignment I've heard Stacy discuss with even a small amount of excitement.

"In that case, I'm sure it's the perfect selection. It's not about what age a book is directed at, it's about the thought it provokes." Handing her back the book, I make a note to read it before I read her report.

She chuckles, a sound that rarely comes out of her. Unlike my other students who are getting rowdy while I'm distracted. "That's exactly what Evie said."

She bends her head and flips to a bookmarked page in the book. Walking back to my desk I survey my students, glaring at Zeke and Ty until they stop goofing off.

Sitting at my desk, I plan out my evening while my students work. All my marking is complete. Most of my classes have two major assignments left and then exam prep. With a month left of the school year, I can feel their focus drifting which is why I try to select projects they will enjoy more.

Glancing at my phone, something I'm not in the habit of doing, I notice a reminder from Mom that I promised her I would go see Dad this afternoon. Not that I need the reminder, but I haven't seen him since the end of April. It's been almost four weeks.

Not wanting to think about that until I have to, I contemplate instead about what Stacy said about the book. I guess I'm not surprised Evie would have that thought about the book. In order to work in a library her love of books must be deep. Especially if Lola is allowing her to pick the weekly recommended reads.

Lola is a toned-down version of me. At least she used to be when we were in school. Often we were partnered together because she was one of the few people who could tolerate working with me.

We even dated briefly the summer after high school, but it fizzled out as quickly as it began.

I can't imagine dating someone like Evie. I prefer women who are organized and orderly, just like me. Dating Evie would be like coming in to work every day and having a new job description. You would never know what is coming and how exactly to proceed.

Every day with Evie would be different. I doubt that woman plans anything out in her life.

Flipping to next week in my planner, I highlight Friday night's block and fill in my dinner plans with Guy and Darcy. My entire week is filled with highlighted boxes and notes about my every waking hour. I like to be scheduled.

The bell rings, dismissing my class. Shocked, I realize I just spent the last twenty minutes thinking about Evie. I don't like the way she has invaded my life, throwing it off its axis. I need to be in control of where my thoughts are, not losing blocks of time pondering a woman I hate.

Hate is a strong word, but I hate anything and anyone that disrupts the order I've created in my life. Everyone I interact with on a regular basis knows my routine, and they leave it alone. My colleagues know I like things a certain way, and they respect that. They may roll their eyes at me behind my back, but at least I can come to work and comfortably know what's going to happen every day.

Mom and Dad have always allowed me to have a schedule. In fact, my entire life was scheduled since they both worked and my spare time was filled with a variety of activities.

Evie doesn't fit into that, it makes me uncomfortable, and for that I hate her. I hate feeling like something in my life is about to implode at any moment, and that's the feeling she inspires within me.

Implosive.

The hospital smell hits me, immediately making me uneasy. My father is my idol, and there is no lack of guilt on my part in the fact I haven't seen him as often as I should, but the fact that he is mostly bedridden and can hardly speak hurts me. Seeing him as less than the man I grew up with saddens me.

I am well aware that as he gets older he's going to change, and I will need to accept that, but having it occur this suddenly has been tough.

When I walk into his room and see him standing there, with a smile on his face, my heart starts racing. I know Mom said he was doing better, that he was more mobile, but I never expected this.

"Charlie." His voice is still slurred, but it's clear his mobility isn't the only thing that's improved. He walks up to me, the effort of every step apparent in the focused look on his face. Hugging me, he pulls back and smacks me upside the head. The force is nothing compared to what it should be, but his point gets across. "This is hard on all of us. I need you to be here for me."

The words come slowly, his voice different than it used to be, but the effect is no different than when I was a child.

"I'm sorry." The words don't mean enough, but only my future actions can show how truly sorry I am.

He simply nods, gesturing to the chair next to Mom before he lays back down on the bed. It's obvious the effort to walk and talk as normally as possible is exhausting. My father never gives up, though, which is why he's made such immense progress from the last time I saw him.

Mom fills me in on what's been happening, lighting up when she tells me he gets to come home in a week.

Dad cuts her off as she starts getting technical. "Let's not discuss this medical shit. I live it too much. How are you, son?"

"Overall, things are good. Sebastian is good, I just took him to the vet the other day and she said he's healthy. The guys are good, up to the usual. Work is wrapping up for another year. I'm planning out my summer right now." Shrugging, I trail off. My life is pretty much the same all the time. Exactly how I prefer it. Except this year I feel like sticking close to home.

Usually, I take Sebastian to Mom and Dad's so the guys and I can go on a road trip. One that I carefully plan and schedule in advance.

My thoughts stray back to Evie. I can't even deny that she's part of the reason I want to stay home.

"Your mother tells me you have a tenant in the rental house. First one. How's that going?" They exchange a look. It's one of those parental looks that as a child you have no clue how to decipher it, but as an adult you know exactly what they're saying to each other.

"It was going well at first. Things were quiet. However, now that I've met her a few times, Mom, I have no idea what you were thinking when you said she was a good fit. I knew within minutes of meeting her that she is completely different than the picture you painted for me." Glaring at my mom, I cross my arms when she laughs.

"Charlie, there is nothing wrong with Evie. She has a good, stable job. She's quiet. She gets along well with the neighbors. Besides, I think it's time you loosen up a little bit and Evie seems like a fun woman." Dad smirks as he watches us.

"I'm sure to some people she is fun, but I find being around her to be too stressful. The people in our life should be compatible to us. She is nowhere near compatible to me."

"You're twenty-nine years old, by now you must realize not everything is going to fit into the world as you see fit." She crosses her legs as I lean forward ready to argue.

"That may be true; however, the people I surround myself with should fit in some way." This isn't the first time Mom has told me she thinks I need to loosen up. I think she thought I would grow out of it, but I like structure and order in my life.

"Darcy and Guy push your boundaries."

I have no argument for this. It's true, they do.

"But you're not suggesting I have a romantic relationship with either of them." My pulse picks up at the idea of being romantically involved with Evie. It frustrates me that I'm physically attracted to her.

They smile at me knowingly.

Dad sits up, adjusting his pillows. "When I met your mother, she had the same reaction to me. Sometimes the people we don't think fit into the future we see for ourselves open up so many more possibilities."

Mom reaches over and holds his hand. Thinking about it, I can see the differences in their personalities. Mom is more reserved, like me. Dad brings out her fun side, something that as a child I've always appreciated. I love the balance they have.

"It doesn't matter. I don't look at her like that."

They let me change the subject. I don't want anything more with Evie, despite the amount of time I've been thinking about her.

Chemistry and *Comfort Zones*

Evie

PLACING THE FINAL book on the display, I step back to examine my handiwork. Every week I choose several books for the weekly recommended reads. I try to find something for everyone, which is an impossible goal, but I strive to do my best.

With the increase in e-book popularity, it's easier for us to have enough copies each week. People think libraries are going out of style, but I disagree. Libraries just need to adjust to the times.

One of the things I love about our team here is the openness to trying new ideas.

Adjusting the display one last time, I walk over and join Everett at the counter.

"Looks good." He leans against the counter.

I look at him and frown. I haven't spent much time with him today, but his lips are drooping in a rare sulky look.

"What's wrong with you today?" I know it's not Natasha. They tried going on a date and both decided they're better off as friends. I wrack my brain, trying to think of anything that may have happened over the weekend, but I can't think of anything.

"Nothing." He sighs.

"Ev, I'm a woman. I know what *nothing* really means when it's accompanied by that tone of voice." I lean back against the counter and arch a brow.

"It's dumb," he mumbles.

"Stop." Rolling my eyes, I refrain from laughing. People say women are moody, I stand by the fact that men are just as moody as women.

"I was playing *Dark Souls* last night and my console died on me. Now I need to buy a new one and I lost a ton of progress." His lower lip pushes out. He could rival the pout on a toddler, he even has a slight quiver.

Fighting a smile, I walk over and wrap my arm around his shoulder. "That would be devastating."

He glares at me. "I don't appreciate your sarcasm."

Laughing, I tighten my arm around him.

I start to tease him when I notice Charlie walk into the library. The words fall from my lips as our eyes meet. He nods at me before disappearing into the stacks.

Everett smirks at me. "What's going on with you and Mr. Perfection?"

Laughing again, I drop my arm. "Mr. Perfection?"

"Yeah, I don't think I've ever met someone so—uptight. Anyways, I saw the look you two exchanged. What's going on there?"

"Nothing. He's my landlord. We can't stand each other." Glancing in the direction Charlie went, I busy myself with straightening around the desk.

"Uh huh. They say opposites attract..." Everett smirks, his depression over his gaming system forgotten.

"I'm pretty sure the small confines of the order he lives in prevents him from having room for anyone else. Besides, all he does is judge the way I take care of his house. He drives by every day to check on me." Rolling my eyes, I grab the few books that need to be shelved and walk away from the counter.

I'm in the historical fiction section when I run into Charlie. Literally.

"Shit. I'm sorry." Stumbling back, Charlie reaches out to stop me from crashing into the shelf behind me. Sparks fly up my arm at the contact. Physical attraction is a bitch, and right now she's mocking me.

Stepping back, I look to the book in his hand for something to do, my brows scrunching together when I see the title.

"No."

"No what?" He looks at me confused.

"No, I'm not letting you borrow that book. You won't enjoy it." Reaching out to take it, I scowl at him when he steps back.

"How do you know? We hardly know each other, and I happen to like historical fiction." He tucks the book under his arm, his eyes boring holes into me.

"That may very well be true, but even from the short time we've spent together, I can guarantee that you won't like that book." Reaching out, I snatch it from him. "Follow me."

"Give me the book back. Seriously, do you treat all the patrons like this, or is this behavior reserved just for me?" He reaches over my shoulder to take the book back, but I duck out of the way. I lead him into the fantasy section and scan the shelf looking for the book I'm going to force him to read.

Finding it, I hand it to him.

"*The Lions of Al-Rassan?* I don't really enjoy fantasy novels." Standing tall, I glare up at him as he argues with me.

"I'm sure you think you don't." I take the book back, flip it over and set it back in his hand. With a sigh, he starts to read.

He holds it out to me. "I don't think so."

"Oh. My. God. Reach a hand out of the small box you live in for a moment and give something different a try. Leave your comfort zone and enjoy this damn good book." I push his hand and the book back into his chest.

He looks at me stunned. "You're actually serious right now? You're holding the book I want to read hostage and forcing another one on me?"

"Yes. I understand you have some neurotic need to control everything in your life, but this is reading. Delving into fictional worlds to escape real life. Can't you suspend your ridiculous need to plan and control everything around you for the short amount of time it takes you to read the words across these pages?" My chest is heaving by the time I'm finished, drawing his eyes down.

I'm not the only one impacted by whatever chemistry we have. I take what little comfort I can from that fact.

"I will let you borrow this book, which will be really disappointing in comparison to the one in your hands." Holding it up, I waggle it back and forth.

He drops his eyes to the book in his hand before growling, "Fine. I will give it a shot."

"You could sound a little more excited about it."

"You're bribing me to read something I have no interest in so that I can borrow the book I actually want to read." He takes the paperback I finally give back to him.

"Yep. And I will be questioning you on it to make sure you read it."

We walk out of the stacks together, a safe distance between us. Everett watches us walk up to the counter in amusement. I'm grinning over the palpable irritation exuding from Charlie.

Leaving him in Everett's capable hands, I walk over to Lola's door and knock.

"Come in."

Opening the door, I enter her office and close the door behind me.

"Did I see Charlie Greene checking out a fantasy novel on the security cameras?" She tilts back in her chair, folding her hands on her lap.

"Yep. I refused to hand over the historical he wanted to read, which I know he will hate, until he agreed to read *The Lions of Al-Rassan*." Sitting in the chair opposite her desk, I peruse the spines of the books on her desk.

"Huh. Interesting."

Picking one out of the stack, I flip it over. "Why is that interesting?"

"I've known Charlie a long time. We spent a lot of time together in high school. Dated for like a month after we graduated, and then parted ways. He doesn't give in to anyone. Not over anything." She grins at me. "Okay, that's a lie. His buddies, Darcy and Guy, occasionally coerce him into leaving his bubble, but that's usually after he's had a few drinks."

Putting the book back on the pile, I mentally note the title to read for next week's recommended reads. Shrugging as I look back up at her. "It's just a book. Anyway, I had an idea."

"Shoot."

A knock on the door interrupts me before I can even begin. Before Lola can answer Charlie's head pops in.

"Hi, Lola. How are you?"

I watch his arms flex as he talks, the smooth timbre of his voice caressing my skin. Looking away, I glare at Lola when I see the laughter glinting in her eyes.

"I'm good. How are you?" Lola looks back over to Charlie as I flip through the rest of the books on her desk. None of the others interest me. The blurbs on the backs lackluster.

"Good." Lola looks over to me. I can feel Charlie's gaze boring into my back.

Sighing, I turn back around.

"I just got a call from Mrs. Jesperson. She's going out of town to visit her son this weekend and she wanted me to ask you if you could water her flowers."

"Oh. Why didn't she just call me?"

He looks at me confused. "She said she didn't have your number."

Lola covers a laugh with a cough.

"Sneaky old woman. I will go over there tonight and talk to her." Rolling my eyes, I smirk. Not only does the woman have my phone number, she rivals Natasha in how much she texts me.

He nods, shutting the door as he leaves.

Lola bursts into laughter. She doesn't say anything, just gestures to me to continue with what I was saying before we were interrupted.

I brief Lola on my idea for a weekly book club. Thoughts of Charlie rolling around in my head. Lola's comment about him not bending to anyone, not even a book, stands out.

Why would he concede to me? He hates me.

That thought kind of bothers me. He irritates the hell out of me, but I take back the thought that I hate him. It's too strong of a word. He just challenges me in a way that I dislike.

Huh, probably like I do to him.

It's an interesting thought, but too much time is being spent on someone I don't even get along with. I mentally roll my eyes at myself. What the hell is wrong with me?

"Evie?"

Jolting, I realize that I've completely stopped talking.

"As I was saying, I thought it would be a good way to draw in new patrons."

"Sounds good." She nods. God, I love my job. "Now, tell me. Have you and Charlie hooked up?"

"You're kidding right?" She just looks at me, her eyebrows raised in expectation. "No. We can barely tolerate each other."

"Sometimes the best sex starts with someone you can hardly stand. Trust me, that's how I met my husband." Lola's husband is a long-haired, tatted and pierced, motorcycle club member who owns the pool bar in town.

I simply laugh. "What is with everyone in this town and matchmaking? I'm pretty sure even if I made a move, Charlie would run screaming in the other direction and then tape an eviction notice on my door the next day."

"There is a fine line between love and hate, my dear."

Shaking my head at the cliche, I excuse myself from her office without responding to that and join Everett at the counter. Heather and Sophie have just come in for their shift.

"Hi, girls." Grabbing my purse from the cupboard, I drape the strap over my shoulder and smile at them indulgently.

They're giggling over something on Heather's phone. Both girls are saving up to go to college in the fall. I actually dread the time when they move and we have to find their replacements. Despite their young age, they work hard and the kids who come here after school like them.

Everett and I walk to our cars together, as per our usual ritual.

We're both stuck in our own little worlds. He's probably thinking about his video games, and my mind is stuck on Charlie... again.

Two Steps Forward,
Three Steps Back

Charlie

I CLOSE THE book and set it on my desk. Well crap.

It's been a week since my trip to the library. A week since Evie forced me to borrow a fantasy novel and bust out of my comfort zone. And damn it if she wasn't right. I read the historical novel first. It was a bust. If I'm being honest, they've all been busts lately, and I think it's because that's all I've been reading.

I finished it within a couple days but avoided starting the fantasy.

My avoidance of the book didn't prevent Evie from harassing me about it all week. In the past week, I've run into Evie several times. I went six months without noticing the woman. Within the past month and a half I can't seem to avoid her.

A couple of days ago we ran into each other at the grocery store. Of course she cornered me and asked about the book before criticizing my selection of produce.

She then made me promise to start the book that night, and I haven't been able to set it down. The character development was incredible, and the world that Guy Gavriel Kay built was magical, complex, and intense.

Packing up the marking I need to complete, I lock up my classroom and head to the library. It's not until I've parked my car in the library parking lot that I realize I forgot to tidy my classroom.

That's never happened before.

Grabbing the books from the passenger seat, I head into the library.

Evie is alone at the counter, scanning books before placing them on a cart. I feel an odd weight in my stomach as I watch her, it's something I've never felt and it's uncomfortable. She makes me uncomfortable, yet for some reason I can't seem to stay away. When she's around, I'm drawn to her.

I hate feeling out of control. The unknown creating immense discomfort.

I close the distance between us and set the books on the counter.

With a sigh I admit, "You were right. It was an incredible read."

The smile on her face is brilliant, but not smug like I was expecting. It's the smile of someone who loves literature and sharing that love of books with others.

It's the first time I've seen her look at me without that hint of irritation and mischievousness that makes me uneasy.

She scans the books back into their system, arching a brow when I don't leave the counter.

"Do you have any others you would recommend?" Tucking my hands in my pockets, I scan the library while I wait for her response. There are quite a few people lounging throughout the library.

A sign that wasn't here last week announces the start of a Mistik Ridge book club. That's a clever idea. If I could guarantee they would pick books I would enjoy, a book club is something I would be interested in.

She hasn't said anything, so I look back over to her only to find she's gone. Before I can get irritated she pops up from behind the counter, startling me.

She grins as she sets a stack of books on the counter. "I set these aside for you last week."

"That was presumptuous of you."

She simply shrugs and pushes the books towards me before going to help a young boy. I flip through the stack of books. None of them are historical. There is a mixture of fantasy, science fiction, and even a paranormal. All of which I would never choose for myself, but maybe she's right and I need to branch out in what I read.

Evie finishes up with the boy. "Well?"

"Okay, I will give them a try. Oh, and I wanted to read that book—*The Crystal Drop*. You recommended it to one of my students." She nods and disappears once again, returning with it in hand.

As she scans the books, I try to think of something to say, but she speaks before I can.

"So, I wanted to ask you something about the house." She finishes scanning, handing the books to me before bracing herself on the counter.

"Is something wrong?" I filter through anything that could possibly need work.

"No, everything is fine. I was just wondering if I could build a little reading nook in the backyard." She pulls out her phone and shows me a photo she's saved.

It's a rustic lean-to, with a bench inside decorated with cushions. It's actually very tasteful, but I'm already shaking my head as I look.

"No." The response comes automatically. I know I'm being what most people call unreasonable, but it's one more thing I would need to maintain.

"Charlie, I will pay for it. I will build it. It wouldn't cost you anything and it's not that big. I thought I could build it underneath the kitchen window, next to the deck." Her voice is pleading.

Sighing I say, "That's fine for right now, but it's more for me to maintain in the long run. I don't want any major changes to be done around the property, as stated in the rental agreement, and that's a major change."

All the friendliness disappears from her face, her eyes narrowing. "You have got to be kidding me."

"I'm not."

"So let me get this straight. I've signed a two-year lease. I have a year and a half left of that lease, but in that time I can't make any tweaks to improve it to my tastes? This is a four foot by six foot lean-to. I'm not asking to knock walls out inside the house. I don't understand why you can't be flexible on this." She pushes up, crossing her arms.

"You signed the lease and expressed no concerns." Planting my hands on my hips, I glare back. Why is this so difficult for her to get? It's all there in print.

"I didn't realize there was an inflexible jackass behind the lease."

"That's uncalled for."

"No, it's not. I think your inflexibility is uncalled for. I understand you like things to be done in a precise manner. I feel like I've been an excellent tenant. I look after the house, I care for the yard. All I'm asking for is a nice place to read outside." Her face flushes, her voice cracking as she attempts to not draw attention. "You know what. Whatever. It's like talking to a fucking brick wall."

She storms away just as Everett appears for the first time since I arrived. She doesn't even stop, just disappears into the stacks.

"Whoa." He joins me in looking in the direction Evie disappeared in. "What's up with her?"

"I pissed her off."

"Well, I deduced that much." He laughs, looking at me.

I've known Everett since elementary school. He's a good guy. Someone I've always gotten along with, but for some reason we've never spent much time together. Probably my fault, the only reason Guy and Darcy are in my life is because they bulldozed their way in and wouldn't leave.

"She wants to build a reading nook in the backyard. I told her no and she got mad," I say matter-of-factly.

He gawks at me before bursting into laughter. "That would do it. I would think she would know by now that you're inflexible to change."

Recoiling, I relax when I see he's not being mean or judgmental. "I am not. I just like things to be done in a specific way. Besides, it would just create one more thing I would need to maintain."

"I know that, but being precise is different than never compromising, and you don't compromise. Everyone in town knows it. Evie just hasn't had as much time to accept it as the rest of us. She will calm down, give her time." Everett smiles in what I'm sure is meant to be a placating way before turning his attention to someone coming into the library.

"Oh my goodness! If it isn't Arianna Kenner. It's been what, nine years?" He moves away from me, catching up with a woman I kind of recognize but I don't have the energy to figure out from where.

His words are taunting me. I'm not that inflexible. I just like things done a particular way. I reject his observation of me, gathering my books and leaving the library.

The Escape

Evie

FIRST MISTAKE WHEN going on a first date, letting them pick you up. Always, always meet them wherever it is you're going.

I'm an idiot.

I watch Brecken's mouth move as I pretend to pay attention, all the while I'm really plotting my escape. Tash isn't free, she has something going on at her inn. Everett hasn't answered my pleading texts. And Lola is on a nice weekend away with her husband.

That is the sum of people I really know in this town. Sad, considering I've been here for the better part of a year now, but that's my reality.

My second mistake, not lining up an escape route.

He just seemed so nice and easy-going at the library.

The reality is—disappointing, and a little revolting.

"—so then the stripper asked me to suck on her tits. I made her come, just from my tongue on her nipple."

Yep, he's been bragging about his abilities to make women come since we ordered our drinks ten minutes ago.

His phone buzzes and he doesn't bother to hide the fact that it's a selfie sent from another woman. *You have got to be kidding me!*

Gawking at him as he leers at the photo before responding, I can't believe I'm in this situation. I usually have amazing creep radar, but he didn't even register.

I ran into him in the stacks right after I stormed away from Charlie.

Glowering, I mentally blame him. It's his fault. I was too pissed off at him to realize what a freak Brecken is.

At least while he's ignoring me, he's not talking about stripper's tits and making women squirt. Disgusting.

The server has come by twice, once to drop off our drinks and the second time to take our orders. However, when Brecken still continues to type on his cell, I'm given a look that says *you can do better* before the server walks away.

Yes, I can do better. However, the only way to get home is if I want to walk across town in five-inch heels. Which, by the way, is sounding better and better. The one cab company has a forty-five minute wait—*Yep, I checked*—and I could walk home in that time. I might lose my feet, but I'm beginning to think it would be worth it.

He puts his phone away, but I'm just dreading the words that are going to come out of his mouth.

"Where is the damn waiter?" His voice grates on my nerves.

Sighing, I look at him pointedly. "He came while you were texting."

He doesn't even react to my words, just leans forward with a slimy grin on his face. "You are incredibly beautiful."

I'm not even flattered. I'm just waiting for the follow-up to the compliment.

"I bet you're a screamer."

There it is.

"Seriously? Okay, let me make this clear. The only reason I'm still sitting at this table is because I have not decided whether I want to walk home or not." Crossing my arms, I clear my throat when his gaze drops to my cleavage.

"Excuse me? Women are honored when I take them out." He actually looks stunned.

"You've obviously been taking out women who have zero self-respect." Standing, I accidentally push my chair into someone passing by. Turning to apologize, I flush when I see Charlie and his friends. Great, witnesses to my humiliation. Mumbling an apology, I turn back to Brecken. "I think I will walk. I can't say it's been a pleasure."

Excusing myself as I push my way past Charlie without meeting his eyes, I'm on the sidewalk when I feel a hand on my shoulder.

Turning, I'm greeted by a large chest. Charlie.

"What?" The word comes out in a whisper. I just want this evening to be over.

"Evie, join us for dinner and I will drive you home after. Brecken is a jerk and no one should end their night like that. He took advantage of the fact you're new to town and haven't heard about his reputation." Charlie doesn't wait for me to respond. He rests his hand on my lower back and guides me back into the restaurant.

Brecken is gone from the table we were enjoying our lovely date at. Cue eye roll. He must have passed by as Charlie and I stood there, but as usual, when Charlie is near I didn't notice anyone else.

His friends are in a booth, smiling at me empathetically as I slide in, Charlie sitting down next to me.

"Darcy, Guy, this is Evie." He gestures to his friends.

"We've met." Darcy winks at me, his brown eyes sparkling with humor.

"Ah, yes. You tried to pick me up in the bar. You were giving off the 'one-night stand' vibe." Smirking, I order a new drink from the same server from earlier. His double take is humorous, but other than that he doesn't miss a beat.

Charlie stiffens next to me as Darcy laughs.

"You're Natasha's brother." Charlie's other friend, Guy, seems to be the quiet one.

He nods, a genuine smile crossing his lips. It's easy to see he's fond of his baby sister. "Yeah. She's a nutcase. Trust me, it doesn't run in the family."

My drink is delivered and we order dinner. Conversation flows easily as I fill them in on the disaster of my first date since moving here.

"You haven't dated anyone since you've been here?" Darcy gapes at me, his eyes flicking between me and Charlie.

Glancing to my right, I meet Charlie's hazel eyes. His face is stoic, as usual. Smiling at him, I turn back to Darcy. "Nope. I was too busy adjusting to the freezing cold of winter and being in a new place."

"I still don't believe it." Darcy shakes his head and I feel Charlie kick him under the table. He doesn't even flinch.

I don't have a chance to respond as our food is being placed in front of us. The guys joke with each other as we take the first bites, and I actually see Charlie smile a little. Apparently they're out celebrating the fact school is practically out for the summer.

"We still have to plan our annual road trip. You've usually already sent us the itinerary by now." Guy grins, teasing Charlie.

For the first time all evening I relax, shocked that it's because of Charlie that my evening is looking up.

Reality Check

Charlie

D ARCY AND GUY laugh at something Evie just said. I missed it because I'm still caught up in the feeling of jealousy I felt when I saw her with Brecken. The fucking idiot.

That jealousy disappeared as she told him off, and it was that feeling that didn't allow me to let her walk away.

I've never felt so conflicted in my entire life.

"Anyway, my professor was speechless for several minutes, a feat with this man, that his entire graduate class showed up dressed like the cast of a Shakespearean play." She's laughing as she tells the story, before falling into an old British accent, reciting quotes from *A Midsummer Night's Dream*.

A laugh bursts out of me at her awful British accent, but I'm also impressed by her extensive memorization of the play.

I stop laughing as three sets of eyes turn to me.

"What?"

"Dude, I can count on two hands how many times I've heard you laugh, and we've been friends for over two decades," Darcy fills the silence.

"That can't be true. I laugh." I'm incredulous. Do people really see me this way? Even my two best friends?

Between my mother, Everett, Evie, and now Darcy, I'm at a complete loss. I know I like things done a certain way, but they paint the picture of someone who is barely tolerable.

Scrunching my eyebrows, I stare at my friends.

"You do. Just not easily," Guy soothes. That's just who he is. Often he needs to moderate between Darcy and me. We're complete opposites, whereas Guy sits more in the middle.

Leaning back in the booth, I set my fork down on my plate, appetite gone.

Evie, sensing my discomfort, distracts them with another story from her graduate studies while I stew.

There is nothing wrong with the way I live my life or wanting perfection. People come and go, the ones worth having will stick around. Why should I have to change just to accommodate people?

Darcy, Guy, and Evie carry the conversation until we finish dessert. Before the server comes to the table, I seek him out and pay for everyone's dinner. Partially to apologize for sulking the last half of the meal, I know Darcy was just giving me a hard time, but also because I wanted to pay for Evie's dinner.

I've seen so many sides to her. The argumentative side that makes me cringe. The vulnerable side when talking about her childhood. Her intellectual side when discussing books. And today I've heard stories of her jokester side. A part of Evie that I find funny, but my gut tells me I would never want to encounter in anything aside from a story.

When the server informs the rest of the table that I've paid for dinner, I get the expected arguments. Instead of responding, I turn to Evie, cutting off her argument. "Ready to go?"

She sighs and nods.

"Thank you for letting me crash your dinner." Guy and Darcy

both hug her goodbye before I lead her out of the restaurant and to my car.

Once we're settled inside, she turns to me. "Thanks again for dinner, for tonight. You turned a terrible evening into a good one."

I give her a small smile, my cheeks stretching a little as her eyes widen at the gesture. Maybe I need to smile more.

"Of course, my pleasure."

Silence descends as she quickly responds to a text, murmuring, "Natasha" as she slips her phone back into her purse.

The drive passes slowly. The last time we were alone together Evie was telling me off. Thankfully, she seems to have let go of that. I would like to be on good terms with her, she is my tenant after all.

Pulling into her driveway, I notice that the grass is freshly mowed, but it still doesn't look quite right. Making a mental note to check it in the morning, I angle my body to face Evie.

Evie opens the door, pausing with one foot on the ground. "Thank you again. Have a good night, Charlie."

"Goodnight."

The door closes behind her. Once she's safely inside, I drive away, my thoughts chaotic as I contemplate the way the evening turned out.

Second Notice

Evie

GRABBING MY BAG from the passenger seat of my car, I heave it onto my shoulder, the weight of the books making me smile. Despite not getting a lot of sleep last night, I am in a good mood today.

Last night was a turning point for me and Charlie. I can feel it. I'm still upset about the reading nook, but with his friends pointing out to him how inflexible and serious he is, maybe I can try talking to him again.

I actually had a surprisingly good time with them. Even Darcy, who I know Natasha dislikes, but I'm guessing that's because two years can feel like a huge age difference growing up. I remember some of the foster brothers I had and how annoying they could be.

Shutting my car door, I lock it. I smile as I check my flowers, pulling a few dead heads off. The pots have filled in nicely, and many of the neighbors have complimented my bright display.

Sighing happily, I turn towards the house eager to start my evening of reading and drinking a glass or two of wine.

Looking up at my front door, my smile drops at the sight of a white envelope taped to it. It's been weeks since I've received one of these. I've been busting my ass to try and ensure he has no complaints about the way I keep the house. And aside from our brief argument, that he won, we've been co-existing nicely.

The closer I get to the envelope taunting me, the angrier I get. So much for a turning point. Apparently last night was just a reprieve until we went back to battle.

Ripping it off the door, I tear it open.

> Ms. Jackson,
>
> I noticed that the last time you mowed the lawn, it was left too long. The lawn mower was adjusted to the proper length, please return it to that setting and correct the lawn. If you have any questions, please direct your attention to your copy of the rental agreement.
>
> Thank You,
> C. Greene

I see red. I get that he doesn't like me. He doesn't like that I push him outside of his comfort zone and that, despite our differences, he finds me just as attractive as I find him. But to fault me on the length of the lawn when I mow it every Sunday like clockwork?

Hold the fucking phone. I mowed the lawn yesterday. That means he probably noticed it while dropping me off last night and didn't bother saying something to my face.

Oh. Hell. No.

This means war.

Storming to the shed, I take out the lawn mower, only to find another note informing me he has corrected the setting. A setting I'm positive I never touched, but whatever.

I'm finishing up the front when Charlie drives by. Meeting his gaze, I smile at him.

A smile that promises I'm going to push his fucking buttons. A smile that says whatever false idea I had that we'd turned a new leaf is gone. A smile that promises he's not going to like what I have planned. And boy, do I ever have a plan.

You see, I found an interesting website the other day and saved it for such an occasion.

He continues driving without a reaction. I expected that, but he won't be so expressionless soon.

Finishing the lawn. I grab my bag from where I dropped it, letting myself into the house and bee-lining it directly to my laptop.

Pulling up the website, I smile as I start to add things to my shopping cart. If I was a villain in a movie, I would be cackling right now with pure glee. A giggle slips out. It might not be an evil laugh, but I can't contain my excitement.

Up until this point, I've knowingly irritated him, but this time I want to piss him right off. I want the confrontation, and I'm going to get it.

The three large boxes on my porch have me racing out of my car as soon as it's in park. I don't even take my keys out of the ignition. Dropping to my knees, I tear into the boxes and burst into laughter. They're even better than I anticipated. The past two weeks have dragged as I waited for this moment.

After opening all three boxes and finding everything in order, I grab my things from the car and haul everything into the house.

Me: *Tash, they came in and they're even more glorious than I expected.*

Natasha: *OMG. I'm coming over.*

There is a knock at my door twenty minutes later. She comes in without waiting, breaking into a huge smile when she sees my living room.

"You're going to get that fight you're itching for."

My living room is cluttered with gnomes. Not just any gnomes. Vulgar gnomes. In a variety of compromising positions.

Some are passed out drunk. Some are in a variety of sexual positions. Each gnome is more vulgar than the last. My personal favorite is the trio of gnomes engaged in a threesome. It's fantastic. Or wait, the one that is urinating has a top spot as well. It's simple, yet effective.

"There is nothing in that damn agreement of his that says I can't decorate the front lawn with lawn ornaments. And I'm going place them on the walking stones so he can't even complain about them ruining the grass. And I've already talked to my immediate neighbors. They think it's a practical joke, but they're all fine with it." Grinning, I walk into the kitchen and grab us each a beer.

"Of course they are. They adore you." Tash takes the beer, popping the top and taking a deep drink. "I've never seen Charlie lose his cool. I wish I could be here to see it."

Apparently it's difficult to get a rise out of Charlie. He is who he is, and people have simply accepted that. That's fine, but I've had enough and he is going to realize I'm not going to accommodate his rigidness.

Compromise is part of being an adult. If he can't learn how to compromise, then it's time for me to up my game.

Now I just need to plan.

Two days later, Darcy and Guy walk into the library. Everett contacted them for me so I could enlist their help.

After explaining my plan, they both agree to help, with one promise from me.

"I guarantee, he will never know your involvement."

We shake, and the final step in my planning is taken care of. Now it's just putting it into action.

Attack of *the Gnomes*

Charlie

"HAVE THINGS IMPROVED with Evie?" Mom hands me a cup of coffee.

Dad is home but sleeping. The move back has been tough for him, but he's shown even more improvement from the last time I saw him, which makes me incredibly happy.

"I'm not really sure." Sipping my coffee, I think back on the look of pure evil she gave me when I drove by the day I left her the note. Things have been quiet in the weeks since, but a feeling of unease has settled in my chest and won't dissipate.

"What do you mean?"

Filling her in on the date I rescued her from, and the books she's been recommending, I then tell her about the notice I left regarding the grass. A note that was effective, might I add. It's been perfectly cropped since.

"Oh, Charlie." Mom sighs. She doesn't say anything else, and she doesn't need to. I can sense her disappointment without the words being spoken. I hate that she feels this way. I hate disappointing her. Part of me blames Evie, but deep down I know this has nothing to do with her and everything to do with what people have been telling me over the past couple of months. Have they tried to talk to me about this before? I couldn't even tell you, but I'm guessing it's come up and I've brushed it under the rug.

Something about Evie has brought all of this to the surface.

Resentment fills me. She's been a thorn in my side for a couple of months now. If she only stayed the quiet renter I had all winter, I wouldn't be having this issue. I wouldn't be sitting here, looking into Mom's eyes and seeing her disappointment in me.

I would be in my comfort zone, living my routine, and being perfectly happy.

Evie has managed to push all my buttons in less time than I thought possible. Even thinking about the purple door, those hideous pots, and the cluttery mess inside the house makes my skin itch.

My phone buzzes, dread filling me when I see it's a group message.

Guy:	*Dude... You're going to want to drive by Evie's...*
Darcy:	*Yeah, man. Just warning you, though, you're going to shit a brick.*
Me:	*The house is still standing, right?*
Darcy:	*Yeah.*

My gut turns. What's she done now?

Before I can excuse myself to go over there, Mom refills my cup.

"You know what I think the real issue with Evie is?" She smiles at me, her eyes crinkling around the edges. Both her and Dad have laugh lines, I can't remember a day growing up where they weren't laughing or having a good time. How I ended up so serious with the two of them as parents, I will never know.

Resisting the urge to roll my eyes, I ask, "What?"

"You're attracted to her, but because she challenges you,

you're resisting it, making you hostile. Maybe you would relax a little if you… you know." She waggles her eyebrows suggestively.

I can't believe my mother is hinting at Evie and me having sex. I've just entered the *Twilight Zone.* My entire circle has completely lost their faculties.

"You can't be serious."

"You're wrong. I'm perfectly serious. I think being with someone as spontaneous, fun, and spunky as Evie would be good for you. I would like grandchildren at some point, and obviously your previous choices haven't been good fits either." Her eyes sparkle when she sees me tense up.

I need to get out of here.

"Well, as fascinating as this visit has been, I need to go." Bending, I kiss her on the cheek and rush out of the house before she can talk more about my sex life, future children, or any other crazy idea she comes up with.

It's a good thing my father wasn't at the table, he just encourages her.

The drive across town is tedious. I catch every single red light, all three of them, and get caught behind a tractor that must have been in the shop getting some repairs done.

As I turn into the neighborhood, all I can focus on is getting to the house and seeing what Evie has done.

My jaw drops as I pull up in front of the house. Slamming on the brakes as my foot slips, I shove my car into park and jump out.

Lawn gnomes cover the front lawn. Scanning, I count ten of them. Ten gnomes in various positions of disarray or vulgarity. Scanning the neighbors in anticipation of them storming out to scream at me, I'm shocked when I see several of them have gnomes in their yards too.

Even Mrs. Jesperson has a trio of gnomes engaging in a threesome. She enlisted the neighbors and successfully convinced them to display gnomes in a variety of compromising positions.

Glancing to the house next to Mrs. Jesperson's, I almost shit a brick, just like Guy said I would. Even Pastor Larry has a gnome on his front lawn. A gnome peeing on his tree. Pastor. Larry.

How does one manage to enlist the help of a clergyman in decorating their lawn with dirty ass gnomes? Where does one even find gnomes like this?

I'm pretty positive it takes dedication and some sort of mythical power to achieve this. But I already knew Evie isn't your typical person. She's managed to get under my skin, and win over everyone around her.

Turning back to the display on the front yard of my house, I take it all in. One gnome at a time.

There is a gnome passed out drunk with bottles at his feet.

Another bent over as a second gnome takes him—or is it a her—from behind.

There is a matching gnome to the one peeing on Pastor Larry's tree urinating on one of the bushes, while another one right next to it is defecating in the shelter of the branches above it.

My head whirls. I can't even comprehend where to start with all of this. Technically she's not breaking any guideline in the rental agreement, so I can't remove them. Her car isn't in the driveway, so I can't even confront her about this.

Growling as I glare at the offending gnomes, I stalk to my car and take off down the street. Once I'm home, I call Sebastian.

He winds around my legs as I measure out his food, before spooning up the soup I prepared last night. Eating at the counter, I rinse the bowl when I'm done and place it in the dishwasher.

My phone dings, pulling me from the roiling thoughts about gnomes and tattooed librarians that make me break out in hives.

> **Guy:**   *Just thought you'd like to know that Evie is home.*

My curiosity about how Guy knows Evie is home is drowned out by my need to confront her. Grabbing my keys from the hook by the door, I shove my feet into my shoes and race out the door.

I've been stewing over this for over an hour, getting angrier.

Pounding on Evie's door, I glare at her when she opens it.

"Charlie." She's not surprised to see me, and steps back allowing me inside.

Slamming the door, I stare down at her.

"Remove the gnomes." Biting out each word, I fist my hands at my sides.

She walks away from me and into the kitchen. Leaning against the counter she picks up half of a grilled cheese sandwich and takes a bite. "No."

Cringing at the fact she is talking with her mouth full, I cross my arms. "They are completely unacceptable. Ignoring the fact that they are inappropriate, they cover the lawn and I do not appreciate the display."

Evie finishes her sandwich, her eyes shining with humor which only feeds my anger. Setting her plate on the counter, she steps into my space. Her soft floral scent surrounds me creating a conflicting chaos of feelings. I hate her and the confusion being around her arises.

"Listen, I have memorized the rental agreement. You did not specify anywhere in there that I cannot decorate the yard. I placed them so they won't destroy the grass. You have no argument here."

Dropping my arms, I growl. "I don't care. Screw the rental agreement. You have been purposely aggravating me and I don't appreciate it." Recounting everything she's done, I can't control the speed of my words as I speak.

What am I doing?

Evie

CHARLIE IS TALKING so fast I can no longer follow what he is saying. I've seen him annoyed with me, but I've never seen him looking at me with such burning hatred. I clearly crossed a line with the gnomes.

I knew he would be upset and I would get a fight, what I didn't expect is the sinking feeling in my gut or that I would experience seeing the anger, hurt, and intense dislike in his eyes.

I wanted to push his buttons, and truth be told there are times I can't stand him, but seeing him this upset isn't providing me the satisfaction I was hoping for.

"Char–" I start to say, but he keeps talking over me.

"—and the neighbors. Even Pastor Larry! How did you manage that?" He takes a breath before continuing, not even giving me a chance to answer his question.

As he rants, he steps closer to me, my nerves igniting whenever his fingers accidentally brush against my skin as he gestures with his hands.

Opening my mouth, I try to interject, but he just talks louder and faster.

Holy hell. He needs to shut up, but I can't get a damn word in edgewise.

Grabbing his neck, I pull him down and kiss him, the movement shocking me as much as him.

We both freeze, our ragged breaths filling the small space between us, and I can feel our hearts pounding in the same rhythm. My stomach knots at the loss of feeling his lips against mine, but I don't lean in again.

"Just shut up." The words come out in a whisper, my eyes locked with his.

The words barely make it out of my mouth before his lips crush mine with a growl, his hands sliding over my lower back and pulling me into him with ferocity.

That was too Easy

Charlie

WRAPPING MY ARMS around her slender body, I moan as she softens into me. Her lips respond to mine with fervor, soft grumbling sounds erupting from her throat as her hands slide up my arms and into my hair.

My body is on fire from a simple kiss. I came here to yell at her, confront her about those disgusting gnomes, and now I can't seem to pull myself away.

I pick her up, humming appreciatively when her legs wrap around my waist. We don't break the kiss as I move to the couch, lowering myself down onto the pile of blankets haphazardly abandoned there. Her lips leave mine dragging a hot trail along my jaw.

She seems fragile in my arms, a feeling completely at odds with her strong personality. She is so small, but she fits easily into me. I groan as she pulls away, her hands still wrapped around my neck, fingers twined in my hair. Our breathing is the only sound in the house, both of us watching and searching the other's reaction for answers.

The reality of how far the kiss went settles like a dead weight.

We drop our arms simultaneously, Evie stumbling off my lap, her hands smoothing her clothes. I follow, leaving a safe space between us. My body aches at the loss of her in my arms, bewildering me. How can my body and my head be so at odds with each other?

I ache to pull her back into my arms, but we have unfinished business. Opening my mouth, I shut it when she holds her hand up.

"Seriously, just listen for a moment. My brain is still trying to process everything you've already said." Her voice is low, a little breathless. She watches me carefully, only continuing when I give her a sharp nod. "I understand that you're upset by the gnomes."

Now that the lust-filled haze is lifting, I feel my anger returning, albeit less forcefully. "That's an understatement. I want them removed from the front lawn."

Her eyes narrow, her lips pressing into a thin line. I can see her analyzing the situation, wondering how serious I am. Clenching my fists at my sides, I wait for her to speak.

"Fine. I will remove them from the front lawn."

My head jerks back, eyes widening. Working my jaw, I can't seem to connect my brain with my mouth and any words that are floating around trying to find some sense of order completely fly away when she steps back into me.

My entire body lights up, eager for her touch, while suspicion filters through the haze in my head. Her breasts brush against me, her arm reaching out. She opens the door behind me, stepping back.

Clearing my throat as she steps back again, her expression closed off. My voice is gruff, "Thank you."

Backing onto the porch, I shut the door with a quiet click, striding to my car without looking at the offending gnomes.

I'm in a daze. The drive home a blur. By the time I have any awareness of my surroundings, I'm sitting on my couch with a beer in my hands.

Evie Jackson is the most infuriating woman I've ever met. She pushes my buttons, something I have no tolerance for. Yet when she was in my arms, everything fell away except the feel of her lips on mine and her pure feminine softness pressing into me.

I've never in my life been so at war with myself. It's no secret Evie enjoys pushing my boundaries. So why did she give in so easily to the removal of the gnomes? That's completely outside of her norm. I may not know her well, but I know enough to realize that Evie is not one who gives in easily.

Locking up my classroom, I breathe a sigh of relief. I love my job, but it feels good to know I have two months of summer vacation ahead of me. Now I can focus on planning my road trip with Guy and Darcy. In the past, we've always traveled the first three weeks in August, but I like to have it planned out and everything booked weeks in advance. This year we're leaving in July, limiting my planning time, and we're only going for two weeks.

"Charlie!" Turning, I watch in confusion as Lainey comes running towards me. She stops, resting one hand on her knee as she catches her breath, the other holding a plastic container.

"Are you okay?"

Lainey has only been at the school for a few months, replacing one of our senior staff members who quit without much notice. Aside from meetings, I never see her since she teaches the seventh grade on the opposite side of the school.

"Yeah, I'm just getting over a cold and don't have my stamina back." She stands, her face still a little flushed. "I never had the chance to say thank you for helping me out when I first got here. I know the materials on my desk were from you."

Cocking my head, I ask, "How?"

I didn't really want her to know it was me, in my experience people don't appreciate it when you butt in without being asked.

"It doesn't take Sherlock Holmes to figure it out. You have a unique way of organizing yourself. It stands out. Anyway, I baked you these to say thank you." She smiles, handing me the plastic container.

Cracking the lid, my mouth waters at the aroma of fresh brownies. "Thank you. It wasn't necessary."

She simply shrugs and turns away, heading back in the direction she came from.

Checking my door one last time, I place the brownies in my bag and head to my car, breathing a sigh of relief as I start the engine.

As I drive the familiar route home, I finally allow myself to think about the events from yesterday. The busyness of the day kept everything that happened at the back of my mind, but now that I have nothing to preoccupy my thoughts there is no reasonable barrier preventing me from turning over the events in my head.

All last night I dreamt about that kiss. I woke up this morning covered in a sheen of sweat, sporting an erection that demanded attention.

When was the last time I woke up like that? I honestly can't remember. But that's what Evie does to me. She draws me out of my comfort zone, kicking and screaming, and loathing her ability to do so.

I've never felt so out of control over my feelings. Everything has been amplified with her. When I get frustrated, it turns into anger. The attraction I feel is tenfold to anything I've ever felt. I hate how out of control I am around her. I hate that she has this power over me.

Slowing as I near the house, I breathe a sigh of relief that the gnomes are gone from the neighbor's lawns. Pulling forward, I scan the yard and relax completely when I don't see any offending gnomes remaining throughout the yard.

Parking, I sink back into my seat. She actually removed them.

Suspicion surfaces. That was too easy.

Mischief *Managed*

Evie

" I CAN'T BELIEVE you took them down." Tash hops up onto the counter. She props one foot up, the other swinging freely as shakes her head at me. "That was probably the most interesting thing to ever happen in this town."

Laughing, I finish loading the books onto the cart, shoving them in Everett's direction. "It was epic, but he was really upset. Besides, you haven't seen the last of the gnomes."

Leaning against the counter, I gulp back some of the smoothie Tash brought for me.

"Really?" She leans forward, her lips curling into a smirk.

"Really."

She takes the smoothie from me, stealing a sip. "Now, let's get back to the juicy part. How was the kiss? That man looks like he can fuck like a god."

Groaning, I turn away and busy myself reorganizing the cupboards. To tell the truth, I had kissed him simply to shut him up, not anticipating the heat that would flood my system and completely take over. There is no denying the attraction we have, but I didn't expect to feel like I was struck by lightning the second our lips touched.

"I just kissed him to shut him up." I keep my face turned away so she can't see the flush I feel in my cheeks.

"Uh huh. Fine, don't tell me. Everyone knows you two are a ticking time bomb."

Finally turning to face her, I snatch back my smoothie before she can steal another sip. "We can barely tolerate being within ten feet of each other."

"We both know you're not going to stop pushing him. There is a fine line you're walking, and one way or another you will cross it. I'm just waiting to see which side you end up on." She lifts her other leg up onto the counter, crossing her ankles as she grabs a paperback and checks out the back.

"My bet is me being evicted and ending up on your doorstep with all my belongings," I mutter.

Tash's eyes flash with worry, before she simply smiles at me knowingly. She opens the book in her hands to the middle and begins to read. Before I can scold her, the bell alerts me to someone coming in.

Grinning, I wave at Stacy and Elliott. They walk over, laughing at whatever Elliott was just saying. "Hey, guys. How does it feel to be high school graduates?"

Stacy smiles, a real genuine smile. "Good. I'm finally leaving this town."

Elliott scowls protectively. "Yeah, she's leaving her best friend behind to go meet her pen pal boyfriend."

Stacy elbows him in the side, shushing him. "Stop. Be my friend and be supportive."

Tash watches them in fascination. Not many seventeen-year-olds could maintain a solid friendship with the opposite sex, but these two have proven it's possible.

"I am supportive, I just don't want to see you end up in the news," Elliott grumbles, crossing his arms.

Stacy wraps her arms around him and looks up. "I will be okay. I promise."

Elliott sighs and hugs her back.

"Okaaaaay." Tash draws out the word. "And what do you have planned, Elliott?"

"I have my landscaping business, and in September, I want to take some night classes. Business, marketing, basic accounting. That kind of stuff. Oh, and counting down the days until I turn eighteen. Forty-five, in case you were curious." His phone rings, so he and Stacy wander away as he answers it.

"Do you think you and Charlie will fuck?"

"Natasha! Seriously?" I peer around her, breathing a sigh of relief when Stacy and Elliott don't turn around.

"What? Like they don't know about sex. Well?" She drops to the ground, inside the counter, snatching my smoothie from me.

"No. Absolutely not."

She grunts in disappointment. "Hate sex is some of the best sex you can have. And you're wrong. You will. It's just a matter of when."

She strokes her chin with her thumb and forefinger, pursing her lips in thought.

Rolling my eyes, I busy myself with the mess I was in the middle of making.

The thing is, a part of me wants to jump his bones and see how the flame would ignite if we allow it to.

"You are so curious," she gloats.

"Shut up."

Dropping my bag inside the door, I kick my shoes off and sag onto the couch. The box of gnomes catches my eye and I smirk.

Rolling off the couch, I drop to my knees in front of the box and start sifting through until I find the one taking a shit.

There is no doubt in my mind that Charlie has already passed by the house. Cradling the gnome in one arm, I head back outside and tuck him into the flowerbed. Examining it, I chew on my lip as an idea forms.

Without bothering to put shoes on, I cross the street and bound up Mrs. Jesperson's steps. She answers after the first knock.

"Good evening, Evie! Do you want to come in?" She opens the door, stepping back.

"Normally, I would love to stay, but I actually came to ask a favor."

"Of course, dear, what is it?"

Laying the book on my lap, I tilt my head back to rest on the armrest.

My foot bobs in the air from where it drapes along the top of the couch. Ever since I was a child I have always read like this. Books are my escape, and they have been for as long as I could read.

Unlike many children in foster care, I wasn't removed from my parents. My father died before I was born, and my mother died while giving birth to me. She had no surviving relatives, so I was thrust into the system day one.

My memories from the early foster homes are blurry, but I vaguely recall someone reading to me. A little clearer is the memory of another woman teaching me to read. I was able to read by kindergarten, and when I was placed in my fourth foster home at the age of six, that ability saved me. My early foster homes have a tendency to blur together until my teen years, but that one stands out because all I can remember is the yelling.

Most of my days there were spent on my bedroom floor with a book in my hands, the only way to drown out the anger brewing below me.

I've never been one to begrudge my upbringing. I am who I am because of my experiences, and it may sound cocky, but I like who I am.

Sighing, I rub my palms over my eyes. I don't know why my mind seems determined to dwell on my past tonight, but ever since I sat down, I find my mind wandering there.

Maybe it's because I finally have a sense of belonging and permanency. Something I have never experienced. I have actual friends, a home, and my two-year plan is right on target.

Dream job—check.

Dream house—check.

Real friends—check.

The only thing missing is something I have never truly experienced.

Family.

My phone rings, causing me to jump.

Rolling off the couch, I walk over to the counter and grab the cordless.

"Hello?" Cradling the phone between my cheek and my shoulder, I open my fridge and scan it looking for something to eat.

"You're a naughty, naughty girl. And you know what happens to naughty girls?" the voice on the other end of the line whispers.

Straightening, I grab my leftovers from last night and pop them in the microwave.

"They get spanked?" Grinning, I lean against the counter.

"Damn straight." There's a pause before Natasha breaks out into a fit of giggles. "I hit the jackpot the day I decided you were going to be my best friend. Too bad you don't have a dick, we'd be perfect together."

"Well, at least we can say we found our friend soulmates. Maybe we should make a pact, if we're both not married by the time we're forty…" I trail off, popping open the microwave when it dings.

"Can I sleep with whoever I want?" I can hear horses whinnying in the background and assume Tash is checking on them before settling in for the night.

"Uh, duh. I love you, but I'm not attracted to you." Grabbing a fork from the pile of clean dishes drying in the drying rack, I sit at the table. Stabbing the tines into a piece of broccoli, I pop it in my mouth, chewing as Tash talks to her multitude of critters.

She finishes murmuring to them, her voice growing louder in the phone. "It's a deal. If we're not married by the time we're forty, we can grow old together. We can even get matching rocking chairs for on my porch and talk about the good ol' days."

We both crack up over the visual of us side by side in matching rockers.

"Now stop distracting me!" A door shuts, and I hear her pop the cap on a beer. "You're asking for trouble, and I'm still betting that it will end up with you and Charlie naked."

I scarf down the rest of my food, dropping the plate in the sink as I go back to the couch. "I have no idea what you're talking about."

"You're so full of shit, but whatever. I don't care what you do as long as you tell me everything."

I can picture her waggling her eyebrows at me, and I just shake my head.

After my kiss with Charlie, I've been trying to sort out how to proceed. I could back off and we will pass the rest of our time as renter/tenant in peace, or I could have fun and try to draw him out of his stuffy routine.

The second option sounds like more fun, and I would be a complete liar if I denied any inkling of hope that future fights end up the way the last one did.

Heat, passion, gratification, these are all things that are missing from my life, and I have never been one to deny my curiosity. Obviously, the attraction between Charlie and I isn't fading, so why not add fuel to the fire and see how brightly it can burn?

I hate Gnomes

Charlie

DROPPING MY HEAD into my hands, I groan before grabbing my beer and downing the rest of it.

"Whoa, buddy. What's wrong with you tonight? Scrap that. What's been wrong with you all week?" Guy drops his cell onto the tabletop and leans forward on his elbows.

"I don't get what you mean." I cross my arms. I know exactly what he means, but I'm hoping to shut this conversation down before Darcy returns from the bathroom.

"Your voice just raised an octave. So spill. You've been distracted, and randomly will groan or growl in frustration. Not to mention your normally rigid routines have multiplied. So something is making you feel out of control, and you're trying to compensate by exerting even more control than usual." Guy picks up his beer, eyeing me expectantly.

Before I can speak, Darcy slides back into the booth. *Shit.* Darcy glances between Guy and me. I'm staring Guy down, willing him to shut the fuck up, but with a simple twitch of his lips I know I'm shit out of luck.

"Charlie was about to tell us why he's wound so tight this week." Guy's smirk becomes a full-blown grin as Darcy zones in on me.

"Finally! What the hell has been going on?" Darcy flags down the waitress and order us a plate of nachos.

Sighing, I down the rest of my beer. "I'd rather not."

"Dude, you know I'm not going to let this go."

"Fine. You know the whole gnome thing with Evie? Well, when I went there to yell at her we ended up kissing."

The waitress drops off a new beer and the nachos, so I grab it and take a big gulp.

"Bro, nice." Darcy and Guy nod approvingly.

"Don't. I don't know what happened, but one minute I'm ranting at her and the next her lips are on mine and we're engaging in the hottest kiss of my life. It's Evie, we all know that's never going to work out." Snatching a nacho, I pop it in my mouth, chewing thoughtfully.

"You're an idiot." Guy and Darcy exchange a knowing look, and for the first time in our friendship they drop the subject.

We polish off the nachos, discussing our upcoming trip. I can't get them to agree on a suitable destination and I need to start plotting our course, stops, and hotels.

"Guys, we need to pick a place."

"You already have a destination in mind, like every year, so just plan it and we will be there." Guy hands back the brochures I have been gathering.

By the time I get home all of the frustration from the past week has built to a boiling point, and guy's night didn't help.

I'm halfway to my front door when something bright red next to one of my shrubs catches my eye. It kind of looks like a—oh shit.

I step onto my lawn, squaring up with the shrub, and the sight before me makes all that frustration boil over.

It's a lawn gnome. One of the disgusting vulgar gnomes from

Evie's front yard. This one is vomiting into the bushes, his pants hanging halfway down his ass.

You have got to be freakin' kidding me!

Grabbing him by his giant red hat, I storm back to my car and drive to Evie's. It's past eleven, but at this point I don't care.

I park in the driveway, next to Evie's car. When I reach the door, I pound on it three times, ignoring the urge to throw the gnome at it.

Evie opens the door with a grin, her eyes sparkling as she sees the gnome in my hand. She steps back, so I brush past her, the zing shooting up my arm at the contact causes my heart to speed up. It's thundering in my chest, the conflicting emotions making me short of breath. The frustration I always feel around Evie thickens the air in the room.

"I thought we were done with the gnomes?" I hold up the offending gnome, gesturing at it impatiently.

"Hmmm, no, I don't think I ever agreed on that. And can you please put Donald down? I don't want you to drop him and break him." She holds her hands out, wiggling her fingers.

"Donald? Seriously?" I hand it over, against my better judgment, and watch her set it lovingly down in front of the window. "Why? Just why?"

"It's funny. C'mon, you have to admit they're cute and hilarious." She flops down onto the couch. I take in the scene before me, the mess around the living room, and my eye starts to twitch.

"No, it's not funny, and I would like you to stop." I grab the plate off her coffee table, stacking a few other dishes onto it, and carry it to the kitchen. I grumble when I see the dishwasher is full of clean dishes and the sink is full of dirty ones.

A few of the cupboards aren't closed fully. I start clearing the dishwasher, putting the clean dishes away.

Evie joins me in the kitchen, taking a plate out of my hands. "Stop cleaning. And, yes, it is funny."

Taking the plate back, I continue tidying her kitchen. "Your sense of humor is messed up. Why is everything so messy? Don't you think it's easier to just keep things tidy rather than letting it build up? How can you live like this?"

She just laughs and starts tidying along with me. I need to release all of this pent up frustration and she's not taking the bait. Every time I'm around her, I lose control and now she's not even letting me do that.

Once we're done Evie hops onto the counter, her legs swinging. "I've been busy. You should learn to let go of your routines once in a while."

"Routines make life better. Maybe you should try to incorporate some routine into your life. When you live life by the seat of your pants, how do you know you're headed into the direction you want to go?"

"You have no idea what you're talking about. Just because I don't plan my entire day doesn't mean I have no direction." She glares at me, finally taking the bait.

"Sure. I can't imagine you planning out anything, aside from how you're going to torture me next."

She tilts her head to the side, eyes taunting. "I don't need to plan that out. I have a backlog."

"Why? Why me? There are over five thousand other people in this town."

"I consider it a public service."

She smirks, turning the tables on me and I'm at a loss for words. My skin itches with the need to release all of this energy and I'm not in the mental space to verbally spar with her.

Growling, I stalk over to her and press myself between her legs. Capturing her lips with mine, I finally begin to release all of the pent up emotions, I lose control in a way I hadn't even planned on.

Chaos. Being near her is chaos.

Why is this so damn hot?

EVIE

H IS LIPS PLUNDER mine, devouring me with the perfect combination of pressure and heat. Moaning, I deepen the kiss, relishing in the feel of his tongue stroking mine.

He pulls me to the edge of the counter, his hips pressing into mine. I feel the power I hold over his body, the power he hates that I have over him.

Twisting my thumbs through the belt loops in his jeans, I wrap my legs around him and press into him.

I have never been kissed with so much passion. His hands are everywhere, leaving scorching trails over my skin. I can feel every frustration he's been holding back, and the desire we both try to deny ourselves. I would never tell him, but in this moment he has as much power over me that I hold over him.

I hate to admit it, but it's fucking hot and I will take this with me to the grave, but I put the gnome in Charlie's garden with the hope that he would come here and this would happen. What does it say about me that I want to antagonize him to the point he comes here to yell at me so we can fight? And after last weekend, I want to antagonize him even more.

The angry make out session last weekend left me craving more.

I'm so messed up.

Charlie slides his hands from my hips to the sliver of skin bared between my jeans and my tank top. Before I can process what he's doing, my arms are lifting and my shirt lands on the floor at his feet.

His lips leave a scorching trail down my neck, over my collarbone, before he lowers the cup of my bra with his fingers. A gasp escapes my lips as he sucks my nipple between his lips, teasing me with his tongue.

"Oh shiiit," I moan out, gnawing on my lip as he moves to the other nipple. I cup the back of his head, arching my back and begging for more.

He straightens, crushing my lips with his in the hottest kiss I've ever experienced. I grasp the hem of his shirt, and lift it over his head, needing to feel his skin on mine. Pressing myself into him, I roll my hips, aching for the friction. His erection strains against his jeans, his hands exploring every inch of my exposed skin. Both of us are caught in this weird moment of anger and desire, walking the fine line between giving in and waiting for the splash of cold reality.

My body is on fire as I anticipate where this is going, hoping to stay in this bubble. I slowly trail my hand down his torso, tracing his abs until I reach the button on his jeans.

And my phone rings.

Charlie jumps back, his eyes glazed as they caress me before my phone rings again. He shakes his head, clenching his eyes shut. "What are you doing to me?"

He crouches down, grabs his shirt, and he's out the door before I can respond.

The phone rings again.

"Hello?"

Sniffles come through the line. Soft whimpers replacing the words that should follow my greeting. Holding the phone away from my head, I check the caller ID.

"Tash?"

"Ev—Evie. I'm in trouble."

"I'm on my way."

Thirty minutes later, I'm on the incredible wraparound porch that surrounds her inn armed with a bottle of wine, two wine glasses, and a bag full of chocolate. I'm about to knock on the door when I see Tash curled up on the porch swing.

My heart cracks when I see her tear-stained face, the quiver to her lower lip, and the way her arms are wrapped around her legs, holding them to her chest.

"Oh, sweetheart. What's wrong?" I put down the goodies I've brought, sit next to her, and wrap my arms around her. The bench creaks as I release her and bend over to crack open the wine.

I fill Tash a glass, handing it to her before I fill my own.

Handing her a tissue from my purse, we sip wine in silence as she composes herself.

She shakes her head, sipping at her wine. Her cheeks glisten with her tears.

"Tash, talk to me. Is it a guy?"

She shakes her head, squeezing her eyes shut. "So much worse."

"Family?" I don't know much about Tash's family, but they've always seemed pretty normal to me.

"No," she chokes out.

I wrack my brain. What else could be causing her issues? "The inn?"

She nods, sobs wracking her shoulders as she loses the little control she's been clinging to. Unable to do anything else, I wrap my arms around her and just hold her until her cries quiet.

"What's going on?

"I think I'm going to have to sell the inn." She downs the wine, grabbing the bottle from the porch and filling up her glass again.

"Wait—what?" I can't stop the shock from filling my voice. Tash has never mentioned being in financial trouble. She always talks about her future plans and the inn is always a major part of them. "I don't understand."

"I've been struggling for a while. I had to replace a chunk of the roof last year, and since then it feels like every single issue that could arise has. I don't tell anyone because I don't want to admit I'm failing."

I sit there unable to form any words. I know she's said that this spring business has been slow, but I didn't realize she was in so much trouble.

"Evie, I can't keep up with the maintenance and the bills are piling up. I've had to shut down two more rooms that desperately need renovations, which I can't afford. That's less income. It's a vicious cycle. I've tried to be positive, tell myself it will all work out, but I'm just not sure anymore."

A tear runs down her cheek as she talks. The porch lights are bright and I look around me with new eyes. I see the broken boards on the porch, the stain that needs to be refreshed. And as I scan through the few times I've spent the day with Natasha at the inn a few things come screaming back to me.

The kitchen appliances that desperately need replacing. The walls that could use a fresh coat of paint. The rooms that need decor updates.

"Oh my goodness, Tash. I'm so sorry. Is there anything I can do to help?"

She fills her glass for a third time, so once she settles back onto the swing, I top up my glass and tuck the wine away.

"No. I just need to sit down and come up with a business plan. I've been trying to avoid getting a loan, but I might need to remortgage the inn, and take a leap of faith. If that doesn't work,

I am going to need to sell." She accepts another tissue, wiping her face.

"I'm sure it will all work out."

"Honestly, I don't want to talk about it anymore. I just needed to tell someone, and I can't tell Guy or my parents, they would just try to fix it. I need to figure this out on my own." She drinks the rest of her wine, looking down at her feet for the bottle. I hand her the bag of chocolate instead. "Thanks. Now, tell me something to distract me from my stupid problems."

"When you called I was half-naked with Charlie in my kitchen." I arch a brow at her as I sip my wine before snagging one of the chocolate bars from her.

Natasha's jaw drops, opening and closing a few times. I smirk at her as she tries to speak.

"Why the hell did you answer the phone?"

"When the phone rang he jumped away from me like I stabbed him." Shrugging, I search under the bench and find the near empty bottle of wine.

She nods, her expression thoughtful.

We drink our wine, crickets chirping the only sound until Tash turns to me.

"Evie, do you like Charlie? Or are you taunting him simply for amusement?"

I think about the question, turning over the past couple of months in my head. It started out as a way to antagonize him because he pissed me off, but in the time we've spent together since then I actually find myself enjoying his company.

He still drives me bonkers, but I weirdly like it. I like walking the tightrope between hating him and not hating him. It's thrilling, and it's spontaneous, and it's combustible, but it fills a hole in my life I didn't even know I had.

"It's not just for amusement. I like not liking him. Does that make sense?"

She laughs. "You're the strangest person I know, but I guess I know what you mean."

I top off our glasses, tilting the bottle to get the last drop. As we drink, we sit in the quiet, lost in thought but enjoying the comfort of each other's company.

I haven't been in Mistik Ridge long, but I've already made these lasting connections that I don't know how I've survived without. I feel like Charlie plays a part in why I ended up here, but I'm not sure who has more to learn, him or me.

Welcome to Denial, Population: One

Charlie

P ACKING UP MY laptop and notes, I shove my feet into my shoes and lock the front door. Walking around my yard, I search for another gnome. I've been on edge for the past three days, just waiting for Evie to hide another one, or call me out for my actions at her house on Friday.

I circle my car, ensuring all the tires are intact before getting inside. After I check my mirrors and adjust my seat, I back out of my driveway and head towards the library.

I've never felt such an explosive passion with someone, never felt so out of control. All my previous partners never ignited me the way she does. I've always been in control of my actions and feelings.

I hate feeling like my life is spiralling in a direction I didn't plan.

It's crucial I avoid further conflict with Evie. It's better if I don't spend too much time around her. I don't even like her or want to be around her, so it should be simple.

My cell rings as I'm parking my car. Checking the screen, I groan. He's been teasing me about Evie every day since Friday.

"Hi, Darcy."

"Hey, man. I took a personal day; do you want to hike the trails with me?"

"I can't. I'm headed to the library to plan our trip."

Silence greets me on the other end of the line.

"The library, huh?"

I can't quite read the tone to his voice, but knowing Darcy, this question is heavy with unspoken words.

"Yeah…"

"Your internet down at home?"

"Um, no." I open my car door, grab my bag, and step out onto the asphalt.

"Interesting."

"What's so interesting about it?"

"For someone who is hell-bent on avoiding a certain sexy librarian, it's interesting that you're going to her place of employment to plan our trip rather than from the comfort of your own home. But I'm not one to judge the method to your madness."

"Okay, first of all, the library is a great source for information. They have a ton of guidebooks and maps to look through. It's a great way to research the places I've found for us. Second of all, I might not even see Evie."

Darcy laughs. "All of that shit is online. Try again."

"You know I hate having to move between windows. This way I can spread out, have everything right in front of me." I fight the urge to hang up on Darcy.

"You've never felt this way in the past. We've been doing these road trips for ten years and this is the first time you've ever felt the need to utilize the library's resources." I can still hear the laughter in his voice as he mocks me.

Frowning, I struggle to come up with an argument that will

shut Darcy up. It's impossible to argue with Darcy when he sets his mind to something.

He takes my silence as concession, speaking before I have the chance to argue some more. "Well, have fun at the library. Call me later."

He hangs up before I can respond.

I check to make sure all my doors are locked before heading inside.

Ever since Evie came crashing into my life it feels as if it's been everyone's mission to make fun of my routines and judge the structure of my life. Like everything that has tilted my world on its axis, I blame Evie. She's set this wave in motion, unleashing control-shattering events that I don't know how to handle.

No one is at the desk when I step into the library. I release the breath I didn't know I was holding, and hide away at one of the tables hidden in the back of the library.

As I'm organizing my stuff on the table, I catch a glimpse of Evie. She's laughing with Everett as they put books away. Her tattoo is vibrant against her creamy skin.

The sound of her laughter shoots straight into my gut, and it's not until they disappear into the stacks that I realize I've been staring at her for a full five minutes.

Rearranging my laptop and notes so I face away from her, I sit down and get to work. Picking a destination was challenging this year because we only have two weeks. Previously we have gone for three, coming home right before I need to return to work, but this year I told the guys I only wanted to do two and I want to be home for most of August. I was razzed about that for over an hour.

They're mistaken, though. Evie has nothing to do with why I want to shorten our road trip. I have been meaning to landscape my backyard and this is the year. I've hired Elliott to design and landscape it. The kid has talent.

Connecting to the library's Wi-Fi, I start out with planning our route. From Mistik Ridge to Glacier National Park in Montana is about an eight-hour drive. Not the longest time we've been on the road, but with the decision to shorten our trip, I thought it best to choose somewhere closer.

Opening my notebook, I note the time it will take to get there if we drive straight there and the number of miles between the two locations. Examining the route closer, I note the major cities we will pass through. For an eight-hour drive, I like to stop three times.

Selecting the cities, I make note of the best place to stop for fuel, get coffee or food, and if there is anything of interest we may like to see. I always plan the second stop as the time to eat, so I search for local restaurants, noting the rating of each one before choosing my top three.

Losing myself in the planning, I finalize my notes and open a blank document to write out our entire itinerary. My fingers fly over the keyboard as I type it out, all thoughts of Evie pushed to the back of my mind.

"That's a pretty detailed itinerary. Aren't vacations supposed to be spontaneous?" Evie's voice in my ear causes me to jump. Awareness trickles down my spine as I tune into her fingers gripping the back of my chair, her chest pressed into my back.

Swallowing hard, I ignore the way my body is immediately on fire and continue typing. "Spontaneous is just a fancy word for out of control."

"No, it's a fancy word for fun and adventure and letting go."

I continue to type, hoping she will go away. When her body heat disappears and she wanders off, I frown at the disappointment I feel.

My fingers are frozen on the keyboard, but before I can analyze the influx of conflict that always arises when I'm near Evie, she's back with a stack of books in her hands.

"I set these aside for you. You should read them."

Instead of walking away again, she sits down next to me. I scan over the titles of the books, I'm familiar with none of them.

I take the top one off the pile. *The Divided* by Bria Starr. As I read the blurb on the back of the book, Evie angles my laptop towards her. I can see her biting her lip out of the corner of my eye, but it doesn't stop the giggle from escaping.

With a sigh, I set the book back on the pile and turn my laptop back towards me. "I know you don't get it, hardly anyone does, but I like being organized and having a routine."

Her smirk falls and she reaches out to rest a hand on my forearm. The muscles jump beneath her palm, and I stare at where it rests as she speaks. "I'm just teasing. I mean, I do think you need to relax a little, but no one expects you to throw away the way you do things entirely. You're just missing out on a different level of living when you limit yourself. It's about balance."

"What do you know about balance? You're the complete opposite of me with no organization, no planning, no structure." Feeling defensive, I lash out. She thinks I have so much control, and usually, I do, but she strips it away. Steals it from me.

I inhale sharply when I see her eyes gloss over, opening my mouth to apologize. She doesn't give me the opportunity.

"When you grow up being moved from foster home to foster home, you learn to adjust. You learn to be flexible because each new home is different. Each set of parents has different rules and expectations. Different feelings on how you should speak or behave. I learned early on that I have no real control, so yeah, I choose to live spontaneously. My mother died giving birth to me. She never got to hold me in her arms. I don't know when I will take my last breath, so I live life to the fullest.

"But you're wrong if you think I don't organize or plan. I graduated high school against the odds. I completed my undergrad, master's, and doctorate in seven years through accelerated programming. You can't accomplish that without structure and routine.

"I'm twenty-seven years old and I have my dream job. I live in a house I love, and I finally have friends I can count on. That's all part of my two-year plan. So just because I don't empty my dishwasher right away. Or I don't fold my blankets in a precise pattern. Or don't schedule my entire life, it doesn't mean I don't have a plan. It doesn't mean I don't know how to organize my life."

She shoves her chair away from the table, walking away from me with a rigid spine. Most people would miss the slight tremble in her hands, but I don't. Nor did I miss the single tear that fell down her cheek as she turned away from me.

Well, shit.

An hour later I'm done planning the trip, so I abandon my laptop and take the stack of books Evie left to the front counter. Everett is manning the desk.

From the glare he shoots in my direction as I walk towards him, I'm guessing he either overheard what Evie said, not implausible considering by the end she had raised her voice quite a bit, or she had come and told him what had transpired.

"Everett." He nods in response, no hint of a smile. "Evie found these books for me, I'd like to check them out."

Without a word, he starts scanning them, his lips pursing tighter with each beep of the scanner. Guilt floods me. Evie is always so tough, so unflappable, that I forget my words have the power to hurt her.

"You could do a lot worse than someone like Evie Jackson." Everett hands me the books, his gaze piercing. "I know she doesn't exactly fit the picture of what you think you want in your head, but that woman is one of a kind. This entire town has allowed you to live your life, doing things your way without really considering those around you, but I think it's been to your detriment. If someone doesn't fit into your square box, you disregard them. At some point that's going to get awfully lonely, Charlie."

"I know." The words slip out before I can consciously acknowledge that he's right. We stare at each other shocked.

"Interesting."

"What is with people using that word? What's so interesting?"

"You will figure it out, man. And the rest of us are just going to enjoy watching it play out." Everett turns away from me, waving at Heather and Sophie as they come in to relieve him and Evie.

I head back to my table, emailing Guy and Darcy the itinerary before packing up my belongings. As I head out the door, there is no sign of Evie. It feels like stones have settled in my stomach.

Thoughts clutter my head. My complete confusion over Evie. Every time I'm near her I go through the entire spectrum of feelings. Varying from complete hate, to confusing lust and affection, I begrudgingly admit I've felt them all.

Then Everett's words echo what I've been hearing from everyone lately, a little harsher than all the others, but the same nonetheless. I don't know how to assimilate this information, but maybe it's time to admit I need to think about my life.

Decisions

M Y CAR MAKES a clicking sound as I turn the key. Slamming my hands on the steering wheel, I cringe when the horn blares. Oops.

Somehow I've given Charlie the power to hurt me with his words. How someone has come to influence me so much in such a short span mystifies me, but somewhere between the first week of May when he dug up my flowers to now, two months later, he has invaded my entire life.

He owns the house I live in. I see him everywhere around town, even if we don't run into each other, I see him. He comes into my work. He intrudes in on my dreams and my thoughts.

The worst part of it all, I like it. I like him. I like picking fights with him. I like being around him. I like kissing him. It doesn't matter what it is, I've come to crave any interaction with this irritating, uptight, sexy man.

The back of my head hits the headrest in my car and I close my eyes. I didn't wear the best shoes for walking home, despite the fact that it's only a short walk, and I had planned on getting groceries.

A smirk pulls at my lips when I think about Charlie's ridiculous itinerary. While he was checking the books out, I scrolled through it again.

I roll my head towards the window when a knock pulls me out of my thoughts. Charlie opens the door when I make no move to roll it down. I would, but sadly my car has decided today is the day it wants to give up.

"Evie, I think I owe you an apology."

That gets my attention. "Okay."

He crouches down, getting to eye level. "You're not the only person who has been 'suggesting' I loosen up."

I can hear the quotation marks when he says suggesting, my lips twitching in response.

"I guess after ignoring the comments, or telling myself I don't need to listen, I got a little defensive. I shouldn't have said what I said. I don't really know you, or much about your life, and that wasn't fair."

I swing my leg out, waiting for him to stand and give me space to exit my car. He's looking at me inquisitively when I grab my purse and lock the door.

"Don't worry about it. I'm tough, I've heard worse and survived."

Charlie steps into me, resting a hand on my shoulder. His touch is light, but I feel the weight of it throughout my entire body, all the way to my toes. He bends down to meet my eyes, his face close to mine as he stares at me. "Evie. I'm sorry. And just because you've heard worse doesn't mean I want to contribute to that."

I release a shuddering breath as he drops his hand, his fingertips gliding down my arm before falling away. I wonder if that was intentional, or some instinctual movement.

"Apology accepted." I start to walk away before I do something stupid, like leap into his arms. That seems to be the end result of any amount of time we spend together and why I had to walk away from him in the library. It was either jump him or walk away and deal with my emotions.

I chose the latter because I love my job and I'm sure screwing someone in the stacks is frowned upon.

He follows me.

"Where are you going?"

"My car won't start, so I'm walking home."

Charlie captures my hand in his, engulfing it. "Let me give you a ride home."

He doesn't wait for me to respond, instead he leads me to his car and opens the passenger door. After I'm seated, he walks around the vehicle inspecting it before joining me inside the car.

I'm grinning and he quirks his eyebrow. "It's important for passenger safety to ensure all tires are intact, and there is nothing wrong with the exterior of the car. That's one of the first things they teach you in driver's ed."

"I know. I don't think I've ever actually seen anyone do it, though."

He grunts in response, ignoring me as he checks his mirrors and adjusts his seat.

"Have they changed since the last time you got in your car?"

"Your posture shifts as the day progresses. Haven't you noticed you need to tweak your mirror as the day passes?"

"Uh, no."

He grunts again, my grin widening into a full-on smile as he starts his car and backs out of the stall.

"How did I not notice you doing this the night at the restaurant?"

His brows crease as he merges into traffic. "I don't think I did."

I can see the wheels turning in his head as he drives me home.

My hand rests against the door handle, but Charlie drives right by my house. "Umm, where are you taking me?"

"I'm going to cook you dinner."

"Why?"

"I don't know."

He looks so perplexed; I fight the knee-jerk reaction to provoke him.

"Make something up."

"Excuse me?"

"Make up a story or a reason as to why you're taking me home for dinner."

He glances at me out of the corner of his eye, not replying as he signals and turns into his driveway. We sit in silence as he shuts the car off, angling his body to look at me. I expect him to fight me on this, to tell me I'm being ridiculous. My request is so un-Charlie, but I wait expectantly.

"Okay." He plants himself back in his seat, his brow furrowed as he thinks, and all I can do is stare in awe that he's taking me seriously.

"I'm cooking dinner for you because something you said registered with me today, and while part of me wants to disregard any contradiction to how I live my life, a part of me can acknowledge that I need to relax. I had the random idea as we turned onto your street to bypass your house and followed it on a whim." He turns his head, his hazel eyes boring into me.

I bite my tongue, holding back my teasing. Instead of making something up, he told me the real reason, but I know that while Charlie is always honest, for him to act on a whim is completely out of his realm.

"May we go inside now? Or do you feel the need to sit in the car for a while longer?" The bite of his tone makes me smile.

Instead of answering, I open my door and step out onto the driveway. Following him into the house, my eyes widen as I look around. I knew Charlie was a neat freak, but his house is spotless. Everything in its place.

I want to move something.

"Sebastian," Charlie calls as he walks into the kitchen.

I'm about to follow him when a black streak comes running down the stairs and cuts me off. The cat winds around Charlie's legs, purring up a storm.

"You have a cat." This surprises me.

He picks the cat up, and it climbs up his chest to rest its paws on his shoulders, curling its head into Charlie's neck. "Yeah, I found him curled up in my flower bed when he was a kitten. It was freezing and he was shivering, so I brought him inside. That was five years ago."

He sets Sebastian down.

I watch in fascination as Charlie opens a cupboard that appears to be dedicated to Sebastian. He opens a plastic container and measures out some food into a clean dish before setting it on a mat inside the kitchen.

Once his cat is fed, he opens the fridge and starts pulling out dishes. One has chicken that's been marinating. Another has fresh vegetables.

"May I help?"

"No, it's ready to go, I just have to cook it. Would you like something to drink?"

He opens the fridge once more, rattling off what he has. It's obvious he feels uncomfortable with me watching him, so I accept a beer and ask if I can look at his backyard.

"Sure, it's a disaster right now. A student of mine that graduated this year owns his own landscaping company, I hired him to redo the back."

"I know Elliott. He's a great kid with a good head on his shoulders."

"I didn't realize you knew him." He leans against the counter, nursing his beer.

"Yeah, I met him when you came with your class that day. Since then he and Stacy have been coming in a couple times a week. We will probably see him a little less now that Stacy has moved."

"Stacy moved?"

"Yeah, she met some guy online and is moving to be closer to him. Elliott was pretty pissed." I watch him process this information, worry etched on his face.

"He's been her protector for so long and her best friend for even longer, I bet it kills him to be unable to do anything."

He turns back to the counter, picking up a knife and starting to chop up some veggies with vigor. It's obvious there is nothing I can say so I leave him in the kitchen, stepping through the patio doors onto a massive deck. I was expecting him to be exaggerating when he said the backyard is a disaster, but he was spot on. There is spray paint outlining the different things happening, tools tucked up against the house, sections of fence missing, and piles of branches from a tree that was cut down.

"Dinner will be ready in ten minutes." Charlie leans against the railing, gazing out into his backyard.

"This looks like a huge undertaking. What do you have planned?"

He points to all of the different spray-painted areas, explaining the different flower beds he wants to put in.

"We're rebuilding the fence first, to six and a half feet tall. Once the flower beds are in, and the pond, he will build a fire pit area out of stone. I want part of the stone patio covered by a pergola. There will be stone paths leading throughout the yard. The final step will be the sod. Elliott is incredibly talented for how young he is and will likely do this all on his own."

"That's incredible. It will be a beautiful place when he's done."

Charlie shifts in place as he nods, a sigh whooshing out of him as the timer beeps. I smile as I follow him back inside, his discomfort palpable.

My smile widens as I watch him mix the stir-fry he made into a serving bowl. We sit at the table, dishing up in silence.

As we begin to eat, Charlie becomes even antsier. We've spent time alone, but usually we've been arguing. This is the most time we've spent together by choice. I love that he's out of his element. I love that his routine has been blown out the window. And I love sitting here and watching him squirm as he tries to figure out what to do with me.

"I borrowed all those books you found for me."

He finally breaks the silence. For a guy as put together as he is, it's shocking how much something changing can affect him. Anxiety is a bitch, and I've come to recognize that's what his issue is.

"Yeah?"

"You have good taste, and it has actually been nice to branch out. I'm enjoying reading again." He gives me a small smile causing my heart to stutter.

He's good-looking when he's stoic, but when he smiles he takes my breath away. I wonder if I will ever see a real, full-blown smile. Part of his appeal is that he doesn't seem to realize how attractive he is.

His words are touching, and in that moment I realize two things.

One: I could actually fall for Charlie, if I let myself.

Two: I want to let myself.

"Wow. Thank you. That's one of the reasons I wanted to become a librarian, I wanted to help people find books they love. Help them explore new worlds, new authors, and experience the magic of the written word."

We finish dinner, relaxing as we talk about work and books. Safe topics, but right now he needs to feel safe and, for once, I am not taken by the need to push him.

He clears the table, and begins to clean the kitchen. Tucking my heels against my bum, I watch as he rinses the dishes before putting them in the dishwasher. He moves through the chore quickly, obviously having a specific order he likes to do things.

Finally, he picks up Sebastian's empty dish. He washes it, dries it, and then puts it away.

Standing, he takes one last glance around his house. Despite how orderly it is, it's surprisingly cozy and comforting. Before I can delve into the feeling of wanting to settle in, I pick up my bag off the floor.

"I think I'm going to walk home. Thank you for dinner, Charlie."

He walks me to the door, opening it for me. Tilting up on my toes, I rest my hands on his shoulders leaning in to kiss his cheek. He turns his head, capturing my lips with his.

The kiss is soft, questioning, and completely at odds to our fevered, angry kisses of the past. It's over as quickly as it started, but its impact is lingering. Neither of us has any power over what is happening here. One action, one word, could topple us in one direction over the other.

As I pull away, I search Charlie's eyes. They are intense, dark, and conflicted. Stepping out the door, I look over my shoulder one last time. "Goodnight, Charlie."

I'm only two houses away when he appears at my shoulder.

"I'm walking you home." His hands are tucked in the pockets of his jeans, his hair messier than when I walked out the door.

"Why? It's two blocks down."

"It's late."

"So, then you will have to walk home alone. And don't tell me it's because I'm a woman." I pull the sleeves of my jacket over my hands, the breeze is making the night cool and it gives me something to do.

He starts to speak, before snapping his jaw shut with an audible click.

"This could start a vicious cycle. Maybe I will need to walk you home to make sure you get back safe, and then you will need to walk me home, and so on and so forth. Are we just going to spend the rest of our night walking back and forth?"

"You're ridiculous."

"You like it."

"No, I don't."

"You're not a very good liar but tell yourself what you need to."

He sighs audibly but doesn't say anything. Verbal banter: Evie for the win.

Reality Check

Charlie

KNOCKING ON MY parents' door, I smile as Mom opens the door.

"Surprise."

Kicking my shoes off, I hug her tight before joining Dad in the kitchen.

"Charlie, we weren't expecting you." He stands, his movements smoother than I have seen since before his stroke. "This is nice. You never just pop in."

Mom hands me a plate with some pancakes on it, before sitting next to Dad and taking his hand. They're so happy and have lived through so much. As we eat and chat, I realize what I'm missing from my life. At twenty-nine, my parents had been married for four years and had me.

I've never even been close. It hasn't even been on my radar, but lately all I see around me are happy couples or people moving forward with their lives. I've been in the same place for the past four years. Sure, I love my career. Yes, I have my dream house. But lately it's felt like something has been missing.

I go through my day, and everything is good, but empty.

"Have things settled down with Evie?" Dad shoves his plate away, leaning back.

I nod as I finish chewing. "Yeah, I guess. I mean, she still drives me insane. Last night I cooked her dinner, and after she left, I discovered she had moved a bunch of things around in my living room. I don't even know when she had time to do that."

Shrugging, I take another bite.

Mom cocks her head. "You don't seem overly upset by it."

"What do you mean?"

"You smiled."

"I did not. It was annoying. Every time I think we find level ground, we fight about something else. I'm just choosing to bypass this one." I finish my pancakes, standing and collecting all the dishes.

"You're bypassing it? She moved your stuff. When I cleaned your room when you were eight, you didn't let go of it for several months." Mom grins, and I finally see where she is going with this.

"Stop. Stop trying to set us up."

"I'm not." She looks sidelong at Dad. "I don't think I need to."

Shaking my head, I smile at my parents. "You two are unbelievable."

We visit for a while longer, and by the time I leave I feel refreshed. It felt good to pop in, I never just drop by. I drive home, and before heading inside, I roll the trash can to the side of my house. That's when I notice the gnome. Another damn gnome.

Picking it up, I roll my eyes. I know what she's doing and I'm not going to take the bait. As I step onto my porch, another gnome sits in front of my door.

"Seriously?" Groaning, I unlock my front door and pick up the other gnome. I feed Sebastian. My kitchen smells amazing with the ribs I have cooking in my slow cooker, but instead of devouring them, I grab my keys and the gnomes.

At this point, I think it's a good thing for my fuel tank that I live less than five minutes away from Evie. I park in what I'm starting to think of as my spot, grab the gnomes, and stride onto the porch.

The door opens before I can knock, Evie reaching out and yanking me into the house.

Holding the gnomes up, I look at her and sigh. "Seriously?"

She smirks, her eyes heating up as she grabs the gnomes and throws them onto the couch. She doesn't even glance behind her when one falls on the hardwood floor and breaks.

Our lips crash together, Evie grabs onto my shirt and starts backing us through the house towards her bedroom. She pulls away, lifting her shirt over her head. By the time she pushes me onto the bed, there is a trail of clothes on the floor in the hall.

My heart pounds, this is the most I have felt in so long. Evie's lips feel so right against mine, the softness of her skin against mine is an incredible sensation, and the fire I feel whenever we're together is something I can finally admit I crave.

She draws me out of my routine, something that is so uncomfortable to me, but the more she does it, the more I need it. I hate to admit it, but I enjoy the banter and the fighting and the frustration. It fills a void in my life that I didn't even know was there.

Where is this going? I have no idea. But for once, I'm okay with that. I don't know if I will still feel like this tomorrow, but right now, with Evie in my arms, I want to embrace spontaneity.

Wrapping my hand in her hair, I pull her head back and stare into her eyes. Bracing my arm around her back, I lift us both off the bed. Crushing my lips against hers, I move forward until her back hits the wall and thrust into her. Hard.

Evie's moans spur me on as I move in and out of her at a bruising pace. I pour everything into devouring her. I revel in the way we feel together, and the fact that for probably the first time in my life I'm not worrying about tomorrow.

Her pussy clenches around me as she comes, the tightness of her clenching around me throws me over the edge as I still inside of her. We're covered in a sheen of sweat, our breathing labored.

Pressing my forehead against hers, we just stare at each other in silence.

"I hate that I like what you're doing to me."

"I'm pretty sure you just did me."

I laugh and set her on her feet.

"Umm, we're not done yet. You had it your way, I get to have it my way now."

Evie walks back into her bedroom with two steaming cups of coffee. She looks stunning wearing only my t-shirt, her hair is rumpled and there is a vulnerability to her that I've rarely seen.

She's a walking contradiction, I've never met someone who evokes so many different feelings in a short span of time.

"Here." She hands me one of the mugs as she sits on the foot of the bed.

She eyes me over the rim of her mug.

"What?"

"I'm just waiting for the freak out."

"Why would I freak out?"

"Well, the last time we were heading in this direction you ran like I told you I wanted you to dress me like a baby and spank me."

Labels

Evie

H E GAWKS AT me.

"How do you come up with the things that come out of your mouth?"

"Don't change the subject. And I'm a creative person." I finish my coffee, and set the mug on the floor, smirking when he cringes.

"I'm not going anywhere, unless you want me to leave. Besides, we still haven't discussed the fact that you're hiding gnomes at my house now."

"You told me to remove them from my yard. They need a yard to be happy, Charlie."

He groans and runs a hand down his face. Crawling over to him, I straddle his hips and curl my fingers into his hair. He moans as I massage the base of his skull, eyes watching me.

"You drive me absolutely insane."

"But you're starting to like it, aren't you?"

He doesn't bother denying it, his lips twitching a little as he fights a smile. That is until his need to organize everything into a category kicks in. "So—are we going to talk about this?"

"No." This time I'm the one biting back a grin.

"Okay, why?"

"Because. You live for order, routine, and labels. I don't want to label this. I want us to react purely on instinct." I roll off him, hugging my pillow to me as I watch him process this.

"But…"

I cut him off. "No 'buts.' Charlie, live a little outside the box."

"I…"

"Nope. No excuses."

"Ev…"

"Live. Outside. Your. Comfort. Zone."

He covers my mouth, allowing himself to smile at me. "Stop interrupting me. I was just going to say that I will try."

"Oh." The word is muffled by his hand, and for the first time since I've met him his small smile turns into a full-blown, "take your breath away" smile.

I was right, it transforms him.

"I better go. We leave early for our road trip tomorrow." He stands, walking into the hall to gather his clothes, coming back into my room with his pants on, the button undone, and his glorious torso on display. "I'm going to need my shirt back."

I finger the soft material before removing it with reluctance. "I will see you when you get home."

He wavers for a moment in the middle of the room, the t-shirt hanging from his hand. I hold my breath waiting to see if this more relaxed version of Charlie stays, or if he shuts down.

When he pulls the shirt over his head and turns towards the door, I feel my face fall. He doesn't turn around, and I wrap myself around my pillow when I hear the front door close behind him.

My cell buzzes, so I roll out of bed and find my jeans in the hall.

Natasha: *What're you up to? I can't sleep.*

Me: *Come on over.*

I throw on some sweats and a tank top before heading to the kitchen and turning the kettle on. The water has just boiled when Tash lets herself into the house.

"Do you want tea?"

"Yeah, that sounds good."

She comes into the kitchen and drops onto a chair. I hand her a mug with steaming water, and the box with my selection of tea. As I sit next to her, she finally takes in my appearance.

"You had sex."

"What?" My voice raises a pitch.

"You totally screwed Charlie, didn't you?" She picks up her tea and settles the bag in the water.

"Yes." I smile, remembering how intense he was, shockingly in tune to my body.

"How was it?" Tash tucks one leg underneath her, cupping her mug in her hands.

Gnawing on my lip, I stir some sugar into my tea. "I don't think I've ever enjoyed sex that much. He was—attentive, intense, and passionate."

She grins at me. "Does this mean you guys are?"

"Nah."

She shakes her head. "Whatever works for you."

The topic is changed as she fills me in on a series of bank appointments, all of which have not solved her financial problem. I wish I could do something to help her, but even if I had the kind of money she needs, I know she would refuse my help.

Time passes in a blur. It's not until we're both yawning to the point our eyes are watering that we decide to call it a night.

"Do you want to crash here?"

"No, I need to do chores and try to figure my shit out."

I walk her to her car, giving her a hug before sending her off. As I lock up the house, the broken gnome from earlier catches my eye. My body is tired, but as soon as I lay down I know I will lie there awake, so I set about cleaning up the living room.

When I'm done and my thoughts still haven't settled, I clean the kitchen. It's three o'clock in the morning by the time I crash.

Road Trip Madness

Charlie

ARCY LOADS HIS things into the back of the SUV I've rented for our trip.

"Dude, I know you like to get on the road, but don't you think six in the morning is a little ridiculous?" He slams the door, buckling in.

"No. You have the itinerary, it's not my fault you didn't pay attention." I hold up my laminated copy, checking off the first stop.

Guy is already waiting at the bottom of his driveway, looking just as tired as Darcy. He doesn't say a word, just hands us travel mugs of coffee.

I set my GPS for our first stop, and soon we're pulling out of town. The guys drop the sullen acts as soon as they've ingested their coffee.

Guy reads over my itinerary, asking questions about some of the places we will be checking out.

"Wait. Can you read over it again?"

"Dude, don't you have this thing memorized?" Darcy snatches it from Guy, looking it over.

131

"No. I finished it, but got distracted, so I didn't review it after."

"Wait. *You* got distracted?" Guy and Darcy gape at me.

"Yeah." They continue to stare at me. I don't want to tell them why I was distracted, but they won't let this go for the entire trip. "Evie brought me some books, and then I may have upset her. So after I finished it, I went to find her."

They exchange knowing looks, before smirking at me and saying in unison, "Evie, huh?"

"Shut up. Now read the damn thing again."

Darcy goes over it. I may not have memorized it, but it's different than I recall. How did I not notice the shift in times and details? Things are missing in some places but added in others.

Then it dawns on me. "Evie. Evie changed it when I was checking books out at the counter."

I stare out the windshield, the scenery passing in a blur. I faintly hear Darcy and Guy in the background, but I have no idea what they're saying. This should upset me. Why isn't it? I mean, yes, I'm annoyed, but overall I find it—funny.

Guy and Darcy stop talking when I laugh.

"Maybe we should pull over. I think you're having a breakdown." They look at each other, then back at me in concern.

"I'm fine. Am I annoyed, a little. It is kind of funny, though, isn't it?"

"For normal people, yes. For you, no." Darcy hands the itinerary back to Guy.

"I don't think you should be driving right now." Guy tucks it next to his seat, not removing his eyes from me. "Clearly you're in the midst of a crisis."

"Don't be idiots. We will just follow the new itinerary."

"We're fucking doomed," Darcy wails dramatically.

This continues well after the first and second stops. They finally quit as we cross the border into Montana, excitement about arriving at our destination outweighing their need to tease me until I snap.

We drive deeper into the mountains, their looming shadows cast on the road before us. I navigate the car to our campground, eager to forget everything but this annual getaway.

We reach the lake, dropping to the ground and sprawling out.

"I thought I was in better shape than this." I'm panting. We just hiked seven miles to reach this spot, and it was gruelling.

Guy yanks off his hat and wipes his brow. "We shouldn't have been so ambitious on the first day."

When we're finished resting, we return to the trail that follows the shore of the lake. Evie pops into my mind. I feel like she would love this. With her history, I wonder if she's ever had the opportunity to take any trips like this.

The water glistens through the trees, sunlight catching the water creating a sparkling appearance on the surface. It's a calm day, so the water doesn't even have a ripple. I can imagine Evie skipping rocks, creating the ripples that are absent.

By the time we get back to the vehicle, we're exhausted and ready to get back to the campsite for dinner. Evie has been on my mind since the lake, and she refuses to go away.

I wonder if she's thinking about me.

I wonder if my yard has been invaded by gnomes.

I wonder—

"Yo, Charlie. Would you like to come back from Evie-land and give some input on this?" Darcy waves his hand in front of my face, Guy grinning as he drives.

"Huh?"

Darcy shakes his head, brows high on his forehead. "Oh, man, you've got it bad. We were saying that we should head home a day early…"

I perk up, waiting with piqued interest. "Yeah!"

"And stop overnight at the hot springs in Banff." He finishes his thought, barely containing his glee at getting my hopes up.

"Oh. Yeah, that would be fine." Resting my head against the headrest, I roll my head and stare out the window. "The only reason she's on my mind so much is because I'm dreading what she's doing to my house while I'm away."

"Yeah, man, we didn't ask." Guy parks in our site, chuckling.

"I have to admit; I like seeing you this out of sorts. You're forgetting all your annoying habits." Darcy swings his backpack onto his shoulders, sauntering to the tent and tossing it inside. He zips the tent shut again and turns to face me. "We have twelve days left, maybe we should bet on how long it is before Charlie breaks the no cell phones rule."

Glaring at him, I grab the axe and start chopping wood. "Why am I friends with you dickheads?"

"Because we're the only ones who find your nuances amusing." Guy and Darcy high-five. Rolling my eyes, I turn my back on them and start building a fire.

Attack of the Gnomes 2

Evie

ELLIOTT COMES FROM Charlie's backyard covered head to toe in dirt. He raises an eyebrow, but doesn't say anything. He tried when I first arrived over an hour ago, but gave up. Smart kid.

"What time does Mr. Greene get home tomorrow?" He returns from his truck, a sandwich in hand.

"I have no idea." I bend to tweak one of the gnomes. I wish I knew. If I did, I would be here taking pictures of his reaction. I may have purchased a few more gnomes. My entire collection is now spread out over his lawn.

"I hope I'm here." He grins.

"Take photos. Please." We laugh as he finishes his sandwich and I pack up my things. Snapping a quick picture, I send it to Tash. As I head to my car, I turn back to Elliott. "How is Stacy doing?"

He smiles. "Good. Apparently *what's his face* is amazing. They look cute together and she looks happy. Which is what she deserves. I miss having my best friend to talk to, though; I sure could use her these days."

"Just because she isn't close by doesn't mean her best friend status is revoked. Call her. Talk to her." He nods, waving goodbye as I get into my car and start the short drive home.

Tash is waiting for me on my front steps with two bottles of wine in hand, a bag of junk food at her feet, and her overnight bag at her back.

"Girls' night?"

She nods, gathering her things and waiting as I unlock my front door. We change into our sweats and pop a movie into my Blu-ray player. Until Natasha, I never really had girls' nights. I was too focused on finishing school and finding a place to finally settle down.

As the first movie comes to an end, I turn to her. "So are we celebrating my epic gnomevasion?"

"That, and we're also mourning the fact that after five separate bank meetings no one will approve me. My only option is to either find a buyer to invest in the inn, becoming a forty-nine percent owner, or sell it completely." She grabs a fistful of popcorn and stuffs her face.

"I'm so sorry. Have you made a decision?" I lean forward, muting the TV.

"No. I can survive for a while yet if I make some cutbacks." She shrugs her shoulders, eyes filling with tears. "I don't know what I would do with myself if I didn't have it. I also don't know if I could handle someone coming in and changing things."

I jump over to her and wrap her in my arms. "It will work out. I promise."

She wipes her tears, sniffling as I top off our glasses and put in a new movie. I'm glad she's here tonight. I need the distraction from thinking about Charlie and his return tomorrow. I've missed seeing him around town these last two weeks, and I'm curious where we will pick up from when he returns.

It's a good thing I'm not at work today. My head is not in the space to be around people, and the only thing keeping me sane is the fact that I've cleaned my house from top to bottom. Something I only do when I'm stressed the fuck out. I'm pretty sure I could eat off my floor if I was inclined to do it.

Having Charlie be inaccessible for the past two weeks has been a good thing. It gave me a chance to evaluate what this is and come to terms with it.

I want more. I told him we would see how it goes, but I want a label. I miss him. More than the pranks and the fun I have aggravating him, I miss the serious moments we've shared. I want to get to know him. I want more intimate moments.

He's like no one I've met, and I like the balance he brings to my life. A balance I didn't know I needed, but one that I've grudgingly grown to appreciate.

We're so different; this could either blow up in our faces, or be absolutely incredible. If I live by anything, it's a willingness to take risks.

Charlie is a risk I want to take.

It's dark by the time I hear the quiet knock on my door. I set the book I'm reading down and try not to rush to the door. Flinging it open, I smirk when I see a gnome in his hands.

He steps inside without saying a word. He looks like his usual stoic self, but as he searches my face, I see his change so subtly that if I wasn't staring at him I would miss it. He looks relieved.

"I think you're missing about nineteen other gnomes."

He fights a smile. "Yeah. I've decided to hold them hostage."

Wait, what?

"Seriously?"

"Yep. You may have this one back, but you need to earn the others." This time he actually smiles. It feels weird seeing him smile more frequently, but I like it.

I take the gnome and set him on the front windowsill. "He's

watching you every time you drive by, judging you for holding his friends hostage."

I grin at Charlie as he shakes his head. "I can't believe you're not mad about the gnome invasion. What happened on your trip?"

"I had two weeks to prepare for what chaos awaited me." He shrugs, looking around as he kicks off his shoes. "What happened in here?"

"What do you mean?" I look around the room but can't tell what he's referring to.

When he sits down on my couch, I tilt my head. What is happening? This is atypical to almost all our previous interactions. I was expecting him to come storming in here, angry about the gnomes. We would yell and argue and then end up in bed together.

Then I was planning to tell him I want more. This is throwing me off, and I don't like it.

"I don't think I've ever seen your house so—orderly."

I go into my kitchen and grab us both a bottle of water. I need my wits about me, this is a side of Charlie I've never seen before. He's changing his strategy in dealing with me in this weird back and forth I think we both crave.

"I clean when I need to think." Handing him the bottle of water, I sit next to him. We maintain a safe distance as we watch each other, both searching for something. The familiar tension builds in the air, but we resist it.

The silence stretches out, and for the first time in a long time, I feel uncomfortable with it. "How was your road trip?"

"Good. We hiked around fifteen miles a day. That reminds me. My itinerary, you made some—interesting changes." He cocks a brow, glaring at me.

Biting back a smile, I shrug. "I actually thought you would catch it before you left. The original is saved on your desktop. I couldn't resist the opportunity when it presented itself."

He stares at me, and I'm positive I'm not imagining the humor. This is not the Charlie from May, I mean, he's still the same guy but not so quick to react. What's causing this change? Could it possibly be me?

Looking away, I quickly deny that thought. People need to want to change, another person can't change someone.

Charlie finishes his water, setting the bottle on a coaster. He takes my half-full bottle from me, setting it next to his. On another coaster. I grin. I've never used those things and I'm sure he knows that.

He settles back onto the couch, then reaches over and lifts me so I'm straddling his lap. The air rushes out of my lungs, and for the second time tonight, he's left me speechless.

Wrapping his hand around the back of my neck, he meets me halfway in a kiss that sends fire down my spine.

Two Way *Street*

Charlie

P ARKING MY CAR, I grab the gnome I brought with me. I can't believe I'm trying this no label thing, but the entire two weeks away all I thought about was her. I want to know her, I want to try and be more spontaneous. I want to let go and live a little. Because she's right, life is short.

My dad was lucky and got a second chance. Her mother wasn't so lucky.

Going against years of routine, structure, and a set way of thinking isn't easy. I still like things to be done in a precise manner, but that doesn't mean I can't find a balance.

I spent the day doing laundry, which leaves me too much time to think. This morning Evie seemed like she wanted to say something, but never got around to it. When I asked, she said it wasn't important.

Knocking on the door, I hold the gnome behind my back. I open the door when there is no answer, letting myself in. Evie is nowhere to be seen.

The living room looks a little messier than it was this morning when I left, but one thing stands out. Her coffee mug is resting on a coaster.

"Evie?" There is no response.

I wander into the kitchen and check out the backyard. Evie is sprawled out on a blanket in the middle of the lawn. She is barely covered in a pair of shorts and a tiny tank top. She's on her stomach, a book in her hands. Her brow is furrowed as she reads, making me curious whether it's the book that's frustrating her or something else.

I step out onto the deck, checking out the backyard. I guess I can admit it's pretty boring. The shed is to the side of the house, holding all the tools she could need, but aside from that and a hedge lining the back fence, there is nothing else to the yard, but that makes it easy to care for and maintain.

Shaking off the doubt, I walk over to where Evie lays. She only looks up when my shadow falls over her.

"You really should lock your door if you're not in the house."

She glares up at me. "There are like five thousand people in this town. I'm sure I'm okay."

"That doesn't matter. For your safety, and for the sake of all my furniture, please lock your door."

"Fine," she growls out.

I sit next to her and hand her the gnome I brought with me. This one is one of the tamer ones, it's giving us the finger. Where she found these things, I have no idea.

I lean back on my hands and watch her reaction.

She holds him in her hand, looking between me and the gnome. "To what do I owe the return of this fine hostage?"

I shrug. I really should hold onto these stupid gnomes, otherwise they will eventually make their way back onto my front lawn, but it's kind of fun returning gnomes instead of bringing flowers. It's more fitting with Evie, and these gnomes have begun almost an inside joke. Despite how creepy and nasty they are.

"This is so much better than anything else you might have been inclined to bring." She hugs the gnome to her, her eyes shining with happiness.

"Why are you reading out here?"

She sits up, the gnome on her lap. "I like reading outside when I can and it's so gorgeous out. I want to revisit my question about the reading nook. I would really like to have a cozy place to read, and I would do all the work, or even hire Elliott."

"No." I'm already shaking my head. "I'm not changing the backyard here. Who is to say the tenant after you will want to look after more than mowing the lawn?"

"They would have less lawn to mow if you let me build what I want to," she bites out, her eyes hard.

"This is not up for discussion."

"Why not? Seriously, you're being ridiculous. There is nothing wrong with changing this backyard to make it more interesting. Why can't you be a little bit more flexible?" She stands, grabbing her book and the gnome. She tries to tug the blanket out from under me but fails.

"Be more flexible? I am trying. I didn't get upset over the itinerary, or the gnomes. I think I've done a damn good job at not letting myself get upset over things that make me want to tear my hair out. But it's not good enough. What about you? You keep asking for me to be more spontaneous, but I don't see you trying to be flexible to me. This is a two-way street."

I jump to my feet, picking up the blanket and shaking it out. "You know what, I think I'm going to go home. I don't feel like arguing tonight. I'm not in the mood to go to battle."

Folding the blanket, I drop it on the back of her couch as I pass. I'm out the door and in my car.

How can she not see how much I'm trying? I'm trying to soften the way I do things, but she doesn't seem to realize she's being as inflexible as she constantly tells me I am.

Letting myself into my parents' house, I find them in the kitchen. Mom is baking, and Dad is reading the paper.

"Why must she be so infuriating?" Bypassing a formal greeting, I start ranting about Evie and letting loose all the thoughts in my head. "I hear what you all are saying and I'm trying. Do you think I like knowing that people get annoyed by the way I am, do you think I don't know I'm difficult? But it's not easy to change the way you think. It's easier to know what to expect. It doesn't drive me insane.

"But no, it's not good enough for her. And where is the effort on her part? Why do I need to be more flexible, but when I tell her no she flips the fuck out?"

Mom and Dad stare at me as I finish yelling. Their eyes are wide, but both of them are smiling at me.

"Why are you smiling?"

Mom plants her hands on my shoulders and pushes me towards my usual chair. "Another fight with Evie?"

I drop my forehead to the table, my voice muffled, but I'm too frustrated to care. "Yeah. I didn't get mad when she changed my itinerary. I didn't get mad when I came home to twenty gnomes on my front lawn. But she can get mad when I say no to something we already discussed and I thought we moved past."

The sound of a glass being set on the table makes me lift my head. It's a glass of milk, and next to it are some fresh-baked chocolate chip cookies.

"Listen up, son. Relationships are difficult. All of them. Friendships, marriages, parenthood, coworkers, you name a type of relationship and none of them are easy. All of them take work." Dad leans onto his elbows, his expression serious. "I guarantee that whatever is going on between the two of you, you are both making an effort. You might not immediately recognize her effort, just as she might not see yours, but you will."

What he's saying makes sense, it's why none of my previous

relationships have lasted. I never wanted to make an effort to be what the other person needed, with Evie, I'm trying.

"I just wish she would see the effort I'm making. I get that I'm less stressed now that I'm letting things go a bit more, and I'm not changing just for her, but some recognition would make it easier."

Mom and Dad grin at me.

"So you're into her now?"

Busted. Dropping my head back, I stare at the ceiling. "I don't know why I like her, because she drives me insane and there are days I can't stand her, but I want to be around her and know her."

They laugh, Mom wrapping her arms around Dad. "We have no control over who is right for us. She may not be your person, but obviously you need her right now."

As I leave their house a couple hours later, I can't believe I've gotten to the point in my life where I'm going to my parents for relationship advice.

Not even relationship advice, because she doesn't want a label. I don't like this. Some things need to be labelled.

Books and *Divas*

Evie

EVERETT STRADDLES A chair, snagging a mini pizza. "The divas just came in the door."

Last week we had two new arrivals for book club and Everett informed me in high school everyone called them "The Divas."

Cassaundra and Emery are both tall and slender, with the perfect hair and makeup. They carry that air of confidence that makes many women feel inferior.

"They're not that bad. They just have confidence. It's easy to resent people like that." I don't get the bitchy vibe from them, but I can see how they may have not been well-liked in high school.

"Have you heard from Charlie since he left your place?" Everett tilts the chair onto two legs. Natasha has been busy trying to find ways to earn some extra money, so I was exploding with the need to talk to someone and he got an earful this morning. Our conversation was interrupted by an influx of people, and we haven't had a chance to pick back up until now.

"A couple of texts. Maybe it's a good thing I didn't tell him I want to label this. We're not ready for it. I'm not ready." I stack the books for next month's read. We're still discussing July's book, but I like to provide the book in advance. "Charlie Greene is complicated. He's teaching me more about myself than I thought I had to learn."

A waft of expensive perfume fills my nostrils. I turn to see Cassaundra and Emery eyeing me up. Everett glares at them, but I give him a shake of my head.

"Charlie Greene? Complicated is an understatement." Cassaundra drapes her coat across the back of her chair, giving me a grim smile. "We dated for a bit a few years ago. I thought I could handle him and his—quirks. He didn't have room for me in his life, though. I hope you have better luck."

Emery sits next to her, giving me a genuine smile as she hooks arms with Cassaundra.

"Thanks. It's a good thing I have a lot of experience being let down by people. I don't really have any expectations of this." The lie rolls off my tongue easily. I've told myself for over two decades that I don't care if people let me down.

Cassaundra meets my eyes. In that moment I know she can see through the lie because the look she gives me is full of empathy. A look full of knowing. The look of a woman who tried and had her heart broken.

The rest of the group starts to file in. The club has grown significantly; every week it seems a new face arrives. As we settle into our chairs, Cassaundra's eyes widen as she looks over my shoulder.

Turning, I'm met with Charlie's hazel eyes. I follow him as he rounds the empty chair next to me and sits down. Every person is silent as they watch him lean over and kiss my cheek.

I can practically hear the minds exploding. Everyone in this room, except me, has lived here since birth. As I start, I can feel everyone looking between Charlie and me, speculating.

I falter mid-sentence when Charlie reaches over and takes my hand. He squeezes, so I take a breath and continue. "Okay, before we continue to discuss *The Red Tent,* I want to announce August's read. I drew *The Kite Runner* from the jar. We have five paperbacks, but there are more than enough e-books for those of you who prefer."

The rest of the night flies by as everyone is immersed in the discussion. Charlie remains silent, his fingers entwined with mine the entire time. As we wrap up, I say goodbye to everyone before turning to him.

His lips touch mine before I can say anything. I relax into his arms, every ounce of tension leaving me as his lips move over mine.

"I think I'm going to go before this gets pornographic. Lock up behind you."

We pull away from each other, watching as Everett walks to the front desk where everyone is waiting to check out their books. Voices fade as people leave in small groups. Most of the lights flick off, and I hear the faint click of the doors locking.

Grabbing the back of Charlie's head, I kiss him feverishly. Our bodies press together and we knock a few chairs over as he pushes me towards one of the tables. We break apart as he lifts my dress over my head.

I can't believe we're doing this, here, but as Charlie lifts me onto the table, pushing me onto my back, I forget everything but the way his lips feel on my skin.

I arch into his mouth, loving the way he plays my body, making it sing. Every cell is at his mercy, every thought on him.

My panties slide down my legs, a trail of hot kisses following the path down one leg, then leaving a scorching trail up the other leg.

"Charlie," I whimper when I feel his hot breath on my core, a moan escaping my lips when he sucks my clit into his mouth while teasing my pussy with the light glide of his fingertips. My body aches with need, a soft mewling noise fills the silence of the library.

Charlie slips two fingers into me, hooking them as he sucks on my clit harder. I can feel my orgasm building, and then he's gone. His mouth, his fingers, his body, just gone.

I lift my head as he picks me up off the table and sets me on the ground. Turning me, he presses a hand in the center of my back pushing me down until my chest meets the cool top of the table.

He nudges my feet apart, the tip of his cock teasing my pussy until he can't hold back anymore. He slams into me with a growl.

My hands grip the edges of the table, my body moving with the power of his thrusts. One hand holds my hip, while the other grabs a fistful of my hair and pulls with a delicious amount of pressure.

The noises coming from me are obscene, I'm mumbling nonsense as my orgasm surges through my body.

Charlie's body collapses over me, my body shuddering with the aftershocks of one of the best orgasms I've ever had.

"Can't. Breathe," I gasp out.

He chuckles in my ear before pushing up off me. We gather our clothes, dressing in silence. The last time we were together hangs over us. Charlie helps me clean up and we lock up the library. We settle onto a bench outside, the moon lighting up our surroundings.

"I'm not very good at letting people in," I start. "And sometimes, okay most times, I'm not very smart when it comes to recognizing when someone is putting in effort."

I slide down so my neck rests on the back of the bench. Instead of looking at Charlie, I look at the stars as I continue. "I have a tendency to push people's buttons until they get fed up enough and quit trying, it's something I'm working on."

This time he's the one to kiss me quiet.

He pulls back, his eyes looking between mine. "I think I like when you push me. I mean, I hate that I like it, but it's not the worst thing to try to be a bit more—flexible."

He smiles at me, my lips twitching in response.

"And I can work on being a bit more considerate to you when you say no."

Charlie takes my hand and walks me to my car.

"So, you and Cassaundra, huh?" I lean back against my door, grinning when he props a hand on the roof and leans in.

He grimaces. "You heard about that, huh?"

I just wait, enjoying watching him squirm a bit.

"We went out for around six months, but we didn't click. She's a nice person, but we couldn't get past our differences." He runs his nose along my jaw, sending shivers down my spine.

Swallowing, I try to speak, but only a croak comes out. I clear my throat before trying again. "I wasn't worried, I just like putting you on the spot." He nips the sensitive flesh of my neck.

My hand fumbles with the handle until Charlie reaches out and opens the door for me.

"Goodnight, Evie."

Here we Go

Charlie

SEBASTIAN STRETCHES UP onto his back legs, begging to be picked up. I lift him into my arms and scratch his chin. "Bash, you're such a big ol' suck."

He purrs and rubs his face on my jaw. We walk around my spotless house, and as I look around I realize how empty it is. I've never really felt it until recently, but it's like a shadow is hanging overhead, taunting me with what's missing.

Setting Sebastian down, I grab my keys.

When I get to Evie's house, I don't bother knocking. I know the door will be unlocked. Twisting the knob, I frown when I'm right, but I let myself in anyway.

It's early, so I lock the door and head to Evie's bedroom. She's sound asleep, but rouses when I shut the door and sit on the edge of the bed.

"Charlie?" Her voice is sleepy.

"You really should lock your door."

"You're the only person who comes in here, except Natasha." She yawns as she sits up and tucks the sheet under her arms. "I didn't think I was going to see you today."

I shift closer to her, tucking some wayward hair behind her ear. "I need to talk to you, it can't wait."

She leans into my hand, more awake now. "Is everything okay?"

"Not yet."

"Okay…" She watches me carefully, worry etched on her face.

"I don't want to do this anymore."

You get what *You need*

Evie

H E CAN'T DO this anymore? Hurt stabs through me, my stomach seizing as I try to school my features into a look of indifference. I'm failing. I can tell by the look on his face as his eyes flick between mine.

I recall a time when I had that look memorized. It's a look you master when you're constantly told you're not wanted anymore. Apparently, I'm no longer able to hide the hurt, or maybe it's just with Charlie.

I try to sort through why I'm drowning in disappointment. Charlie and I are so different, I don't know why I thought we could work, but part of me thought we just would.

Throwing the covers off, I wrap myself in a robe and move into the kitchen, Charlie following me wordlessly. The bedroom is too intimate.

Licking my lower lip, I steel myself as I search his face. His expression is tense; I don't know what he's waiting for.

He presses his thumb over my lips as I try to speak. "I don't want to just see where this is going. I need a label. I need more than an open-ended question. Can you give me that?"

He wants a label? I'm finding it difficult to keep up, and when his thumb starts tracing my lips my brain shorts out. He caresses my cheek as he slides his hand to the back of my head, pulling my hair a little.

"Evie?"

Licking my lower lip, I nod. This is a rarity, but he's managed to make me speechless.

He crushes his lips to mine sending heat racing through my veins like molten lava. His free arm wraps around my waist pulling me into him.

We move from to kitchen to the living room, barely stopping to breathe, until we fall onto my couch in a tangle of limbs. Charlie grunts when I accidentally bite his lip but deepens the kiss without missing a beat.

I can feel his relief that I didn't argue, but I want to label this too. I want to be able to know we're on the same page. My life may be spontaneous, but Charlie provides me with the stability that I didn't know I was craving until now.

The morning and afternoon fly by in a tangle of limbs and passion, with only a quick break for lunch and to freshen up. Straddling him, I kiss a path to his ear, nipping at the lobe. "So where do we go from here?"

Leaning back, I trail my fingers over his arms basking in his smile.

"I guess we need to plan our first date." He links his fingers through mine, his thumb rubbing circles over my skin. Tingles shoot down my spine from his gentle touch.

"Let's go out now."

"Now?" His thumbs stop, the smile dropping from his face.

"Yeah. We've made this official, we should go on our first official date."

"Now?" he asks again.

Cocking my head, I slowly smile. "Yeah. Now."

Standing, I pull him up from my couch. He doesn't move as I gather my purse and keys. He's still in the same spot as I slip on my shoes.

"But we don't have reservations. Or an idea of what we want to do. We should at least have a discussion about what we want to do. Are you hungry? What do you like to do on a date? This is a small town, our options are limited."

Suppressing a grin, I walk over and take his hand. He follows me, reluctance written across his face. "C'mon. It will all work out."

I finally get him out the door, pushing him towards his car. "Where am I supposed to drive? We haven't picked a destination."

Shaking my head, I walk around the car and arch my brow until he unlocks the door. Once we're settled inside, I buckle up and wait for him to start the car.

"Where are we—." His words are cut off by a wave of my hand.

"Just drive towards Main Street."

He grumbles to himself, his hands clutching the steering wheel as he makes the short drive to Main Street. He keeps glancing at me as he drives, I just sit back and smile to myself.

We're near the end of the street when I finally tell him to park. He just sighs and does what I say. Stress lines his face. I know the effort it's taking for him to pretend to be okay with this.

I take his hand as we step onto the sidewalk, squeezing gently. His hand engulfs mine; I love the way his fingers wrap all the way around. Even before I got to know him, he made me feel safe and steady. After being tossed aside like I meant nothing for years in the foster care system, that feeling is something I don't take for granted.

As we walk along the quaint shops that line Main Street, I don't miss the glances shot in our direction. It's a small town, word has spread about the gnomes and other arguments Charlie and I have gotten into. It shouldn't surprise me that seeing us walk hand in hand will stir up gossip.

Stopping Charlie outside Liliana's, I open the door and lead Charlie inside. The diner is quaint, with cozy booths lining the front windows, and stools sitting in front of the counter. It's tiny, but the food is amazing.

The walls are a pale green and decorated with old photographs of the town throughout the decades. This evening canvases are set up on the tables for a paint night.

"It looks like they're booked for an event tonight, we will have to go somewhere else. This is why you plan ahead," Charlie teases as he tries to lead me out of the diner.

"I know. I sent Liliana a text on our way here asking her to hold two spots." Smirking, I lead Charlie to a booth, pulling him in after me.

"We're painting?"

"Yeah. I've never done a paint night before, but it's wildly popular and I thought it would be fun."

"I don't know how to paint."

"Neither do I. It will be a fun experience, and they walk us through step by step." Taking his hand, I gently squeeze.

People start filing in, more than one person giving us a double take.

Leaning into Charlie I whisper, "I think we're going to be the talk of the town before the night is out."

He looks around the room, finally noticing the attention we're getting. He smirks a little, his hazel eyes light with amusement as he looks down at me. "The joys of small-town living."

"Maybe we should really give them something to talk about."

Before he can respond, I cup the back of his head and kiss him. The scruff on his chin creates a delicious friction that I love. When I first met Charlie, he had the faintest hint of a five o'clock shadow, but lately he's been letting it grow a little and I love it. It seems so out of character, but completely suits him.

As we part and smile at each other, every other sound seems to fade. I don't know how this is going to work with us, but I want to see where this goes. I'm drawn to Charlie in a way I've never experienced. It's terrifying and thrilling. I've never run away from how I feel, I tend to go with it and deal with the outcome. One day that could bite me in the ass, but for now, it's served me well.

Our instructor comes in and talks us through the first steps. Charlie's forehead creases as he focuses, all my attempts to engage him in conversation prove to be ineffective while he's so intent on getting it perfect.

The scene we're painting is a bridge over a stream, trees in the background. It looks familiar to me. "Where have I seen this before?"

Charlie keeps painting, but replies in a whisper, "It's the bridge in the park."

Now that the connection is made, I recognize it. I dip my brush in the paint, trying to follow along. Charlie's painting looks incredible, while mine is not nearly as good.

"How is yours turning out so—perfectly?" I lean into him, holding his arm away as I look at how well the paints are blending, and how natural his bridge looks. Grunting, I return to my painting, glaring at it.

"I'm paying attention." A small smile appears on his lips as I glare at him.

Resisting the urge to stick my tongue out, I follow the final steps. I'm done while Charlie is still adding little details when inspiration strikes.

Turning my canvas away from Charlie, I pick up my small brush and start adding one final detail.

The sound of people talking becomes a quiet roar as everyone shares their final results.

"What are you doing?"

"Adding something."

"Why did you turn it away?"

Turning the canvas towards him, I show him my complete painting. His eyes widen, before he starts to laugh. The diner falls silent, every person staring at Charlie in shock as he continues to laugh and shake his head.

"You can hardly tell that your trees are trees, how did you manage to paint a gnome so clearly?" He rests his arm over the top of the booth, leaning in to check out the gnome.

It's perfectly done. The gnome is standing on the bridge, a bottle of vodka in his hand. I can't explain how I could not paint a tree, but the gnome looks incredible. It's a gift.

"Who knows, maybe gnomes are my spirit guide, my Patronus charm, my emblem. Maybe gnomes are what have always been missing from my life. And not boring garden gnomes. The dirty, inappropriate ones."

The diner is starting to clear out, so we gather our paintings and head back onto the street. Charlie takes my hand as we meander back to his car.

It's been the perfect first date.

Small town
Chatter

Charlie

C HECKING MY LIST, I turn my cart down the pasta aisle. As I'm deciding what I want to make Evie for dinner, another cart rams into mine.

When I turn around, I sigh as I see Darcy's grin.

"Hey, man." He comes to stand next to me, smirking as I pick out some penne noodles.

"Spit it out."

"The town is abuzz with talk about you and Evie. I hear you were walking hand in hand with her last night and shared quite a few looks."

I take the things I need off the shelf, drop them in the basket, and start rolling my cart away from him.

"Do you seriously have nothing better to do than listen to the gossip in this town?"

"Man, it's impossible to avoid. And whether you like it or not, you two are what's hot. Especially since you're laughing, and painting, and overall being less of a stick in the mud."

He stops to grab a few things off the shelf before continuing to follow me.

"Your point?"

"No point, just thought I should let you know."

We finish shopping and head to our cars. Shutting my trunk, I turn to him. "Are we still on for guys' night tomorrow?"

"Yeah." He turns away before angling back towards me. "We're all rooting for you two. Don't fuck it up."

"What makes you think I will be the one to fuck it up?"

He rolls his eyes, opens his car door, and sits down. "Just don't mess this up."

The door shuts before I can say another word.

That night after dinner, Evie and I are cuddling on my deck, looking over my backyard. It's still a mess, but Elliott has made incredible progress on the yard in a short time. All the sod has been dug up where the flower beds are going and, as per my request, been removed from the property.

With July coming to an end, he's hoping to have the stonework complete by the end of August, so in September he can do the planting and the finishing touches.

"I can't believe how fast he works. His parents must be proud."

"His mom is. His father passed away when he was eight."

Evie curls into me, her features pulling into a frown when I tell her that.

"Poor kid. I had no idea. He doesn't talk about them when he comes into the library."

"Yeah. It's a tough subject."

She nods. She doesn't need to say anything; I know exactly how well she understands not having a parent around. Kissing her temple, I breathe the sweet scent of her shampoo.

"Did you just sniff me?"

Her body shakes a bit as she laughs.

Ignoring her, I lift her into my arms and carry her inside.

"Sleep over."

"I can't, I have to be at work by eight for a meeting, and I don't have any overnight things here." She snuggles into my neck, her arms tightening their hold. Before I can try to change her mind, she's mumbling against my neck, "Screw it, I will wake up early."

She starts kissing my neck, moving to my jaw before claiming my lips. Taking the stairs two at a time, I kick my bedroom door shut and lay her on the bed.

Her hair spills onto the pillow, the dark blonde strands creating a halo around her. Evie smiles at me, her eyes dilating as I lift my shirt over my head. Her fingers trail lightly over my skin causing the muscles to twitch in response.

She sits up, removes her shirt, and tosses it to the floor. The rest of our clothes follow, and not a moment too soon I'm kissing my way up her body.

Evie ignites something within me, a passion I never knew I had. Don't get me wrong, I've always enjoyed sex, but sex with Evie is on a level I never knew could exist. Every sound she makes, every movement of her body is erotic.

As I sink into her, there is more than just the need for both of us to reach our release. I want to worship every inch of her body. I want to devour the way she looks with my eyes and capture her noises with my lips.

Evie's spontaneity, her zest for life, intimidates me. There is no sense in denying that I'm secretly envious of the way she lives her life. I don't think I will ever completely abandon my need for order, but when I'm with her, like this, I can forget everything but being in the moment.

"Did you know the entire town is talking about us?" Evie asks.

I'm driving Evie home so she can get ready for work, our

hands linked over the console in my car. The neighbors gawk, waving with unusual force, as we drive by.

"Yeah, I ran into Darcy at the grocery store yesterday."

She shakes her head, chuckling good-naturedly.

"It doesn't bother you?" It bothers me, not that I would ever say anything. Aside from moving, there is no way to avoid town gossip. Not in Mistik Ridge. It's something I don't think I will ever get used to or appreciate about living here.

She shrugs one shoulder. "Not really. It comes from a place of caring. Don't get me wrong, I know that not every person in this town is nice, it's not possible, but for the most part everyone here cares about everyone else. The sense of community here is so prevalent; I even hear kids talk about it. The size of Mistik Ridge is part of what drew me here."

I park my car, letting it idle a moment as I pull her into me and kiss her goodbye. She runs her fingers through my hair with a smile on her face as she exits the car.

Leaning over the console, I stop her from closing the door. "Speaking of community. What do you think of going to the silent auction at the park? I think there are games and there will be grills set up for anyone who is hungry."

"Sounds fun."

She shuts the door and saunters up the driveway, shimmying a little as she unlocks the door. Once she's safe inside, I head back home, smiling the entire way.

I don't remember ever smiling this much, my face actually hurts.

As I get to my house, I decide to bypass it in favor of going to Mom and Dad's.

I park in front of their house, making a mental note to mow the lawn before I go. Bounding up the steps, I let myself in when no one answers the door. I hear the murmur of my parents talking, so I follow the sound to discover them sitting on the deck.

They turn when they hear the sliding door, both greeting me with wide smiles.

"Darling! What a pleasant surprise. I love this new habit of you stopping in." Mom stands from her seat, enveloping me in a tight hug.

Before he can stand, I've bent to embrace dad.

He's made a remarkable recovery from the stroke. All his facial muscle control is back, and his speech is close to normal. His movements don't come easily, but every day he says they get better.

"How's Evie?" Mom asks as she returns from the kitchen with a plate of cookies and some coffee.

Groaning, I accept the coffee. "Seriously? This town doesn't know how to keep quiet. We went on one date."

"And she spent the night at your house last night. That constitutes two dates," Dad teases me.

"I can't believe I'm having this conversation with you two."

"You're not, you haven't really said anything." Mom smiles at me as she bites into a chocolate chip cookie. "I told you she is the perfect tenant. I just knew she would be good for you."

"Jesus, Mom, don't read too much into it. We're seeing how it goes. We're still very different people." I sip my coffee, trying my best to ignore their prying. They soon give up, but I know the reprieve won't last long.

"You should invite her over for dinner. I see her on occasion around town, but I would love to get to know her, and your father hasn't met her yet." And there it is, I didn't even make it through one cup of coffee.

"I will ask her if you promise to drop the subject of Evie."

I smile indulgently when she concedes.

The sun shines down on us as we visit, talking about anything and everything, except Evie. I update them on how my yard is coming along and give them Elliott's card when Dad says he wouldn't mind getting some landscaping done.

Before I know it, a few hours have gone by and my stomach is growling.

"Why don't you stay for lunch?"

"Okay, but in exchange I'm going to mow the lawn."

I ignore my dad's protests and grab the lawnmower from the shed. As I mow, I find the sound of the lawnmower almost lulls me into random daydreams. All of which Evie is the star. She seems to occupy most of my thoughts throughout the day, especially since I don't have much work to do to get ready for the school year in a month.

It's easy to think of all the things I want to do with Evie. The silent auction event in the park is just one of the many town events Mistik Ridge does over the summer. July is usually a wash for me since I'm gone, but August is busy.

There is the town carnival. The end of summer dance. The talent show. Not to mention events for singles, and events for couples. Like the moonlit carriage ride.

I want to take Evie to all these things. It's become a craving to be close to her. To spend time with her. At first I thought it was so I could keep an eye on whatever scheming plan she could possibly come up with, but now I know it's more.

Shutting off the lawnmower, I'm walking towards the gate when I hear my name. Cassaundra greets me when I turn around. She's barely covered in tight shorts and a low-cut tank top.

"I've been hoping to run into you." She props her hands on her hips, catching her breath.

"Why?"

Ever since we went out, Cassaundra hasn't gone out of her way to talk to me. Cocking my head to the side, I wait to hear what she has to say.

She licks her lips, her eyes flicking between mine as I arch a brow when she doesn't say anything right away. Finally, she sighs, glances away, and then locks eyes with me. "Here's the thing. I like Evie. And I know you and how you are in relationships, yet something with her makes you yield. I just don't want to see either of you get hurt, so be careful. You have some hard limits, and I don't know if she fully understands that yet."

She pulls the rubber band out of her hair, before smoothing it out and tying it up into a messy bun on her head.

"Anyway, I know it's none of my business. But I just spotted you and wanted to say something. I hope things work out for you two. She's softened you in a way I never thought possible."

Without waiting for me to respond she takes off at a jog again, slipping her earbuds into her ears.

Gossip and *Gnomes*

Evie

"**W**HY DO YOU have three gnomes in your window?" Everett sits next to Tash on my couch, propping his feet onto the coffee table.

Both he and Tash gape at me when I hand them coasters, but I ignore the looks.

"Charlie is holding my gnomes hostage. These are the ones I've gotten back. They're sitting in the window until their brothers and sisters are home."

"What she's not telling you is that she has a second wave hiding in her basement."

"Shh. Don't give away all my secrets."

Crossing my legs, I hug a pillow to my stomach and grin at my friends. Charlie is having guys' night, so I thought it would be a good opportunity to catch up with my two best friends.

"Do I even want to know what you need to do to get them back?" Everett asks with a grimace.

Throwing the pillow I'm holding at him, I laugh. "He brings them in lieu of flowers."

I pick up my beer, grinning as I look at the gnomes staring out my window. It's been too long since I've put any in his flower beds.

Chewing on my lip, I look over at my friends.

"What do you say we break out the new batch of gnomes and take a walk?"

Tash's eyes light up, her lips spreading in a slow smile. "Yes. Oh, hell yes."

Jumping up from my spot, I run downstairs to grab the box. Everett and Tash already have their shoes on, ready to go.

"Did you find any new levels of vulgarity?"

"Yes, they have some nasty ones, but kids see them, so I didn't buy the really bad ones. But I couldn't resist the hilarious one that's bent over like he's throwing up."

We open the box and each dig out a gnome. Locking up, we start the short walk to Charlie's house.

The night is clear, the moon lighting our path as we walk. My skin feels sticky by the time we're crossing Charlie's lawn, the humidity in the air making it feel ten degrees warmer.

We bicker back and forth as we place the gnomes in Charlie's flower beds, trying out different spots but not able to agree. Headlights illuminate the street, so we duck behind a tree giggling like teenagers toilet papering a house. The car passes by, and we play around a little more before we finally settle on their spots, we situate the gnomes and start to walk back to my house.

"I still can't believe he's actually giving them back to you." Everett chuckles as he glances back one last time. "That's so— un-Charlie."

Natasha hooks her arms through mine and Everett's, giving him a sly smirk. "We know she pushes his buttons in all the right ways."

Smacking her arm, I laugh. "C'mon. How many people have truly tried to push his limits? He's not as uptight as I thought."

"Oh give me a break. The man is rigid. He's one compulsion away from full blown OCD. He's just yielding more to you than he ever has before. That's why none of his previous relationships have lasted, not because his girlfriends didn't try, but because Charlie would never concede to anything. With you, he's different."

Tash's words send warmth flowing through my veins. He has definitely become more relaxed, while maintaining most of his routines. I see the change, and yet the urge is still there to push him. To see how far I can go.

It's something I know I need to suppress. I tend to push people past their limits so that when they give up on me I can say it's because they couldn't accept me. With Charlie, I see how much he is trying to compromise with me, and for the first time I'm trying to show him the same courtesy.

We may be opposites, but we're the same in that we drive people away with our own cycles.

As we settle back onto my couches, Tash crosses her legs and leans forward. "I can't believe I have to ask this, but aren't you at all curious to hear the gossip going around about you and Charlie?"

I know she's using me and Charlie as a distraction from her own problems, problems which she refuses to talk about by saying "I'm working out my options," but I still shake my head. "Not really."

"Come on!" She bounces on the spot, folding her hands together and holding them out.

"Puppy eyes and begging doesn't work on me." I knock back the rest of my beer, setting the bottle back onto the coaster.

"Whatever, I'm going to tell you anyway." She taps her chin, clucking her tongue as she thinks. "The most bizarre one I heard is that you and Charlie had a one-night stand and now you're pregnant, which is why you're dating."

"Oh, I heard that one too!" Everett chips in. "Although, I

think the weirdest one I heard is that you're not actually dating, that you're using Charlie to make Guy jealous."

"Seriously? Guy? I've spent time with him once, and Charlie was there."

"People are also wagering on when you and Charlie will break up." The humor fades from Tash's voice at that one, but it makes me laugh.

"I'm not really surprised by that one. Didn't you say Charlie's longest relationship was six months with Cassaundra?" I wrap my arms around my knees, resting my chin on them.

"Yeah, she held on the longest. They never had any hope, though, Charlie wasn't as invested in the relationship as she was." Natasha jumps over to the couch I'm sitting on, wrapping an arm around my shoulders. "I don't think I've seen Charlie look at anyone the way he does you."

Locking up the library, I smile when I see Charlie leaning against my car with a gnome in his hands. He holds it out to me, leaning down to kiss me on my cheek.

Tucking a hair behind my ear, he asks, "How was book club?"

"It felt long today. I'm not feeling well, and everyone was exceptionally chatty." I lean my head into his hand as he cups my cheek, my eyes closing as his thumb runs over my cheekbone.

"Why don't you follow me home and I will cook you dinner?" He opens my door for me, taking my bag and setting it on the back seat.

"That sounds really nice."

Once we're at his house, he pushes me towards the couch, covering me with a blanket before heading into the kitchen with the promise of a cup of tea. I sink into his couch, laying my head on the armrest. Sebastian hops up, circling a few times before he settles onto my lap.

I stroke his soft fur, his purring lulling me into a deeper

relaxation. Maybe I should get a cat, it would be nice to have someone to come home to.

The couch dips, a soft touch brushing my hair off my forehead. "Evie?"

"Hmmm." Opening my eyes, I look up into his warm hazel eyes. "I'm sorry, I didn't mean to fall asleep."

He leans down and kisses my forehead, smiling. "I like seeing you sleeping on my couch with my cat. He doesn't like too many other people."

"He's adorable. I've never had a pet. I should add that to my list."

Sitting up, I adjust Sebastian on my lap. He yawns and stretches his paws out, kneading them on my leg.

"I've had Sebastian for five years, I think I've told you that before, and I can't imagine going a day without him now." He looks at his cat affectionately until the timer on the oven beeps, interrupting us. "Dinner is ready."

Following him into the kitchen, I grin at the precise way he's set the table until I notice the candles he's lit and the gnome sitting next to my placemat.

"Two gnomes in one night? Am I forgetting a special occasion?" He pulls out my chair for me before setting a steaming casserole on the waiting mat.

He serves me first, the layers of cheese, veggies, and beef steaming from my plate.

"No occasion, you were just muttering about gnomes in your sleep so I thought I would set one by your placemat." He glances over at it, grimacing. "Maybe we can put it on the floor while we eat, though."

Laughing, I set the vomiting gnome on the floor where Sebastian proceeds to rub his cheeks on it. "Sebastian likes the gnome; I don't understand why you're so adverse to them."

"They're disgusting. What happened to the cute gnomes? The sleeping ones, or the ones with rosy cheeks and red hats."

"He's wearing a red hat…"

"He's also bent in half as he throws up." Charlie looks at me in exasperation as I sit there and grin.

"It's funny." I finish eating, setting my fork and knife on top on my plate. "Charlie, that was amazing. I can't believe you just whipped that up."

"It's really easy. The longest part is waiting for it to bake." He motions for me to stay in my seat as he clears the table. He moves about the kitchen, cleaning up and wrapping up the leftovers.

He turns on the kettle, then sits back at the table watching as Sebastian sleeps next to the gnome. "I guess they are kind of funny."

I widen my eyes, clutching my chest as I feign passing out in shock. "I never thought I would hear you say that."

"Don't tell anyone, I have a reputation to protect." He winks at me, standing as the kettle whistles.

I close my mouth, aware that I'm gaping at him. How is this the same Charlie from three months ago? He still has all the same quirks, his kitchen cleaning routine is eyebrow raising, but he also smiles more and lets little things go.

He hands me a cup of tea. I hold it up, inhaling the comforting smell of peppermint.

"Do you mind if we sit on the couch?" I ask.

He nods, holding his hand out for mine. He squeezes as I slip my hand in his, leading us into the living room. I settle in between his legs, laying back onto his chest.

We fall into a comfortable silence as we drink our tea. The rise and fall of his chest relaxes me as I soak up his warmth and the warmth of the cup in my hand.

My head still feels fuzzy, but for the first time since I was a child, someone is taking care of me and I'm letting them.

Charlie flips on the TV, loading Netflix. We settle on *This Is Where I Leave You,* his hands rubbing my arms as Jason Bateman comes onto the screen. As much as I love this movie, I'm soon dozing off in Charlie's arms.

Meet the Parents

Charlie

EVIE RUNS HER hands over her thighs as we park in my parent's driveway. She gets out of the car, her teeth chewing on her lower lip.

I cup the back of her neck, pressing my lips against hers. "You've already met my mom, and my dad is awesome. Don't be nervous."

"Easy for you to say, you don't need to go through this. Everyone in my life you already know." Her voice is sharp, her eyes narrowing as she lashes out at me.

Cringing, I don't say anything as I lead her to the door. She's right, I don't have to go through the "meet the parents" situation. And any girlfriends I've had I've already known the woman's parents.

When we stop at the door, she turns to face me. "I'm sorry, that wasn't fair."

"No, you're right. I haven't ever gone through this. I know they will love you. My mom was telling me I should make a move back in May."

"I do like your mom." She smiles, finally relaxing as I knock on the door before opening it.

Mom calls us from the kitchen, so I lead Evie through the house letting her check out the photos as we pass. She starts giggling when she sees one of me in a Speedo from my swimming days.

"Man, those are tiny."

She's still giggling when we walk into the kitchen.

"The swimming photo?" Dad smiles.

I grimace and nod. "This is my dad, Bryan. And you've met my mom before."

She shakes their hand, smiling at both of them. "Yeah, the bathing suit is funny, but his little chicken legs were what really got me."

Grunting, I scowl at her and my parents as they laugh. Mom brings over a tray that is overflowing with cookies and squares. Once she's brought us each a cup of coffee, she sits down next to Evie falling into easy conversation with her.

I sit back and watch as Evie fits right into my family. There is no awkwardness as they get to know each other. No weird silences or uncomfortable moments.

My chest seizes with the realization that despite our differences, Evie has seamlessly blended into every aspect of my life.

I hear bits and pieces of their conversation, but I pay close attention when I hear my mom ask, "Is there anyone from your childhood that you still keep in contact with?" Mom has that look in her eyes, the look that says her heart is breaking and I know how hard listening to Evie's past must be for her.

Mom lost her own mother as a toddler, but she at least had her father and her siblings. Evie didn't have anyone consistent.

"No. After I went through the emancipation process, all I wanted was to distance myself from that world. I lived with other kids I got along with, and some that scared the shit out of me. No one I connected with enough to try to maintain contact with, though." She shrugs her shoulders, a sure sign that while she's at peace with her childhood she still wishes she could share stories about adventures with her siblings and parents.

Wrapping my arm around her, I tuck her into my side and kiss her temple.

Mom practically preens as she watches the public display.

"Well, it sounds like you've found some good people here," Dad chimes in, smiling softly at Evie.

Evie leans into me, smiling back. She's not even fazed by some of the lingering issues from my dad's stroke. "I have. I like living in a small town."

She takes another piece of brownie, mumbling her appreciation as she takes a bite. By the time we leave, the plate of treats is almost gone. Mom and Dad both give Evie a hug, inviting her over any time she wants to visit.

As we drive away, I glance over at her. "Well?"

"I love them. Charlie, you seriously have the best parents." She starts talking about all of their amazing qualities, filling me with pride as she speaks.

It's easy to take them for granted, but when I think about the multitudes of "parents" that Evie has gone through, I realize I need to appreciate them a little more.

That's something Evie continues to teach me, not to take anything for granted. I've started to appreciate things more than I ever have before, see things in a different light. It terrifies me how easily she's brought about change in my life.

Many have tried, she's the only one who's succeeded.

I wave at Elliott as I dial Mom and Dad's number. He's digging a trench where a new flower bed is going to go, prepping the area for the stones. When we were going over the design, he encouraged me to go with stones rather than bricks. I was skeptical, but looking at what he's done so far, I'm glad I took his advice.

Mom picks up after the second ring.

"Hi, sweetheart, how are you?" Mom's cheerful voice comes over the phone.

"Good. I'm just watching Elliott work. He's finished one of the flower beds. The stonework looks amazing." I go back into the house, bending to scratch Sebastian on the head.

"I can't wait to see it. So, I need to tell you how much I enjoyed visiting with Evie the other day. I liked her when I met her, but she's so sweet. Both your father and I absolutely love her."

I grin as she gushes about everything she likes about Evie.

When she finally pauses to take a breath I interject, "I'm glad you like her, but I want to ask you a question."

"Oh, sorry, honey."

"Your anniversary is coming up." I pause.

"I know." Mom is trying not to laugh, but she's failing.

"I want to send you and Dad on a trip since you had to cancel your plans this spring." Mom and Dad were going to go to Greece, but with Dad's stroke they had to postpone.

"Charlie, that's very sweet, but it's too expensive." Mom is quick to refuse, which I knew would happen.

"Too bad. It's already booked."

She huffs out a breath, mumbling something about stubborn men. "And I'm guessing it's non-refundable."

"Yes. That would be correct. You leave in a week. It's a three-week holiday." Grinning, I listen to her relaying the information to Dad. I can hear his grumbling voice in the background telling me I shouldn't have.

"This is too much."

"No, Mom, it's not. You guys deserve this after everything.

Go, have fun, and when you get back, we will have a cookout in my newly finished backyard."

Dad comes on the phone, thanking me. We catch up a little, I listen to him rave about Evie for fifteen minutes until we finally hang up.

Heading back outside, I call Elliott over to take a break for lunch. I don't think they've ever went on about one of my girlfriends the way they just did about Evie. What is it about her that makes people so drawn to her?

Powdery Mildew

Evie

SLIPPING MY FEET into my flip flops, I head out into the backyard to work on the garden. I've seen Charlie almost every night since we agreed to become an official couple, but I know he won't excuse me from maintaining the yard.

The backyard doesn't take long to finish, I weed the flower beds and pick the dandelions from the lawn. Once the lawn is mowed, I head to the front.

As I'm working the soil in the flowerbed, I notice a white film developing on one of the bushes. What the hell is that?

Snapping a photo, I text it to Natasha.

> **Natasha:** That looks like powdery mildew. Water down some milk and pour it on the mildew. It should take care of it.

> **Me:** Thanks, Tash. You know how Charlie is. I don't know how I haven't caught it before now.

> **Natasha:** It's because it's been so humid lately. It doesn't look too bad, I wouldn't worry.

Checking the rest of the shrubs, I groan when I notice that another shrub has it and it's way worse than on the first one.

Oh no. My neglect over the past couple of weeks is going to bite me in the ass. Racing into the house, I dig under the sink and find a spray bottle. Mixing up the milk and water, I rush back outside and start spraying.

After I mow the lawn, I check over the leaves despite knowing it's too soon to see any difference.

"Tash, not only did the milk not help, but it's now spread to the third shrub. All the shrubs in the bed have it. What am I going to do?" Cradling the phone between my shoulder and ear, I peek out the window.

I've been avoiding Charlie for the past three days, trying to get the mildew under control. I've told him I'm sick, which wasn't a lie, but I'm feeling better and I won't be able to use that as an excuse for long.

"I hate to say it, you're going to have to dig them out. That shit will spread over the rest of the plants. Get the shrubs out of there before it spreads to the perennials."

Groaning, I head to the shed in the back and get the things I need.

"He's going to flip his shit."

"It's not your fault."

"Tash, you know how he is with those beds. He meticulously planned out the shrubs and flowers." I walk to the front of the yard, halting when I see Charlie looking at the shrubs, his hands resting on his hips with a scowl on his face. "He's here, and he looks pissed. I need to go."

Hanging up, I walk over to him with my supplies.

"What is this?" He gestures to the white film covering the leaves.

"It's called powdery mildew. It's spread to all three shrubs. Tash says I need to remove them before it spreads more."

He clenches his jaw, checking the perennials for any sign of the mildew. "How did this happen?"

"I've been distracted lately, and when I've watered I haven't looked as closely as I should have." Stepping over to him, I rest my hand on his arm. "I'm so sorry."

He steps away, grabbing the shovel I've brought with me.

"Evie, I need you to be consistent with looking after the yard. This is unacceptable. How could you let this happen? The rental agreement specifically states that the flower beds need to be maintained."

"I know." Wringing my hands together, I watch as he digs out each shrub. His movements are jerky, his jaw clenching and unclenching with each shovelful of dirt.

Once all three shrubs are out of the bed and in the compost bin, he cleans off the gardening tools and returns them to the shed.

I'm waiting in the living room, ready for him. "I know you're mad, but it's an honest mistake."

I grab a pillow and hug it to my chest, watching him.

"I need to know I can count on you. Regardless of whether we're dating, you still need to follow the expectations of renting this house. I know you don't think it matters, but these things are important. I guess you wouldn't understand, not ever being a homeowner, but they do. Just because you don't own this house doesn't mean you shouldn't look after it as though you do."

He's pacing the living room as he continues to scold me for my irresponsibility. Cringing each time he reprimands me, I can feel my own anger building as he lists all my flaws.

Is this how it's going to be? Everything is fine, he's relaxing, and then one small thing sets him off? It's almost as though he's just holding in his obsessive need for order and routine just to appease me until it explodes.

"And what is with the mess in here?"

"Stop." Jumping up from the couch, I move to stand in front of Charlie. "I made a mistake, I get it, but you need to quit attacking me for every little thing just because you're upset about the shrubs."

"Okay, you're right, it's your choice if you want to live in a disaster zone, but it's not your choice to look after the flower beds, it's something you agreed to when you signed a two-year lease. And you did not follow through on that agreement." He crosses his arms, his non-apology just pissing me off more.

"You're right, and what you haven't done is given me a chance to rectify that. Now you may own this house, but I still live here, and I want you to leave."

"Seriously?"

"Yes. I have work to do and you need to calm down. I will see you tomorrow at the auction in the park." I cross my arms and wait while he walks away and out the door.

Once he drives away, I grab my keys and head to the Mistik Ridge Greenhouse. Natasha told me they should have the same shrubs to replace the ones Charlie had to dig up.

By the time I get home, my stomach is grumbling. The temporary replacements I bought are similar, but not identical to the ruined shrubs. That's not going to help matters with Charlie.

Sticky Fingers

Charlie

THE PARK IS full of people wandering around and laughing. Guy and Darcy come sauntering over, red Solo cups in hand.

We greet each other, watching the spectacle around us.

"Where is Evie?" Darcy crosses his arms, scowling at me. He caught Evie planting new shrubs last night and then proceeded to call me and ream me out.

"She said she would meet me here." I look around the crowd, maybe we should have given an exact location.

It feels like the entire town is here.

"Darcy tells me you flipped out on her last night." Guy shakes his head at me.

"I might have lost my cool."

Before he can pry further, Evie breaks through the crowd and walks over to us, Tash and Everett in tow. "Hey, guys!"

Evie doesn't come to hug me, but she does smile at me. Closing the distance, I place my hands on her hips and walk her backwards until her back hits a tree. Keeping one hand on her hip, I plant the other one next to her head.

Leaning down, I look into her eyes. "I'm sorry. I know these things happen and it wasn't fair for me to get so mad. And it was really shitty of me to lash out about you as a person. It's not fair for me to expect you to keep your space the way I would mine."

She leans her head against the tree, her eyes flicking between mine.

Holding my breath, I resist the urge to keep talking. My mouth gets me in trouble sometimes, case in point, last night. I think she knows she's making me uncomfortable when she smirks at me.

"Okay. But just so you're warned, you speak to me like that again and the gnome incident will seem like child's play."

She pulls me down for a kiss, her soft lips brushing against mine. Teasing me. We kiss until our friends start cat-calling us, drawing the attention of our friends and neighbors.

Parting, Evie laughs softly as she tucks her hair behind her ear.

"I guess we're giving them something else to talk about. You won't believe this, but someone stopped me as I was searching for you to ask how far along I am." She looks down at her flat stomach, grinning humorously.

"Some people have no boundaries." I take her hand and we walk back towards our friends.

Now that we're all here, we wander through the park. Booths are set up with food, gifts, and games. I buy Evie some cotton candy before we make our way to the auction tables. As we come to the first table, I hear Darcy swear under his breath.

"This year's charity is the inn?" he asks, his tone hard.

Natasha's cheeks flush as she meets all our eyes and nods. Evie doesn't seem surprised, neither does Guy.

"What's going on?" I ask Natasha softly, edging Evie and her away from the crowd.

"Money is tight since I had to replace a section of the roof last year. I need to renovate some of the rooms, but I don't have the funds. When Liliana was organizing the auction, she came to see me and noticed right away that the inn could use some work. The town council voted, and they want this year's profits to go to the inn since it's been part of the town for seventy-five years." She shrugs, trying to appear nonchalant.

Evie suggests taking a look at what there is to bid on to Tash, quickly linking arms with her and leading her away. Their heads are bent together as Evie whispers to her.

"I can't fucking believe it," Darcy growls, glaring at Natasha.

"Dude, chill," Guy warns.

We move along the tables, stopping to bid on different things. I get why Darcy is mad, his family used to own the property and the inn, at that time it was their house. His grandparents sold it when they fell on hard times, forcing Darcy and his parents to move into town.

Five years ago, the inn went up for sale while we were on our annual summer road trip and Tash bought it.

Darcy grumbles but drops the subject.

After we finish with the auction, we make our way to the stage. Mrs. Jesperson waves from where she talks to Pastor Larry. A local band will be playing this afternoon, they're quite good so we settle in to wait for the show.

"Tell me about this band." Evie presses her back into my chest and looks up at me.

"They're called *Wanderlust*. It's a duet, two local girls. They're nineteen and twenty-two, sisters. They're really good and can play a wide range of music." Leaning down to touch her lips with mine, I love how she relaxes even more into me.

The crowd goes wild as Wanderlust comes onto the stage, waving and smiling. As they start to play, Evie sways to the music as she eats her cotton candy. Her fingers are pink and blue from the sugary treat, but she doesn't seem to mind.

It doesn't take her long to devour the rest of her cotton candy. I throw away the plastic bag it came in, catching one hand in mine.

Our friends are watching the show, but I'm watching Evie as I suck one finger into my mouth, licking every trace of sugar from it before moving to the next finger.

Her breath catches as I suck on each of her fingers until they are all clean. Dropping her hand, I weave my fingers through her hair and crush my lips to hers. Deepening the kiss, I revel in the sweet taste of her mouth. A mixture of cotton candy and Evie.

Parting, she grabs my hand. "Do you mind if we go?"

"God no."

Snickers follow us as I lead Evie through the crowd. The walk to my house seems to take forever, but soon we're naked in my bed, Evie lowering herself onto my cock.

She looks stunning as she moves, her blonde hair messy from my fingers. Her lips, a little swollen from my scruff, quirk in a smile, catching me staring.

Her pussy starts clenching around me, her body quivering as she rides out her orgasm. Sitting up, I wrap my arm around her hips and flip her onto her back. I chase my own release, never straying from the lure of her eyes.

After I clean up, I wrap her into my arms and watch her fall asleep. She looks so peaceful, a soft smile on her lips as she sleeps. She frustrates the hell out of me, challenges me in a way no one ever has before, and even though I worry that our different way of approaching the world will be the downfall to this, I can't imagine not being with her. How can I be so committed after such a short amount of time?

Surprises

Evie

CHARLIE HUGS HIS parents, watching them walk into the terminal before we pull away from the airport. The drive back to Mistik Ridge is long, so I crank the music and start singing along.

I turn to Charlie in surprise when he turns it down. "Why did you do that?"

"It's unsafe to drive with the music that loud. I can't hear if there are any emergency vehicles approaching that would need me to move."

Grinning at him, I turn it back up. "You don't need to turn it that low. We would still be able to hear sirens."

He grits his teeth, adjusting the volume once again. "I don't feel comfortable with it that loud. When you drive, you can determine how loud you want the music, but in my car, leave the dial alone."

Tucking my foot under the opposite leg, I leave the volume alone. Charlie didn't give me a hard time about the different shrubs, but he's regressing in other areas and losing much of the flexibility I was starting to see.

189

We drive silently until the town comes into view. As Charlie slows the car, driving down Main Street, I'm surprised when he parks outside of Liliana's.

"What are we doing here?"

"It's a surprise." Staring at him, I follow him slowly to the sidewalk and into the diner. It's set up for another paint night. Charlie turns to me, a proud smile on his face. I'm at a loss for words as we sit in the same booth as last time. One moment he is arguing with me about music in the car and the next he is surprising me with a paint night.

Wrapping my arms around him, I kneel in the booth so I can rest my chin on his shoulder. "This is a good surprise. Thank you."

"It's not the only one I have planned for this evening." He turns his head and kisses me.

Less heads turn this time; we're slowly losing the interest of the townsfolk. It's kind of a relief, if they were still watching and waiting for us to fail I would feel like there is this overhanging doom on us.

We start painting, this time I'm set on doing a better job. As we continue to add layers, I grumble about Charlie's painting looking better than mine. He smirks at my ramblings.

"Yours isn't that bad." He chuckles as the colors that are supposed to blend together mix into a muddy color.

"Don't be a condescending ass." Picking up my small brush I threaten to add paint to his canvas. He fends me off, glaring at me.

Giving up on matching what the final product is supposed to look like, I start adding random things. I paint a couple gnomes, a T-Rex, and a spaceship.

Liliana walks by, doubling back when she catches sight of my additions. Busting out laughing, she leans on the back of the booth to take a closer look.

"I think I like your version better, Evie."

Charlie looks over and shakes his head. He rinses his brushes off, his canvas done and close to perfect. His field of flowers is vibrant and the colors blend together perfectly.

"Charlie, you should let Evie add a gnome to your painting." Liliana laughs, walking away.

Picking up my paintbrush, I wave it in the air. "I think that's a wonderful idea."

"I think we better pack up and go. Our evening has just begun." He slides out of the booth, holding his hand out to help me.

"Where are we going?" I pick up my painting, following him back to the car.

"No hints." He opens my door, taking my painting before closing the door behind me.

We drive out of town, down country roads I've never taken the time to explore. I have to admit this side of Charlie is surprising, although it's clear he has a plan.

I lose track of where we're going, enjoying the fields of canola, wheat, and oats. We turn down another country road, the fields disappearing as trees loom up on both sides of the road creating a canopy of leaves.

Charlie slows the car, turning into a parking lot. Perking up, I look around until I see the sign announcing we're at the Mistik Ridge Botanical Gardens.

The parking lot is full of flowers and neatly trimmed shrubs. Crossing the parking lot, we come up to a cluster of buildings. They look like they belong in a fairy tale with gables, shutters, and window boxes full of flowers.

Charlie leads me to the closest one, paying our way in as I continue to look around. Another building advertises a gift shop, another a restaurant, the other building houses the butterfly garden and the tropical garden.

We pass through the arch leading into the gardens. A hand painted sign points to the different areas. We decide to make our way through the Japanese Garden first. Charlie takes my hand as we walk the path, looking at gorgeous fountains and tidy flowerbeds. The entire trail centers around creating a feeling of peace.

When we get to the end of the trail, I see a large rectangle of pure white sand. There are rakes and stones off to the side.

"Is that a life-size Zen Garden?"

Charlie nods, allowing me to drag him over there. We place rocks throughout the rectangle, before picking up the rakes and creating a pattern through the sand. We make waves and circles and straight lines.

Charlie has a smile on his face the entire time as we work side by side. When we step back to look at our handiwork, I lean into him.

"This is so much fun. I didn't even know this place exists."

We put the rakes back onto their rack and head back down the path. We meander through the rest of the gardens, admiring the flowers, fountains, and decorations.

Charlie checks the time as we're about to head into the Butterfly Garden.

"We have reservations in the restaurant in five minutes. We should head that way."

"But we didn't get to see the butterflies or the tropical garden." I start to reach for the door, but Charlie tugs me away.

"I know, but we can't be late. We have reservations."

"I'm sure it will be okay if we're five or ten minutes late."

"No, we can't be late." A muscle tics in Charlie's jaw.

"Charlie, we can walk through and be right outside the restaurant." Tugging my hand out of his, I open the door and wait.

He clenches his jaw but walks through. I gaze around at the thousands of butterflies fluttering around. The fragrant scent of flowers fills the humid room. There are dishes with sugar water throughout the room for the butterflies.

I've never seen so many different types. I can't name any of them, aside from the monarch butterfly, but they're all beautiful.

Quickening my step when Charlie disappears into the tropical room, I follow him through trying to see as much as I can while keeping up.

By the time we're at the hostess's desk in the restaurant, we're only two minutes late for our reservation and no one is present at the desk.

"See, we're barely late and they're not even here." I sit down on the wooden bench, trailing my fingers over the intricately carved flowers, before turning back to Charlie with a smirk on my face.

"That's not the point. I hate being late. One or two minutes, it doesn't matter. It's disrespectful." He paces away from me, peeking into the restaurant.

A woman comes rushing over to us looking flustered as she grabs a couple of menus.

"Hi, Charlie, sorry. We had a bit of a dishwasher emergency."

She leads us to a secluded booth, the black leather shining under the low lighting of the restaurant. The dark, mahogany tabletop is glossy and smooth.

The woman hurries away.

"Don't be grumpy. It's been such a nice day so far."

"I just wish that you would show a little more respect for my boundaries. Some things I won't change, and you need to be okay with that." He leans back as a young guy in black slacks and a white button-up shirt places two waters on the table.

He nods at Charlie before turning to me and winking. Charlie scowls at him, clearing his throat.

"My name is Matt, and I will be your server this evening. Would you like to hear the specials?" He looks between us, a broad smile on his face.

I nod and listen as he goes over the different specials they have. By the time he's done my mouth is watering. Matt leaves us to decide, but I don't open my menu.

"Okay, I see what you're saying. Next time can you tell me we have a reservation so we can hit all the sights? That way we don't run into this issue again." I reach my hand across the table to cup his cheek. "Can we please not fight anymore?"

He turns his head to kiss my palm, a small smile pulling the corners of his lips up. "Of course."

Matt comes back, taking our orders and then disappearing again.

Now that tension is no longer radiating from Charlie, I look around a little more. The design of the restaurant is simple, yet elegant.

The lights are dim, yet not so dim that my eyes feel strained. The fixtures are brushed glass with little flowers etched in them. The tables are dark mahogany, and the chairs smooth black leather.

To offset the darkness of the furniture, the linens are a pale green and the restaurant is full of gorgeous orchids.

"This place is so beautiful."

"Mmhmmm. They have weddings here all the time, and photo shoots. This is where the graduating class comes for their ceremony."

Matt comes back once more with our dinners. My clam chowder smells delectable, and as I spoon the first taste into my mouth I moan in pure bliss.

"Oh. My. God. This is so good." Resisting the urge to pick up my bowl and just suck the soup back, I savor it spoonful by spoonful.

Looking over at Charlie, his fork is hovering in the air as he watches me eat.

"What?"

"I'm just waiting for you to stick your face in the bowl. If I reach over there, what are the chances you will bite me?" He takes his bite, chewing slowly.

"The chances are pretty high, so I wouldn't risk it." I wink at him, returning to my soup.

As we finish our meal, Matt returns to clear our dishes.

"Are you interested in the dessert menu?"

"Yes, thanks," Charlie replies without looking at Matt.

Charlie leans on the table, his hazel eyes warm as he holds my gaze.

"Why are you staring?" I smile, feeling my cheeks flush a little under his scrutiny.

"You're incredibly beautiful, Evie, why wouldn't I want to stare at you?" He grins as I shrug.

Feeling oddly bashful, I'm grateful when Matt returns with the dessert menu. Flipping through it, it doesn't take me long to decide what I want.

"What are you getting?" Charlie closes the tiny leather-bound book.

"The white chocolate brownie. It looks absolutely scrumptious."

"Good choice."

We place our order, Charlie reaching across to take my hand in his. My body heats up as his thumb strokes small circles over my hand.

The air sparks between us over dessert, the low lights and stars shining through the glass peak in the ceiling creating one of the most romantic environments I've ever been in.

The brownie is amazing, but it loses its flavor when Charlie moves into the booth next to me, sliding my hair away from my neck so he can press a soft kiss just below my ear. My body shivers as he kisses where my neck meets my shoulder. And when he moves the strap of my top to kiss my shoulder, I give up on trying to savor my brownie.

Matt comes with the check, leaving without a word. Charlie pays, helps me out of the booth, and we're on the road home within five minutes.

Charlie holds my hand the entire way home, our earlier spat forgotten. This has been one of the best days I've had. As I look at Charlie's profile, his face lit up in the white light of the moon, I realize that I'm falling for this rigid, handsome, and surprisingly sweet man.

The revelation doesn't frighten me because things with Charlie feel right. Despite our differences, we work, and I never want this feeling to go away.

Jealousy *and Distance*

Charlie

G UY PARKS HIS car outside the library. We grab the paperwork we've brought with us and head inside. Evie has been working long shifts at the library this week and I haven't seen her since our date at the botanical gardens.

Evie is at the desk with Everett, laughing and gesturing as she tells him something. Everett waves at us as we walk in the door, Evie turns and smiles at me before returning to her story.

We spread out at a table close to the desk, I open the binder with my lesson plans and look at the emails outlining new material we need to incorporate.

Evie comes over and wraps her arms around me from behind, kissing my cheek. She talks with Guy briefly about his project and looks at me quizzically when Darcy doesn't do more than say hi before returning to the stack of papers before him.

"Okay then. Are you here for a while?" She rests her chin on my shoulder.

"I'm going to work until your break and then we can go grab something to eat really quick."

"Okay." She kisses my cheek once more and heads back to the desk.

Marking changes in my existing lesson plans, I keep getting distracted by Evie and Everett's explosive laughter. The three of us stare over at them as Evie doubles in half, her hand resting on Everett's arm.

Shaking my head, I try to focus back on my work, but I find myself watching them. I knew Evie and Everett had become close friends, but I've never really watched them interact.

My blood boils when I see her wrap her arms around him in a hug. He says something and her responding smile is so huge I want to knock him on his ass.

I feel a finger jab into my shoulder. Turning to face the table, I glare at Guy who is sitting there and giving me a stern look. "They're just friends."

"I know."

"Apparently your facial muscles disagree." Guy leans back and crosses his arms.

"Shut up." I look over my shoulder, relaxing as I see they're no longer touching or laughing, but actually working. Lola is with them at the desk with a clipboard in her hands, pointing to different parts of the library. "Am I crazy that I don't think she should hug him?"

"Yes."

"No."

Guy and Darcy say at the same time. They stare at each other.

"It's clear that's just friendship. Everett has always been an affectionate guy, and Evie is the same way." Guy looks between Darcy and me.

"I don't know. If I'm with a woman I don't want her hugging on someone else."

I nod, agreeing with Darcy. I've never been fazed by this before but seeing Evie smiling at him and touching him has every muscle in my body tightening.

"Would you feel the same if that was Tash?" Guy points out.

We have no argument for that, and I see Guy's point, but I can't prevent the irritation from sticking around.

Evie disappears into the stacks as Everett mans the desk. Returning to my work, I finally find my focus and make my way through the changes. I add some new projects and take some out. One of my biggest goals is getting my students invested in the novels they read. I try to make the projects fun and informative.

A couple of hours pass until Evie comes back to the table, resting her chin on the top of my head. "I'm on break for the next forty-five minutes, are you ready?"

"I thought you have an hour break."

"I do, but I was talking to Everett in the break room and we lost track of time."

She backs away as I stand, Guy mouths for me to behave as I leave the table. Evie follows me outside, rushing to catch up and walk alongside of me.

"You okay?"

"Yeah." I know I'm being ridiculous, but I can't seem to turn off the jealousy and anger. I'm starting to think I should have invited Guy and Darcy along to keep me in check.

"Why are you walking so fast?"

"You don't have much time." I lead her into a smoothie bar just up the street, stopping when she grabs my arm and pulls.

"Charlie?"

Huffing out a breath, I turn to face her. "I'm not okay with you flirting with other men."

Her jaw drops as she gapes up at me, her eyes resembling a stormy day as she tries to figure out what I'm talking about.

"You and Everett. You've been flirting with each other all morning." I turn and place my order, stepping aside so Evie can do the same.

Once she's done, we face off again.

"We weren't flirting."

"From where I was sitting that's what it looked like."

"He was telling me about a blind date he went on, it was a funny story. And then he told me he's worried about finding the right person, so I gave him a hug and told him when it's right he will know it."

Our names are called, Evie grabs both of our meals and walks out the door. Out on the sidewalk she hands me my panini and starts to walk back towards the library.

Despite her assurance, I still feel jealous of Everett. She's never laughed that freely with me or looked quite so relaxed. Part of her still holds back when we're together, and I don't like it. Which is completely hypocritical because I'm holding part of myself back too, not quite sure we will be able to work long-term.

"Seriously, Charlie, there is not one little part of me that's attracted to Everett. We're friends, nothing more." Evie turns to face me, leaning up against the side of the library. Her face earnest as she tries to appease me.

Giving her a small smile, I take her hand. "Okay. I'm sorry I overreacted."

She squeezes my hand and returns my smile, but I can see she doesn't quite believe me.

Inside the library we rejoin my friends, talking and visiting with them for the rest of her break. I can feel her watching me, but I keep the smile on my face.

Can Evie and I work long-term? Or will our vastly different personalities eventually destroy us?

I don't want her to change who she is, because, truthfully, I really enjoy who she is. At the same time I hate feeling uncertain as to whether I can live with the differences and I worry about feeling jealous when she expresses herself in a way I don't like.

By the time Guy, Darcy, and I leave the library, my thoughts are chaotic and my emotions a mess. I don't know how to deal with these unclear feelings. My entire life I've always known exactly what to do with how I feel. For the first time in twenty-nine years, I don't know if I'm happy with any of the choices I have.

Distance

Evie

TASH JUMPS UP onto the counter while I cook dinner. She has dark circles under her eyes, but she keeps telling me the silent auction will help her keep afloat for another six months to a year. She doesn't know that I see the weight she's lost or the way her hands shake.

All these things are why I made her come for supper.

"So, how's things going with Charlie?" Tash munches on the veggies I set out on the counter.

Dumping the boiling water into the sink, I set the ribs on a pan and start rubbing barbecue sauce on them. Shrugging I reply, "Things are—weird."

"What do you mean?" she asks around a bite of broccoli.

"I don't really know. He got all jealous of Everett—" I pause when she starts choking.

"Really? Everett? And you?"

"Yeah. Anyway, after assuring him he had nothing to worry about he said okay, but since then he's been quieter than usual. I don't know what's going on, but I feel him pulling away and it scares me." Opening the oven, I slide the ribs inside before checking on the potatoes.

"Have you told him you love him?"

"No. I will, I just hope we can get back to normal first."

"Maybe you need to pull another gnomevasion. That way he sees you're not acting any differently." Tash hops down and gives me a hug. "I didn't even know Charlie was the jealous type."

Laughing softly, I state, "Neither did I."

Her words offer some comfort, but I still have an unsettling feeling in my gut. It's the same feeling I used to get right before I was moved from one foster home to another. I'm fighting the urge to push him away, I want to show him I can work through these bumps. It's not easy. My fight-or-flight instinct is kicking in. I've always been a fighter and the urge to push his buttons is high.

"Anyways, enough about that. Is anything else new with you?"

"Aside from Charlie being weird? No. Work is good. Although now that Heather and Sophie have quit, I've been working extra hours until we find a replacement for them. The board wants to shift how we schedule the staff."

The timer beeps, so I start setting out dinner as I explain how they want one person to open, someone to come in to work a shift that overlaps the morning and evening, and another person to end the day.

As we eat, I keep pushing food on Tash until she finally shoves her plate away. "Ev, I seriously cannot eat any more."

Laughing, I get up and grab a container. "Well, you're at least taking some of these leftovers."

She nods, the look on her face telling me she knows what I'm doing and that she appreciates it.

After Natasha leaves, I move about my house cleaning up. It's funny, now that I've been dating Charlie for a while, I see his touch everywhere. In the clean lines of the furniture. The simplicity in the decor. I feel him in this house, I think that's one of the things that I love about it. I love seeing his touch mixing with what I've added. His orderliness with my splashes of color.

Curling onto the couch, I wrap myself in a blanket and pick up the book I'm reading for next week's recommendations.

An hour passes and I'm still not able to focus on the book, despite the fact that it's one of the better ones I've read in a while.

Closing it, I set it aside and make my way to the box of gnomes in the basement. There are four left, plus the six I have upstairs.

Gathering all of them, I drive over to Charlie's and start setting them out. He's out with the guys tonight but should be home soon. It doesn't take me long to position them and get back home.

I pick up my book once more, this time I lose myself in the story. Maybe Tash was right, I just need to show him that nothing is different on my side and he can finally let go of whatever happened the other day.

Fucking
Gnomes

Charlie

T HE FIRST THING I see when I turn into my driveway is that my yard has a ton of fucking gnomes in it. Shutting off my car, I stare at the display before me. I'm pretty sure she's put out every single gnome she had left.

Gathering all the gnomes, I carry them into my house and put them in my closet with the rest that I've confiscated. There must be close to twenty-five gnomes in there.

Looking at the time, I decide to go to Evie's first thing in the morning. I don't doubt the gnomes are a reaction to my odd behavior. It helps me to think clearly when I'm on my own, but everything is still so muddy.

I don't know how to tell what the future holds for me and Evie. One of the reasons my relationships have always failed is because I don't like the unknown. With Evie, that unknown feels bigger because she's so unpredictable.

While I've come to accept the way she pushes my boundaries, I still don't like it. That's not something I think will ever change, and why should I?

The house creaks as I get ready for bed, the quiet noises

reminding me how alone I am. Until Evie, I never minded the noises, but now they seem louder.

Why does everything need to be so muddy? Why can't the answer be obvious?

I hate this. I miss my predictable days, with my predictable feelings. I miss knowing exactly what each day would bring.

The reality is though, that life isn't predictable. No matter how I try to keep everything exactly how I want it, there will always be external factors impacting my day to day.

Evie has taught me how to accept those things with greater ease. She has taught me to appreciate being a little more flexible, but that fear that our mutual attraction won't be enough refuses to go away, though.

Evie opens the door before I have a chance to knock, her arms wrapping around my waist. I hold her close, breathing in the fruity scent of her hair. For the first time in days, I finally relax.

"I made French toast." She pulls me into the house, shutting the door behind me.

"How did you know I would be here?"

She arches a brow at me. "Because of the gnomes."

Following her into the kitchen, I'm taken aback by how clean it is. The counter is clear, the sink is free of dishes, and the table is set for the two of us.

Evie's kitchen never looks this tidy unless she has something on her mind.

"Did elves come clean the kitchen?" I sit down in my spot, smiling at her as she grabs some orange juice from the fridge.

She shakes her head, chuckling good-naturedly. "No, I couldn't sleep last night, so I tackled it."

As we eat, we fall into comfortable silence. I've never appreciated before how Evie can sit with me and not need to fill the quiet, or we can talk about anything and she has insightful input to give.

"What do you have going on today?" Evie finishes her slice of toast. She collects her dishes and puts them in the dishwasher.

I can't help but notice it's empty.

"I was going to go mow the lawn at Mom and Dad's. Sebastian has his annual vet appointment. Then I was thinking about walking the trails along the river."

"Do you want company?" She sits back at the table, filling her glass with more orange juice.

"Don't you have to work?"

"I took the day off."

Shoving my chair out, I put my dishes in the dishwasher and help Evie tidy up. I was not expecting her to have the day off. And while spending the day with her is something I want, I need to remind my brain that it's okay to change up my expectations for the day.

When I look over at her, I cross to her in one step when I see the corners of her lips drooping. "That would be great."

Her responding smile is bright as she reaches up on her toes to kiss me.

"Things have been a little weird, I thought it would be nice to get back to normal."

"That does sound nice. You know how much I like normalcy." I drop my arms as she pulls away, her face soft.

"I know."

I wait while she gathers her things and locks up the house. The new shrubs are nice, and nothing else seems to have been affected by the mildew.

We're soon at my parents. I watch Evie weed their garden while I mow. She's methodical as she ensures every weed is gone. It doesn't escape my notice that she's become more careful in how she does things.

Guy and Darcy have both been on my ass about not appreciating the way that Evie has shown me she cares. She may like to play pranks and push my boundaries, but as I watch her, I realize they're right.

Maybe I've never been open to yielding before, but isn't that what marks long-lasting relationships?

"You look lost in your head," Evie says as she rolls the compost bin towards me.

I empty the final bag of grass-clippings into it. "I find I do some of my best thinking when I'm mowing the lawn. There is something soothing about the sound."

She rolls the bin to the curb and walks with me to put the mower away. "It makes me sleepy."

Taking my hand, we make our way to my house to pick up Sebastian. By the time we return from the vet, it's late afternoon and Evie's stomach has been grumbling loudly.

Guiding her into my kitchen, I push on her shoulders until she sits in the chair. Ignoring her protests, I heat up some leftovers and set them in front of her. We've been on the go since eight this morning without stopping. I heat myself something to eat, sitting next to her so she slows her pace.

Evie's knee bounces as she waits for me to finish eating. She doesn't stop fidgeting until we're walking toward the trails that run alongside the river.

The trail weaves along the water, the only sound is the rustling leaves in the breeze and the quiet rush of the river. The sun beats down on us through the tops of the trees. Mistik Ridge sits up on the bank overlooking the river.

One of the reasons I've never left is because I love its isolation. I love that the surrounding nature is mostly untouched.

Evie slides her hand into mine. We walk in silence, our feet moving in unison.

Glancing down at Evie, I notice the usually smooth skin between her eyebrows is creased. Her eyes are downcast as she watches our feet move.

"You okay?"

Evie's chest lifts as she takes a deep breath. "Yeah. I just have a lot on my mind. I'm worried about Tash. Plus, there are some changes coming at work and I'm not sure what I think of them."

"The town raised a lot of money for her, is she still in trouble?" Looking down, I watch as she licks her lips and closes her eyes, following me blind.

"She says she's got enough to last a while, but I know she's not taking care of herself."

Stopping Evie, I turn her to face me. "Natasha Mulroney is one of the most resilient, resourceful women I know. Probably only second to you. I wouldn't worry about her too much."

"You don't understand, Charlie. Tash is the closest I will ever have to a sister. I don't trust people easily. It's one of the things I promised myself when I moved here. I told myself I would be open to friendships and relationships. It's not easy for me to let people in, to let myself care. If I shut it off, I won't be able to turn it back on."

Cupping her cheeks, I brush my lips across hers. "If it makes you feel better, I will talk to Guy and make sure he's keeping an eye on her."

She nods, wrapping her arms around my neck before kissing me, her tongue stroking against mine. Her words echo in my head as we part and start walking again.

"What's going on at work?"

"They're thinking of only hiring one person to replace Sophie and Heather, which means either Everett or I will have to work a mid-shift, or at least share. It's not a big deal."

She brushes it off, changing the subject to how much she loves living alongside the river.

It bothers me that she's trying to brush off her feelings. She's always been so open and honest, more than most people I know, obviously something else is bothering her.

I drop Evie off at home a few hours later. Promising to return for dinner, I head home to get some work done, an unsettling feeling sinking into my chest.

I Love You

Evie

THINGS FELT OFF with Charlie today, he was preoccupied, and I didn't tell him I'm in love with him. Despite my hopes, he left promptly after dropping me off, but at least he is coming back.

I set about distracting myself, trying to figure out how to tell him how I feel. I've never said those three little words before, they've always held too much meaning and I've never let myself get close enough to anyone.

The sun is shining, the sky cloudless and vibrantly blue. I throw on some yoga shorts and a tank top, cleaning up the garden and soaking up the vitamin D. The new shrubs look good, but the greenhouse has three of the original ones on their way. They should be here tomorrow so I can finally put the flower bed back to the way it was.

It takes me less than an hour to get the gardening done, so I pull out the lawn mower and do that too. By the time the grass is cut, I'm still feeling restless, so I start cleaning the inside of the house.

After vacuuming, I wash the floors. Then I crawl onto the counters and scrub the top of the cupboards. By the time I'm finished, I think it's the cleanest the house has been since I moved in.

Collapsing on the couch, I search for one of my favorite romance novels in my bookshelf next to the couch and start reading. Maybe I can get some tips from Fabiola Francisco on how to do this. She's one of my go-to authors and I soon lose myself in her writing.

My phone rings, startling me. Setting my book down, I answer.

"Hello?"

"Hey, you will never believe what just happened." Natasha's voice makes me smile, I can hear the excitement in her voice, and it makes me happy.

"Well then you'd better tell me." Moving into the kitchen, I turn on the oven.

"You know that horse that someone randomly abandoned in my pasture?"

Chuckling, "Yes. Which I still can't believe, despite seeing the horse with my own eyes."

"I found him a home. And not only that, they refused to take him for free, they're buying him from me. Then on top of that, they reserved a room for the weekend. Things have been so slow this summer because I haven't had the budget to advertise, I'm just so excited to have some guests."

"That's wonderful news."

"Anyway, what are you up to? Did you tell Charlie yet?" I hear the creak of the porch swing in the background.

"No, I chickened out. He was being all weird, but he's coming over in twenty minutes. I'm cooking us dinner and then after dessert I will tell him." I grab the apricot chicken I've prepared and put it into the oven before starting on the rice.

"Sounds perfect."

"I guess. I've never said those words before, so I hope I don't screw it up."

"Evie, there is no possible way to screw up telling someone you love them. Call me first thing tomorrow so I can hear how it went."

We hang up so I can finish the preparations.

Laying out a blanket on the living room floor, I add some cushions to make it cozy. I want to have an indoor picnic, since Charlie won't want to eat outside on the grass. Setting out candles throughout the entire living room, I light them and turn the lights off.

The sun is starting to set, so the candles give the dim light in the living room a soft glow. Rushing to my room, I quickly change into leggings and a flowy top that sits off one shoulder.

Tossing my clothes in the hamper, I look around my bedroom one more time to make sure everything is tidy. I hear the front door open, Charlie calling my name.

Leaving my room, I enter the living room. He looks incredible in jeans and a plain black t-shirt that hugs his biceps. My heart picks up a little as he looks around.

When I first met him I never thought we would be here, but despite our differences he makes me so happy. He understands me in a way no one ever has and provides the stability and balance I've always craved.

Wrapping my arms around him, I lift onto my toes to kiss him. When he moves to pull away, I wrap my hand around his neck and pull him back down. Pressing my body into his, I moan when he deepens the kiss, his arms holding me close.

The timer beeps, interrupting us. With a sigh, I pull away and go take the chicken out of the oven. Loading our plates, I bring them into the living room where Charlie is still standing looking at what I've done with the room.

"I thought we would have a romantic picnic indoors." I hand him his plate, then take a seat on the blanket, patting the floor next to me.

He steps towards me, slowly sitting down. We start eating, the chicken is perfectly cooked, and the apricot sauce is the right amount of sweet and tangy.

"Did you get all the work done that you wanted?" I look up at him, proud that my voice is steady despite my nerves.

Charlie eats slowly, adjusting his plate several times. He finishes chewing before he answers. "Yeah. I've done all the prep I can do until I head back in two weeks."

He moves a candle from the floor onto the coffee table, before taking another bite.

Watching him carefully, I finally sense the tension rolling off him. He keeps looking at all the candles between each bite. Taking another bite of chicken and rice, I watch as Charlie sits there, awkwardly balancing his plate.

He's not enjoying this at all. I should have known better, but I wanted to try something new, something outside our routine.

Sighing, I stand and hold my hand out for his plate.

"What?"

"You're not enjoying this, so let's move to the kitchen."

He jumps up and starts blowing out candles. "Candles are a fire hazard, as nice as they look. I don't know how you can relax without worrying about fire or wax getting everywhere."

I bite my tongue, reminding myself that I want tonight to be perfect and if blowing out the candles and eating at the kitchen table is what Charlie needs, I can deal with that.

Isn't that the whole point of loving someone, loving every part of who they are? Charlie will never be the picnic type of guy. I don't know what I was thinking trying to do something differently.

We get situated at the kitchen table, helping ourselves to seconds. Charlie is visibly more relaxed and we finally start to really enjoy our evening. He still seems distracted, a little more like the stoic Charlie I first met.

"Did I tell you how someone abandoned a horse at Natasha's a couple weeks ago?" I try to lighten the mood, maybe divert him from whatever is on his mind.

He leans back in his chair, smiling at me for the first time since he walked in the door. "Really? No, I didn't hear about that."

"Yeah, she got up one morning and there he was, in her pasture. Thankfully the fences were still intact, otherwise he could have done a lot of damage to her gardens. Anyway, I guess she found someone to take him. Who would just leave a horse at someone's house like that?" I take a sip of wine, watching him carefully.

"Who knows, people are weird and unreliable."

We finish eating, Charlie starting to clean up the kitchen as I put the leftovers in the fridge. Topping up our wine, we settle onto the couch. I curl into Charlie, loving the way his arm wraps around me.

Still not ready to take the leap, I suggest we watch a movie. He picks a World War II epic. I don't care for it, but I'm too busy trying to figure out how and when I want to tell him. Should I tell him on the couch? Or when we go to bed? What if he doesn't want to spend the night?

I've never been so nervous to do something. I've stood in front of a judge and explained why I thought I should be allowed adult status at the age of sixteen. I fought caseworker after caseworker to get the support I needed when fighting with foster parents.

I stood in front of a panel and fought to complete my doctorate in an accelerated program. But this, this is terrifying. Opening my heart to him, basically handing him the power to hurt me is the most challenging thing I will ever have to do.

Getting up halfway through the movie, I pop the apple crisp I made for dessert in the oven. Leaning against the counter, I try to amp myself up.

My gut is churning, and I don't know why. I want to tell him. I want this relationship to progress. I feel like I'm reading too much into how quiet he's been because of my nerves. Maybe once I don't have this hanging over my head I won't read too much into every perceived weird look.

Charlie joins me in the kitchen once the apple crisp is done, serving us both.

"Are you okay?" he asks. "You seem distracted tonight?"

"Yeah, I've just been doing a lot of thinking about us and where we're going." I scoop ice cream into my bowl, spooning up some delicious apples and ice cream.

My heart pounds as he sits up, leaning onto his elbows. "I've been doing the same thing."

"Really?"

He nods. Maybe we're on the same page and I've been stressing for no reason.

"Maybe we should talk?" Charlie takes a bite, grumbling in appreciation.

"Here goes. I know we're very different people, and there have been some kinks and arguments, but at other points we work so well it surprises me how this has just flowed."

He starts to speak, but I hold my hand up to stop him.

"No, please let me finish."

"Okay." He pushes his empty bowl away, watching me carefully.

"I know I have a tendency to push people's buttons. And if I'm perfectly honest, I like playing pranks and testing limits. It takes a unique type of person to tolerate that."

I gulp back the rest of my wine, trying to regroup. I don't even know where I was going with that.

"That's beside the point really. Charlie, I know that you like things done a specific way, and I kind of go with the flow. You've given me something I didn't know I needed; you've given me a sense of balance. Despite our obvious differences, I don't have any doubts. What I'm trying to say is, I love you. I'm in love with you." I repeat it twice, because saying the words out loud feels so good.

I'm glad I didn't say them until I found someone I am certain about. My heart knows that we can overcome our differences.

Charlie stares at me, his eyes flicking between mine. When he doesn't say anything, I reach out and rest my hand on his arm, thinking, hoping, that maybe he thinks he misheard me.

"Charlie, I love you."

He looks at my hand resting on his arm before pulling it away and looking deep into my eyes. "I don't."

Hindsight is *Twenty–Twenty*

Charlie

MY FRONT DOOR opens, Guy coming in with Darcy on his heels. Their arms are full of the groceries I asked them to pick up. When Guy asked about guys' night, I suggested we have it here and sent him a list of what I needed to make my famous chili.

"Holy shit. What happened in here?" Darcy looks around my kitchen, eyes wide.

"I'm finishing my kitchen renos. I want at least one room in the house complete."

I haven't left my house since I got home from Evie's four days ago. This weekend I tore out the old linoleum and began painting. My cupboards are new, my countertops top-grade granite, but I was waiting for the perfect tile to come in before I put the finishing touches on the renovations.

The tile has been ordered, it looks like natural stone with varying shades of gray throughout, and each tile looks different so it will give it a unique effect. To balance out the dark flooring, dark cabinets, and dark countertops, I'm painting the walls a cream color to match the new backsplash which is a cream stone.

Guy grabs a roller and we finish the final coat of paint while Darcy looks at the backsplash and tile samples. Once we're done, I wash the brushes and put everything away.

When I rejoin them in the kitchen, I start laying out the supplies in the order I need them while the guys go out back to check Elliott's progress on the yard. By the time they both come back in, the chili is simmering on the stovetop.

"Wow, that kid sure has skills." Darcy lifts the lid to the pot and peeks in. "How long until that's ready?"

"It's best if it simmers for a couple of hours." Opening the fridge door, I grab three beers. "Elliott will be done by the end of the week and is looking for more work if you want anything done."

Darcy hums, sipping his beer as he watches me. "So, what's up? The last time you started renovating your house was when your dad had a stroke. I just saw him yesterday and he's fine."

Guy stares out the window at my backyard, his back tense. I knew Evie would call Tash; I didn't expect her to tell Guy.

"Evie and I broke up." Crossing my arms, I watch Darcy process what I just shared.

He downs the rest of his beer before slamming it onto my kitchen table. Glaring at him, I swipe it off the table and toss it into my recycle bin. We stare each other down as I grab the dishcloth and wipe off the ring of condensation from the otherwise pristine wood.

"You fucking idiot. How could you let her go?"

"Hey! How do you know it's me?"

"Of course it's you, you dingbat. You're an insane person and whenever you feel the remotest connection with anyone who challenges the way you look at the world, you flee before you have to really examine yourself and your feelings."

Guy finally turns around, his lips twitching as Darcy mutters at me under his breath before turning his glare onto Guy. "Don't you want to chime in?"

"No, you've got this. Besides, Tash told me within twenty-four hours of it happening that this fucktard screwed things up. And what else did we expect? Evie loves him and it scares him that he feels the same way." Guy watches me, his eyes twinkling as I process his words.

"No, see that's the problem. I don't love her. How is it fair to lead her on?"

"No, the problem is that you do, but you're going to cling to the fact that you both have such different personalities that it could never work and you're going to lose the best woman for you because you don't see it. You chose your sad life of denial and burying your feelings in renovating a house you share with your cat rather than trying to hold onto anything real." He walks into my living room and picks up my remote, surfing through the channels until he finds something he wants to watch, obviously done with the conversation.

Darcy glares at me and points his finger in my face. "Hindsight is twenty-twenty, and a bitch. Have fun cleaning up this mess." He pretends to drop a mic before turning and walking into my living room, joining Guy on my couch.

Returning to my chili, I stir it while arguing with them in my head. It doesn't matter that I miss her. At some point our differences would tear us apart. The fact that I've never felt so strongly about someone before her isn't enough to make things work.

Look at the picnic. It's a clear example of our differences. It doesn't matter that she set it up inside, or that she let us eat at the table in the end. It doesn't matter that when I think about her everything else fades away, even my need to organize everything in my life.

How long could she keep that up before she got tired of it, because at some point she would want to have someone who is exactly like her.

No matter how much I love her, that risk is too great.

The spoon clatters into the pot, disappearing into the bubbling chili.

"Well, I think reality just sunk in." Darcy and Guy appear at my side.

Fishing out the spoon, I drop it into the sink and replace the lid before collapsing onto a chair at my kitchen table. Hindsight is a bitch. I'm a level-headed person, how could I behave so irrationally. Okay, stupid question, because Evie and I don't make sense, except now I realize we make perfect sense. Something I would have seen if I let myself.

I look back on that night with fresh eyes. Evie moving to the table instead of pushing me to finish on the floor. When it really counts, she backs down from whatever scheme she's come up with to push my buttons.

Rather than appreciating what she does for me, I threw it back in her face.

The hurt in her eyes after I said those horrid words haunt me. The way her face crumpled as I stood and walked out the door.

"Crap." I look up at my friends. Their faces vary from pity—Guy—to straight up judgment—Darcy. "I need a plan."

They both throw their arms in the air. "Dude!"

"This is how I do things, okay. Now, are you going to help me?"

Guy shakes his head. "Nope. Not this time."

Darcy's eyes widen, usually Guy is the first to let me get away with shit, but obviously not this time. "Let's watch a movie and you can think on this later. At this point, one more day isn't going to hurt."

I set the timer on the stove, and we settle in to watch some horror flick Darcy finds on Netflix; my mind is running a mile a minute so I don't protest the choice.

I don't know if I will be able to come back from this, but I'm going to try.

———————— ♥ ————————

My alarm goes off at seven, not that I was asleep. Jumping out of bed, I ignore my exhaustion and throw on some clothes.

Rushing through my morning routine, I grab my keys and with a quick pat of Sebastian's head, I'm out the door and heading to the rental.

When I get to Evie's several things hit me at once. All the gaudy flowerpots are gone from the front yard, the shrubs that she had planted after the mildew incident have been replaced with ones that match what was originally there, and her car is gone.

Parking in the space next to where she usually parks, I go and sit on the steps of her porch, faltering when I see the front door has been painted back to its original white. What's going on?

Mrs. Jesperson comes around the side of her house, a watering can in hand. By the look on her face, I can tell she's heard the news. I wonder who won the bet.

"Why are you just sitting on the step?" She crosses the street but stays on the sidewalk.

"I'm waiting for Evie to come home."

Her eyes widen and she backs up a step. "Charlie, you may want to just go inside."

I'm taken aback as she turns and returns to her yard, avoiding further eye contact with me. Finding the house key on my keychain, I unlock the door and step inside.

The keys fall out of my hand as I look around the living room. Every personal touch Evie had put into this room is gone, right down to the feature wall which now matches all the other walls. The furniture is laid out exactly as I had it before Evie moved in and changed everything. Her books are gone, her knick-knacks, her pillows, her blanket, everything.

I try to catch my breath as I stumble across the room into the kitchen, only to have it stolen again when I find the same thing. It can't be. In denial, I check the rest of the house and the backyard before returning to the living room and sitting on the couch.

All traces of Evie are gone, except a faint hint of her perfume, just like she promised would happen if she ever moved out.

How does one small person accomplish so much in four days? Shaking my head, I answer myself. She has a flair for recruiting people into whatever she is doing.

Me: *Did you know Evie packed up and moved out? The house looks like she never even lived here.*

Guy: *Are you really surprised?*

Looking around at the house now devoid of Evie, I rush to the door and outside unable to stomach seeing the house so empty. It doesn't matter that it's full of furniture, there is no color, no life.

That is what Evie did for me; she made my life more than my daily routines. She brought color to my world, made things interesting, and even though in the moment it was a struggle, I now realize how much I needed it. And I threw her away. I threw away the person who brought happiness to my life.

Opening my car door, I shut it and slam my hands into the steering wheel, pain ripping through my chest as I race away from a house I can no longer bear to look at. This is my doing. In a moment of panic, I made the biggest screw-up of my life. I won't stop until I fix this, but I doubt anything I do will work for me.

I can't fix this by following my normal patterns. I need to think outside my comfort zone, I need to think like Evie would.

Projects

Evie

B ALANCING MY LAUNDRY basket on my hip, I open the door to the room Tash is generously letting me stay in until I decide what to do. Despite my requests, she refused to put me in one of the rooms she closed down because they need to be fixed up. It was a big argument, but in the end, she won because she's as stubborn as I am and I appreciate her giving me a place to stay, so I didn't push as much as I normally would.

When I see Tash sitting on the edge of the queen-size bed, I try to smile. By the look on her face, she sees right through me.

"It's okay to be sad, you know." She pats the bed next to her, wrapping her arms around me when I sit down. "What do you want to do today?"

"I know, I just hate not feeling like myself. And I hate him for being a coward. All I want to do is find some projects I can focus on so I'm not sitting here as this sad puddle of a person. Tash, I've never told anyone I love them before. Why would anyone put themselves through this?" I'm rambling, but I'm a chaotic mess of feelings and it's proving to be impossible to lock them up.

"I'm so sorry." She rocks me back and forth as I bite back tears. She's seen me cry enough already.

I was crying when I sent her the text asking her to come over. I was crying as we put all my belongings in boxes. I was crying as we painted the walls back to their original color. I was crying through it all. Now it's time to move forward. I don't think I've ever shed so many tears in my entire life.

"Tash, you know how much I appreciate you, right?" I finally hug her back, allowing myself to absorb her comfort.

"I do."

"Can you please let me help you around here? Lola gave me the week off, and I just want to keep busy." I release her from my grasp, leaning away until she does the same.

"Why did you take the week off if you want to keep busy?"

"Lola made me. Please. There must be something I can help you with," I plead with her.

Tash sighs as she looks up, thinking. "I was going to tackle one of the rooms that is still open today, touch up the paint and rearrange the furniture. I have those people coming to get that horse and I want them to enjoy their stay."

I reach out and squeeze her hand. "They will. Let me help you get it ready."

She finally agrees and we spend the morning and most of the afternoon making the suite shine. It's the most recently renovated room with a huge state-of-the-art bathroom, a sitting area, and a king-size bed.

"When I bought this place it needed a lot of work, but I thought I could do it slowly and the things to fix just kept piling up. I was able to renovate three suites, but I should've done one suite and three bedrooms. This place hadn't been a functioning business for years, but it's taken me a long time to realize it's going to take a lot of work to get it to the point it's earning me money."

I look up from where I'm scrubbing the giant tub. "You will get there."

She wipes her forehead with her forearm as she finishes with the walk-in shower. "I hope so, I just need to stay afloat."

It's late afternoon when we finally finish cleaning, moving furniture, and setting out the new decorations Tash found on clearance. We stand back to examine our handiwork. The freshly painted walls are a pale green that makes the dark mahogany furniture stand out. Two plush armchairs face each other in the bay window, a vase of fresh lilies on the table between them.

The bed is a simple sleigh bed, the new linens a darker version of the green on the wall. Tash found a handmade quilt with a star design to match the metal stars now decorating the walls.

It's cozy, classy, and ready for her guests to arrive first thing tomorrow morning.

"I think we've earned some fresh chocolate chip cookies." Tash hooks her arm through mine, closing and locking the door behind us.

It's been four days since I told Charlie I'm in love with him. Four days since he told me those feelings were not reciprocated. With the help of Tash, Guy, and Everett, we moved me out and put everything back the way it was.

Every night I went to bed too exhausted to think of anything else. When I woke up this morning with the knowledge I had nothing else to keep me occupied, the feeling of despair was crushing.

Thankfully, Tash seems to see how much I need busy work. After we eat cookies, we walk around the property tying ribbons around dead trees that need to be cut down. We talk about books we're reading and focus on anything that will keep thoughts of Charlie at bay.

By the time I crawl into bed, I fall asleep as soon as my head hits the pillow.

The cutest couple I've ever seen finishes checking in as I come in the front door. I couldn't sleep so I got up with the sun, took a book outside, and read under the canopy of a massive willow tree. The grounds the inn sit on are vast and beautiful.

Large trees cover most of the property, but surrounding the house are stunning gardens with different themes. I can't wait to explore them, and hopefully convince Tash to let me maintain them for her while I'm here.

Tash looks up when she hears me, smiling when she sees the book in my hand.

"Evie, these are our guests. Lia and Alex." I shake their hands, not missing the protective arm Alex has around Lia.

"It's nice to meet you." Lia smiles at me.

"You too. How long are you two staying?"

"Just two nights, I have to get back to prep for a horse show. I wish we had more time, but it's a busy time of year for us."

"Only because you're insisting on doing the horse show," Alex rumbles, kissing her cheek with such love and affection I need to look away to collect myself.

"He's mad because he lost the argument. I may be pregnant, but I'm not an invalid."

We chat for a while longer, learning that Lia and her family own a ranch several hours west of Mistik Ridge. Alex's arm stays around her waist the entire time we chat. He's friendly but quiet.

At Alex's insistence, they finally excuse themselves to go settle in. Tash directs them to their room and Alex starts to guide Lia away. She rolls her eyes, grinning at us over her shoulder.

They disappear up the stairs, talking and laughing the entire way. I sigh as I turn to Tash.

"I thought I had that. I hate feeling like this. Turning off the feelings I let myself feel for him isn't working. Maybe that's not a bad thing, I like knowing I can meet someone and feel that way, but right now it sucks." I jump up onto her front desk, pushing my lower lip out. "I need another project."

"Evie, letting people in will always open you up to hurt, but the hurt doesn't last forever. I've already been thinking of things we can do. I need to do some painting outside, so unless you're tired of painting, you can help me with that." Tash continues to list all the things she wants to get done today.

We spoke at length last night about me helping her out around here. She refuses to let me pay for my room, so I told her I would move out if she didn't at least let me earn my keep. Thankfully, she didn't argue too much. I know she needs the help and I need to stay busy. It's a win-win.

Hopping down from the desk, I follow her outside to a run-down shed. We collect everything we need and haul it to the sign at the front of the driveway. The sign is the original and it doesn't look like it has had a fresh coat of paint in years.

We talk about random things as we work, skirting the subject of Charlie. It's fascinating to me how we never seem to run out of things to talk about, and how random our trajectory in conversation is.

This is the first time in my life I have a friend I can count on to listen when I need it or distract me like she is right now. Her hips sway back and forth as she starts to sing "Baby Got Back." After the third time, I dip my paint brush in the forest-green paint and swipe it down her arm.

"Oh, it's on." She chases me around the sign, tackling me and straddling me as she tries to paint my forehead.

I laugh and yell at her as I wave my paint brush in my attempts to fend her off.

I faintly hear the sound of tires on the gravel, but I can't look away from her as she continues to get paint on my forehead, cheek, and neck.

"Screw mud wrestling, I think I like paint wrestling better. Am I the only one getting a little turned on?" We freeze, turning our heads to see Darcy hanging out the window of Guy's truck, a giant smirk on his face.

"Dude, that's my sister." We laugh as Guy yanks him back into the truck and smacks him on the back of the head. Tash rolls off me, holding her hand out and helping me stand.

"What are you doing here?" She drops her paintbrush into the tray and walks over to the truck, propping her hands on her hips, while I gather up the painting supplies.

Seeing them reminds me of how sad I'm trying not to be. I hate sounding whiny and pathetic. I don't let people get me down. I don't cling to hurt feelings or disappointment. I come back swinging. It's one of the reasons I tend to fly by the seat of my pants. With no planning comes little chance of being let down.

"We thought it would be a nice night for a bonfire. I know you need a bunch of trees cut down and wood chopped, so it kills two birds with one stone. We brought food, we are the manpower, all you need to do is show up." I can hear the smile in Guy's voice. I look over at them, giving him a small one in return.

Tash doesn't fully appreciate her brother, but he's one of the sweetest men I've ever met. He's over here at least three times a week trying to help her. She's constantly getting mad at him for it, I know it's because she feels bad, but I wish she realized how lucky she is.

Darcy slaps his hand on the side of the truck with a smile as they drive away, turning down the driveway to park at the back of the inn.

"You should invite Lia and Alex," I suggest and start heading back. "Maybe she will suggest coming here to her family and friends. Word of mouth is the best advertisement for your business."

"I was thinking the same thing."

Tash drags out the hose to wash off the brushes before we attempt to get the majority of the paint off ourselves too. Once we're clean, she runs everything back to the shed while I wind up the hose.

The wood of the porch creaks as someone walks over.

Looking up, I see Lia approaching with a wide smile. I greet her as I finish my job.

"Do you live out here too? Or are you just visiting?" Lia leans on the railing of the porch, smiling down on me.

"I'm just here for a while. Things didn't work out at my rental and Tash said it was her best friend duty to give me a place to stay." I climb the steps and sit on the porch swing next to where Lia stands. "We're having a bonfire tonight, you and Alex should join us."

Her eyes pierce into me, but she doesn't pry. "We would like that."

The sun is low in the sky by the time we all make our way to the fire pit. Alex joins Guy and Darcy as they lay out the food they brought while Lia joins Tash and me where we sit by the fire.

"How did you make out with the horse?" I ask Lia.

"Good, she's pretty skittish, but she will come around. I'm hoping to gift her to my apprentice, Nella." Lia explains to us what she does, and it's fascinating to me. A whole world I knew nothing about.

The guys join the conversation, Darcy sits next to me and hands me a hot dog.

"How're you doing, Evie?" He rests his elbows on his knees as he watches me.

Chewing on my lip, I glance at Tash before meeting Darcy's gaze once more. "I'm doing okay, I guess. I don't really want to think or talk about what happened."

"I just—I wanted to tell you that I think he is a fool. And no matter what happens, you brought the best out in him." Darcy looks past my shoulder, his eyes narrowing.

Tash plops onto my lap, nearly knocking the hot dog out of my hand. She looks between Darcy and me before sticking her tongue out at him. "Dude, what's with the scowl?"

He mumbles something neither of us hear. Grateful for the

distraction, I look into the flickering flames of the fire as I eat, the low hum of chatter comforting and distracting me. It's not easy being around Charlie's friends, knowing they've talked to him and knowing I can't ask any questions.

It goes against my nature to hold back, but, in this instance, I don't think my heart can take the answers to my questions, so I leave it alone.

Operation: I'm a Dumbass

Charlie

I'T'S BEEN A week and a half since I made the single-most idiotic ass of myself, and I haven't seen Evie once since then.

I might be more likely to see her, but I can't seem to bring myself to leave the house for anything but more reno materials. Driving past her house is a constant reminder of the person missing in my life. Gone with two words.

Guy finally broke down a few days ago and told me she's staying with Tash and that she had last week off from work. He gave me a heads up that she's done being sad and is now pissed off.

I don't blame her. I completely screwed up what we had, and I hate myself for it, it would make sense for her to hate me too. Especially after she told me she doesn't open herself up to people because she's been thrown away ever since she was a child. Taking her "I love you" and throwing it back in her face was the worst thing I could have done.

The drive from my house to the library passes quickly, the only reason is because I know I will be seeing her soon.

Parking my car, I am grateful that Darcy and Guy are waiting for me outside the library. It's the weekly book club meeting and Evie is back at work and running it. I'm uncertain if they are coming to support me or keep me in check, but either way I'm grateful they've come on board with helping me.

"Are you sure this is a good idea?" Darcy asks as I join them at the doors to the library.

"No, but I need to see her." While I know she's not going to be happy to see me, a small part of me hopes I can talk to her tonight and sort this out.

From the moment I left her house I haven't been able to sleep. My house is a disaster as I've begun to tear apart the master bathroom now that the tile has been laid in the kitchen and the backsplash glued to the wall. I miss Evie and with school's start still a week away, I've been pulling all-nighters redoing my house trying to occupy my thoughts and fill the void letting her go has created.

When she first came into my life, I thought she was a curse, now I realize Evie is exactly what I need. I still can't wrap my head around how we fit so well together, but I see it more now that she's been gone than I ever would have before.

Taking a deep breath, I lead the way into the library. Evie's voice soothes my nerves as we make our way to the back where she usually hosts the book club. It sounds like they've already started, which surprises me since I made sure we were early.

Rounding the final stack, I'm facing Evie's back. She's in a sleeveless top that shows off her slender shoulders and the stark contrast of her pale skin and the ink marking it. Her legs are bare, her calves flexing from the monstrous heels on her feet.

Seeing her makes my heart pound and the empty ache in my stomach settle. Self-loathing mocks me as I watch her gesture and talk to the crowd.

As the three of us stand behind her, we're gradually spotted by the crowd of people sitting around the room. It doesn't take long until the only person who hasn't seen us is Evie.

The looks range from outrage to curiosity to disbelief. Everett finally stops scowling at me and catches Evie's attention from reading the excerpt no one is paying attention to. Except me. I don't hear the words; all I hear is the sound of her voice. I soak it in, my eyes hungry to see her face, even a look of hatred, any emotion. My biggest fear is that she will look at me and be devoid of feeling. Shutting down what she finally allowed herself to feel, closing herself off like she did when she was a child.

She finally turns, her face passive as she sees me, no emotion. My chest feels like it's going to cave in until I see her eyes. They darken, becoming a storm as her emotions run through her, betraying her careful expression of indifference.

That one sign gives me hope that I haven't completely screwed things up, that I have a chance to make this right.

I'm acutely aware of the crowd of people watching us, waiting for an explosion or some sort of drama they can spread through the town grapevine, but I ignore them while I wait for Evie to decide how she wants to deal with me.

She straightens her body and turns back to everyone else. "If you're joining us you need to take a seat."

Her response surprises me. I know she's at work, but I was expecting a little more reaction. Maybe a quip or a cutting remark. Evie doesn't hold back, but I know she's biting her tongue right now. As I sit in the nearest available chair to her, she finishes the passage she was reading, and they start discussing it.

I can't tear my eyes away from her, but as she smiles and interacts with everyone else, she avoids any further eye contact with me. It sears my heart that I hurt her so badly in one moment of fear and denial.

By the time the book discussion is over, and the next book is chosen, I'm just counting down the moments when everyone starts to clear out so I can talk to her.

Evie wraps up the night, but instead of leaving like they usually do, every single person stays in their seats and continues to visit.

Guy and Darcy smirk next to me as Evie cleans up while laughing at something Everett is saying to her. It sounds wrong, like she's forcing it out.

"We're going to go wait outside," Guy says. I look away from Evie to acknowledge him. From across the room, Cassaundra watches me and shakes her head with a frown on her face as I glance at her before looking back at Evie.

I sit back as Evie finishes cleaning up. I would offer to help her, but there are already too many people getting in her way. It's not until she has her keys out and everyone is walking with her that I realize they're not going to let me talk to her alone.

Evie has become a Mistik Ridge resident; she's beloved by everyone who meets her, I should have known this wouldn't work out for me.

I follow a few feet behind them, but when I pass Evie as she holds the door open, I turn my back on the posse of people guarding her and look down at her bent head.

"Evie, I was hoping we could talk—alone."

She looks over my shoulder at the crowd, a small smile on her face before it falls away as she finally looks up at me. The mask she's been wearing all night slips as she searches my face. Her eyes glisten, but no tears fall. She's so strong, I hate that she needs to guard herself against me. "No. I know what you're going to say, Charlie. It's written all across your face. Words aren't going to be enough."

"Evie, please."

She rests her hand over her heart, one tear slipping before she regains composure. Her eyes are ice as she looks up at me. "I love words, I love the power behind them and what we can do with them, but sometimes they're not enough."

She shuts the door, locks it, and walks away from us all to her car. No one moves as she gets in, starts it, and drives away, her taillights disappearing as she turns the corner to drive down Main Street.

Turning to face the crowd, they are all staring at me again.

Three. Two. One.

Voices fill the silence as every single person starts in on me. It's hilarious, less than a month ago they were taking bets about when we would break up. Now that we have, they're angry about it.

I stand there for a moment listening to the voices blending together.

"Enough." Done with their diatribe, I look into each of their eyes. "Stay out of this, it's none of your business and it will never be your business."

Pushing my way through them, I join Guy and Darcy at my car.

"I hate small towns."

"No, you don't. You just usually aren't on this end of things." Guy laughs.

"How about you stop tearing apart your house and actually fix this?" Darcy chimes in.

Giving them the finger, I get in my car and drive home where I promptly change into my work clothes and start hauling the garbage out to the large dumpster that now sits in my driveway.

Evie wants actions, I need to think of something that would show her I'm serious. It's three in the morning by the time I finish demolishing my bathroom.

Throwing the final garbage into the dumpster, I kick it in frustration. I still have no idea what to do.

The solution comes to me two nights later when I'm in my basement gathering the supplies I need to outline the changes I'm making in the bathroom and I stumble across all of the gnomes I've been holding hostage. Somehow, over the course of knowing Evie, I've accumulated close to thirty gnomes.

For the first time in close to two weeks, I start to laugh.

Gnomes. Of course, it would have to be the gnomes. She knows how much I hate them. Now I just need to see if I can recruit as many people to my cause as she was able to recruit to hers. It won't be as easy for me, but I think once I make my case I might be able to get some help.

Loading the bucket I've been using to haul my tools back and forth, I head upstairs and start making some phone calls. I have less than a week until I'm back in the classroom, I need to get to work.

Things are
getting weird

Evie

WALKING DOWN MAIN Street with Tash, we head to Liliana's for pie and coffee, laughing as we talk about a date Tash went on.

"It's really tough dating when you live in a town where you know every single person. You've seen them go through puberty, you know their dating history. It felt like I was back in high school and that is definitely not a good feeling. I was a little awkward in my teens."

"Maybe someone new will move to town, someone who didn't see you through the awkward stage." I hold up both hands, crossing my fingers. I'm grateful to have something to distract me from my own thoughts, which seem out of control lately. It took all my strength not to throw myself into Charlie's arms the other night. I don't think I was imagining the remorse I saw, but pretty words won't make up for the way he made me feel.

"One can only hope." Tash laughs.

We fall silent as we come up to Liliana's. As Tash opens the door releasing a wave of mouth-watering scents, something catches my eye in the flowerpot outside her bakery.

Sitting amongst the Creeping Charlie, underneath the Calla Lilies, is a gnome smoking a pipe. Staring at the little gnome, my pulse quickens as I take in the black pants, blue shirt, white beard, and red hat.

Why would a single gnome be sitting in there? Main Street is quaint and designed to be the hub of Mistik Ridge. Murals are painted on the brick walls, trees canopy the street, and flowers line the sidewalk. This single gnome is out of place.

I follow Tash inside, thankful when she leads us to a different booth than the one I shared with Charlie. The planter with the gnome is right outside the window, straight across from me. I can't resist the urge to look out at it, but when I do the gnome is gone.

"Okay, I'm going crazy." I shake my head, staring at the empty planter.

"Why?"

"I could've sworn I saw a gnome in the midst of those flowers, but now it's gone."

She follows my gaze, her lips twitching in response to my random hallucination. "Maybe you're imagining things that remind you of Charlie because you're finally ready to talk about it."

Rolling my eyes, I smile at her. "You're pushy, you know that right?"

"I sure do," she sings.

Shaking my head, I look back out the window. "I told myself I was going to stay mad at him, I wasn't going to forget how he made me feel, but here's the thing, when you love someone, really love them, you don't stay mad for long. What is love without forgiveness and letting go? Without those things, love becomes conditional and who wants that? Who wants someone to love them under certain conditions? So, I'm letting it go."

Pausing as Liliana brings us our food, I finally meet Tash's eyes. She gives me a small smile as Liliana walks away, waiting for me to continue talking.

"This doesn't mean I'm going to beg him to take me back. If he wants to fix this, I need to see it. I need to feel like he's in it for good and will work hard at it. I don't know if that's what Charlie wanted when he came to see me, or if he was just trying to talk to me about breaching the lease, but I'm not angry anymore. And I can't stop loving him just because he doesn't feel the same way."

Rather than share my suspicion about the impromptu attendance of book club, I give her what I feel comfortable sharing. It would be humiliating enough telling Charlie words aren't enough and have him questioning what I mean without letting anyone else in. I don't know if I saw what I want to see, or if I'm right in my assumption he regrets the haste with which he left things, but I'm holding onto that glimmer of hope. Clinging to it like it's my last breath.

"Charlie is uptight about that agreement, but you know he would have sent you an official notice if it was regarding the house."

We laugh as we dig into our pieces of strawberry rhubarb pie. Liliana bakes the pies fresh each morning, among other things, and it's the best pie I've ever eaten. I could easily come here every day if I let myself.

"That's true."

"I guess we just need to wait and see what happens." Tash winks at me. I know she's on my side no matter what, despite knowing Charlie her entire life. I've never met someone as loyal as Tash is.

Later that afternoon we're leaving the spa from a few hours of pampering when I spot another gnome. This one is peeking out from behind a tree. Tash is looking at the window display in a tiny jewelry shop. Turning, I call her.

"What?"

"Look, another gnome." Turning back, I point where the gnome was, but it's gone again. Growling I say, "What the hell?"

I look up and down the street, but no one is around. How is this even possible?

"Someone is probably playing a prank on you. The entire town knows how much you love gnomes." She hooks my arm with hers and leads me away from where I'm staring. "Maybe Charlie?"

"Yeah, right? Can you imagine?" I shake my head. Charlie being behind the gnomes is something I can't even fathom.

"You're probably right. That's not a Charlie move."

The entire rest of the way I can't help but look around searching for more gnomes. Of course, by the time we reach her car I haven't seen any more.

Laughing it off, I accept Tash's prank theory.

Together we head home, and I spend the rest of the day in her garden, pulling weeds and listening to an audio book to keep my mind distracted. By the time I crawl into bed, the melancholy I fight all day hits me. I don't want to show the townspeople how sad I still am.

I've heard the whisperings. *They were only together a short time.*

I think even Tash thinks that to an extent, not that she would ever belittle my feelings. In fact, I've even had the same thought. A tear streaks down my face as I end another day without talking to Charlie. I miss him. I miss his quirks. I miss the way I can push him and he gets this small smile as he tolerates it.

Maybe love is the wrong word to describe how I feel about Charlie, but it's something I had never felt until him. And the pain of missing him is something I feel through my entire being. It's not something even the smallest hope that he wants to fix things can cure.

Sleep starts to take over, the weight lifting from my chest a little. Tomorrow is another day of pretending I'm okay. Pretending I don't miss him as much as I do. Pretending I am as strong as people think I am.

Lola comes out of her office, a grim look on her face. "That was brutal."

All morning she has been on a conference call with our board of directors, defending her proposition to maintain two daytime staff and two evening staff. Exhaustion lines her face as she joins Everett and me behind the counter.

"Why don't I go and grab you a smoothie?" I offer, hip checking Everett as I pass him.

Lola nods, giving me a small smile. "I could use the pick me up."

Grabbing my purse from under the counter, I head out the door and down the street. The sun beats down on me, the fresh air relieving the headache I'm fighting, so I slow my usual stride and enjoy the short walk.

Everett has been hovering, watching me for any signs of distress. I just want to do the job I love, but lately it's taxing. I'm still not sleeping, so my usual patience is wearing thin and even selecting our weekly recommended reads has become tiresome.

The bell above the door jingles as I enter J's Smoothies, smiling at Jessica as she comes from the back.

"Hey, Evie! How are you?" She leans her elbows onto the counter, smiling at me as I approach.

"I'm good. How are you?"

"Fabulous, as always. What can I getcha?"

"I need Lola's usual. A strawberry mango for Everett." Pausing, I search the menu for something I haven't tried. "And a nutty monkey for me, please."

She mixes everything up, the sound of the blenders running eliminating the ability to chat. As she works, I turn and look out the window. Staring at me from the bench on the sidewalk is another gnome.

I search the sidewalk for any indication of where they are coming from. There is no one around, at least no one I can see from my position inside. Something ignites inside of me as I watch this simple gnome sitting on the bench. A spark of intrigue.

"Evie, your smoothies are ready."

Smiling at Jessica, I slip her a ten before picking up the tray and head back onto the sidewalk where I glance at the bench to look at the gnome once more. It's gone.

Turning in a circle, I don't see anyone who is carrying a gnome or hurrying away from me. I wish I could commend whomever is doing this on the creativity of their approach. It's distracting me from being sad, although the gnomes are a daily reminder of Charlie, simply because I appreciate the spontaneity and randomness of when they appear.

It's a game, a puzzle, and I love to play.

Back at work, I set the smoothies onto the counter, taking mine and hopping onto the counter to enjoy a quiet moment with Lola and Everett. School starts next week, teachers heading back at the end of this week, and it's been significantly quieter in here as parents prepare for the new term.

"You look—refreshed," Everett observes, jumping up to sit next to me.

Lola glares but lets us stay where we are.

"Maybe I just needed a walk." Wrapping my lips around my straw, I sigh at the mixture of chocolate and banana.

He looks at me, skeptical. "You have a glimmer in your eyes. A hint of mischief that I haven't seen in a while."

Lola looks between us, a smirk on her face. Only two people knew I was going to get smoothies, and they're both sitting right here. Narrowing my eyes, I look between the two of them. Could they be behind the gnomes? And if they are, why?

"Really? I can't imagine why. It was a typical walk to J's." I watch them carefully, but they don't give any indication that they know anything out of the ordinary happened.

This can't be a random coincidence.

Allies

Charlie

ELLIOTT AND I walk through my completed backyard admiring his impeccable work. Three brand new elm trees provide shade, with sprawling flower beds around them. Elliott spent time researching placement of each perennial to ensure it was put in the proper spot.

Rather than grass, he planted different varieties of thyme anywhere there aren't flowers or shrubs. A stone path weaves throughout the yard leading us to the new pond and the dug-in fire pit.

There is only one thing missing.

"Elliott, you have an incredible talent. I just need you to add that one feature we were talking about. I think the secluded corner next to the pond would be perfect."

We turn back to the house where Elliott proceeds to draw out his design. We hover over it for close to an hour making tweaks and settling some details. Once the design is finalized, I give him the envelope with the remainder of what I owe him and a hefty bonus.

"Thank you so much, Mr. Greene."

"I'm not your teacher anymore, you can call me Charlie." He's been calling me Mr. Greene all summer, so he looks at me in surprise when I correct him.

Losing Evie was eye-opening in more than one way. I've been working hard at being more relaxed and giving a little.

"I'm going to go buy the supplies for this now and get started right away." Elliott folds his design and sticks it along with the envelope I've given him into his bag. "I will see you tonight."

"Wonderful. I'm hoping this works."

After he's gone, I don't give myself a chance to relax. Every inch of me aches, but I'm putting the final touches on the bathroom. My entire thought process has been on how I can show Evie I made a mistake and that I want her in my life.

Part of that is turning this house into more of a home. Something I thought I had until Evie taught me what having a home really means.

Once I'm done caulking the new shower and tub, I pack everything up and examine my work. I love renovating. It keeps me busy; I can design it and follow a plan to get a beautiful end result. My bathroom is huge, the original layout was not meant for more than one person.

Now it features double sinks, more storage, a giant walk-in shower, and the biggest Jacuzzi tub I've ever seen. I even added a vanity where I can picture Evie doing her hair and makeup. Everything, right down to the paint, was thought of with Evie in mind. I think the paint specialist at the hardware store almost had a heart attack when I selected a pale sea foam green instead of my usual neutral colors.

My phone dings with a text distracting me from nitpicking the final touches in the bathroom. It's Darcy confirming our plans for this evening.

I shoot him a quick response before pulling up the final number I need. The one person who I desperately need on my side, and the one I will have the most difficult time convincing.

The phone rings a few times before she finally picks up.

"Charlie." Her tone doesn't leave any room for guessing as to how she feels about me calling.

"Hi, Natasha. I need—"

"Let's get something out of the way before you start asking me for help." She pauses, waiting for an argument from me. "What you did was really shitty. You're a lot of things Charlie, but I never thought you were a coward. Relationships take work and open communication. If you really want Evie back, you're going to have to learn to tell her your worries. I won't help you if you plan on using some lame ass excuse to end things with her again, especially when it's obvious you're in love with her too."

Shame fills me as she talks.

"You're right. I let my doubts about how different we are cloud my head. I'm working on not being such an uptight ass. It's not easy. I like things done a certain way, but I miss the way Evie balances me out. I won't make this mistake again." Putting aside my pride is something I've gotten really good at lately, and I hope she hears the sincerity in my voice.

After forty-five seconds of silence, I check my phone to make sure the connection didn't drop. Still more silence greets me as I press it back to my ear.

"Tash?"

She sighs. "What do you need?"

Relief fills me as I fill my lungs and let go of a deep breath. "Thank you so much. I need you to come to Ridge Hall this evening. And I need to know what her schedule is like. Something is in the works, but it's been hard to pinpoint her whereabouts lately. I'm hoping after this evening things will be a little clearer."

"Hold on. Are you behind the gnomes?" Her voice is incredulous.

"Yes."

She starts laughing. "Well, I'll be damned. You obviously mean business if you're pulling that off."

249

"I'm dead serious. I don't think I've ever taken anything so seriously as figuring out how to show Evie I want her back."

"I'm glad you've finally realized that you two complement each other. A year ago, you wouldn't be doing this. That's why I'm helping you. You two bring out the best in each other, and sometimes it takes your complete opposite to do that."

We say goodbye, the final weight lifting from my chest.

I can't believe it took such a foolish moment to realize Evie was bringing out the best version of myself. Letting Evie go is that moment for me. Changing my way of thinking isn't easy, and I will always like to plan and organize, but like Tash said, we are our best selves when we're together.

Later that night I'm standing at the sidelines looking out at the majority of the town, ready to eat humble pie. The murmur of the crowd fades as I step onto the stage, my heart pounding.

Licking my lips, I look out at them. "Thank you for coming today, I know that I'm not the most favorite Mistik Ridge resident and I'm beginning to understand why."

Darcy and Guy hold their thumbs up in support. Tash smiles at me as I take a deep breath. The rest of the crowd is silent, waiting to see where I'm going with this, their faces skeptical and disappointed.

"I'm not the easiest person to be around. I like things done a certain way, and until recently I never bothered to understand anyone else's point of view. In May, I met someone who didn't tolerate my bullshit and pushed my boundaries. As you all know, I kind of fucked that up."

The crowd laughs, many of them leaning forward to listen more intently. A few, like Cassaundra, are leaning back with their arms crossed.

"Before I get into that a little more, I need to make a couple apologies. First off, I want to apologize to the book club members for my outburst the other day. It was inappropriate of me to lash out, and I respect the fact that you were trying to look after Evie.

"Second of all, I want to make a general apology to the entire town for my overall lack of leniency and respect to you. I am making a sincere effort to think before I speak and act."

A collective breath is released as people look at each other. Shock permeates the room as the majority of them have never heard me apologize for my behavior.

Sweat drips down the back of my neck as I try to formulate the next words I need to speak. Anxiety overexposing my vulnerability makes the room spin before me, but I center my focus on my friends to ground myself before turning back to the people I'm about to bare myself to.

"For the longest time, I didn't really appreciate this town and the benefit of living in a place where everyone knows you. And now, here I am, pleading with you to forgive me for that because I need your help.

"I've always thought I didn't need anything from anyone, but I was wrong. I even tried to fix this without asking for anything, but I know I can't do it alone. That being said, I'm here to humble myself before you and ask for help.

"I love Evie. I miss her, and I miss what I had and took for granted. I let fear of our differences and the way she makes me feel cloud my head, and I broke us. I can't get her back without your help and support. Please, help me."

The room fills with noise as people begin talking over one another, to one another, and yelling at me. Standing straight and tall, I take it because I deserve it. I've treated most of these people with disdain and here I am asking them to help me.

The rush of talking fades as Everett stands up, his arms in the air motioning for people to be quiet. I wait for him to berate me, but instead he helps Old Man Johnson up from his seat.

He coughs into a handkerchief before levelling a cold stare at me. His voice is gravelly, but strong. "And why do you feel we should help you? Because you apologized?"

He wavers on his feet as I open and close my mouth to answer him, when I'm cut off.

"That's what this town does. The person doesn't matter, but we help each other, and we should show the same love to Charlie now."

My eyes are wide as I follow the voice to where Emery stands, her hand on Cassaundra's shoulder. It's no secret that she hates me, apparent in the way the entire town has now turned to gape at her.

Cassaundra stands, her arms crossed. "Emery is right. This town thrives on kindness, and I for one will help Charlie with whatever he needs."

Several others stand, including Elliott, Mrs. Jesperson, Jessica, Lola, and Pastor Larry. I smile at them in appreciation.

"What about Evie? I don't want to see her hurt again." Everett helps Old Man Johnson back into his seat, his eyes narrowing on me as he straightens back up.

"It hasn't escaped me that Evie's and my relationship was something of a topic. Between bets on when we would break up, to the shock others felt that we were together in the first place. I'm going to level with you, give you some insight into why I can say with absolute certainty that I'm not going to screw this up again."

Chairs scrape as everyone sits down, the hum of chatter fading once again.

"From the moment I walked out of Evie's house, something has been missing. I lived in denial for a couple of days, but it didn't take me long to figure out it's because I let the best part of my life go. Evie and I couldn't be more different in our personalities, but we just clicked. We balance each other out and that is what I couldn't see until I was so off-kilter I couldn't even sleep. I haven't slept more than a few hours every night since that night. I'm not going to promise I'm going to become some easy-going guy or promise that no one will ever feel irritated by me again, but I can promise you that Evie brings out the best in me. I don't ever want to feel like this again, and that is why I can promise you I won't hurt her again."

Everett stares me down, I hold his gaze not moving a muscle as I wait for his verdict. I thought Tash would be the most difficult person to convince, forgetting completely how protective Everett is of Evie.

Every set of eyes is watching us. In my peripheral vision, I can see the smirk on Tash's face, but I accept that this is the price to pay for acting like an entitled prick my entire life.

When Everett gives the slightest nod, I almost collapse in relief.

"Okay. What do you need us to do?"

Pressing my hand to my heart, I smile as I begin to let myself hope this can work.

Evie walks into the grocery store, her eyes scanning the list in her hand. Nodding at Mrs. Jesperson, I watch from my car as she scurries to the exit door and situates a gnome right in line with Evie's car before she hustles to the other side of the concrete median to watch for Evie.

Tomorrow, everything will all come together, two days before I need to be back in the classroom prepping for the new school year. All I can do is hope that this works.

Giving up Evie and realizing how much I want and need her in my life has been eye opening. In the time we've been apart, I've learned how I can still be spontaneous but have control in the important aspects of my life. Balance. Something I've never really had before.

A sharp whistle draws my attention, Mrs. Jesperson waving her hands at me in what I'm sure is an attempt to signal that Evie is at the cash register. Chuckling, I wave at her and watch.

Sure enough, Evie comes out with a cart full of groceries—I wonder how she conned Tash into letting her shop. She turns towards her car, her steps faltering as she sees the silly gnome I found online. This one is sticking his tongue out at her.

Evie looks around, only moving forward when she realizes no one is around.

Halfway to her car she glances back, but Mrs. Jesperson has already taken the gnome and is hiding behind a stack of pallets. My heart stutters when Evie turns back to her car, a small smile on her face.

Once she drives away, I start making my way through the list of people who are helping me out. By the time I get home I've delivered twenty boxes of gnomes.

Tash texts me once Evie is back at the inn for the night so I can start working on my yard.

Gnomevasion

Evie

EVERYONE HAS BEEN acting weird all day. The library is empty, and Lola and Everett keep glancing at the clock. All our work is done, but they're moving around the library like there is still a ton of work to be done.

"What is with you two today?" I finally corner them by the front desk.

They look between each other before shrugging in unison. "Nothing."

"You're both full of shit." Narrowing my eyes, I point my finger and flick it between them. "I know when you're up to something and right now you're having a tough time even looking me in the eye."

Lola looks at me and holds my gaze. "Sorry, we're really not doing anything. I'm just eager for the end of the day."

"Yeah, me too," Everett pipes in as he saunters over to me and drops his arm across my shoulders.

Shaking my head, I roll my eyes at them. "Whatever you say."

Walking away from them, I take my notebook and start jotting down books I want to read in planning for my next set of recommendations. Over the summer I've been putting out weekly instead of monthly recs and with a little less than a week left until the kids are back at school, I want to have some amazing books for the upcoming week. I really hope the increased traffic we've been seeing continues as the school year starts.

By the time I'm done doing my walk around the stacks it's time to head home. Lola is nowhere in sight and Everett is dragging his feet.

"Aren't you coming?" My purse is over my shoulder, keys in hand, but he's still standing behind the desk.

"No, you go ahead. I have an appointment up the street in half an hour so I'm just going to hang out here." He settles onto a chair, his cell in hand.

Standing there, I watch him flip through his phone before I finally turn to leave. My gut twists as I walk to my car. Something is going on and it's making all my friends behave strangely. It feels like the days leading up to finding out I'm being taken from one foster home and put into another.

My stomach turns over as I remember being let go like I was nothing. Foster home after foster home. None of them saw anything special in me, something worth holding onto. Before I can stop myself, the sinking feeling settles into my heart as I picture Charlie standing up and walking out.

That was a thousand times worse than all the foster homes combined. Which is why when he came to book club I didn't let myself believe the look I'm sure was on his face. It's different in a small town, he can't pretend I no longer exist like those families used to do.

With him, I let myself believe I could have more, that someone out there would want me forever. It's difficult to have faith in that when my entire life has shown me otherwise.

As I reach my car, I see something out of the corner of my eye. A gnome.

Less than ten feet away from it is another gnome. They are twin gnomes, their fingers pointing in the same direction as they look back. Opening my trunk, I toss the sweater I wore this morning inside. When I straighten, the gnomes are still there.

Curiosity piqued, I toss my keys into my bag and follow where they're pointing. Maybe I will meet the devious mind behind the disappearing gnomes. I don't see another gnome until I reach the corner. This one isn't looking at me, but he's looking down Main Street. Turning, I start walking. My momentary lapse into feeling sorry for myself is forgotten as I scan the street looking for another gnome.

It's not until I reach one on the next corner that I realize there is no one in sight. Main Street is typically busy with townspeople, but I have not come across a single person. My stomach fills with butterflies fluttering around as I follow the gnome's guidance to cross the street.

When there is no gnome on the corner, I continue walking straight into the neighborhood. My old neighborhood. Typically, there are people working on their lawns, but again no one is in sight. As I get closer to the house I rented from Charlie, my heart starts pounding at the sight before me. Every single yard around me has gnomes in it.

Gnomes mowing the lawn. Gnomes sleeping. Gnomes reading the paper.

Every house on both sides of the street has gnomes.

As I reach my old house, I force myself to look at the home I loved.

My heart falls. No gnomes.

How could I let myself hope that this was Charlie? The sense of fun starts to fade as I wonder if this is some cruel joke. Straightening my shoulders, I push myself forward. I will get to the bottom of this.

Continuing to walk down the streets, the gnomes continue to cover the lawns of the houses. As I get to the corner, the abundance of gnomes disappears leaving me looking at a single gnome pointing to the street Charlie lives on.

I stand frozen on the corner, the butterflies stirring up again, my heart picking up speed. Is this some elaborate joke on Charlie and I just got caught up in it?

Needing answers, I step off the curb and start walking down his street. Gnomes begin to fill the yards again, some of them looking like they are in the midst of a yard party.

Part of me wonders what everyone is going to do with the gnomes once this plays out. I should've been counting how many I've seen. I'm sure there are hundreds between all the houses. Stopping, I count the gnomes in the yard next to me. Fifteen of them.

Continuing up the street, I feel my pulse race as I get closer to Charlie's house. It sits at the end of the street on the curve, impossible for me to avoid.

Inhaling, I keep walking and checking out the random displays each house has put out. It's really incredible. Like something you would see in a movie or read in a book.

Looking up, I catch my first glimpse of Charlie's house. My breath catches in my throat.

I must be imagining this.

His entire front lawn is full of the vulgar gnomes. I see them all, laid out in an array of activity. My steps pick up, the other houses falling away as I rush to reach his house.

I don't see him, so I step onto the lawn and look at each of my little gnomes, free from being held hostage. When I glance at the door, I see a white sheet of paper on the front.

My heart is beating so fast it feels like I ran the entire way here. It's telling my head to go look, it hasn't given up hope, despite my best efforts. Looking around, I still don't see a single person, so I make my way up the steps.

Evie,

I request your presence in the back yard.

Charlie

His crisp, neat handwriting reminds me of our early days, and I can't help but smile at the memory of those first encounters. Folding it, I slip it into my purse. He doesn't know it, but I've kept all his little notices.

Stepping back down off his stoop, I cross the yard to the gate which now sits open. A stone path lies before me, leading me into the now complete yard.

My breath is stolen as I look at the newly planted trees, shrubs, and flowers. It's serene, isolated, and simply perfect. A single gnome sits at the Y in the path, pointing me to the left. Stepping carefully on the stones, I walk along the path to an arch covered in vines.

Sliding my fingers over the leaves, I go into the corner of the yard. It's completely enclosed with shrubs creating a secret garden feel. Following the trail, I turn when the path leads me around a tall shrub.

In front of me sits Charlie inside an exact replica of the reading nook I asked him to let me build only a couple short months ago.

My vision blurs as he stands but stays in the shade of the thatched roof. I can't catch my breath as I walk over to him, taking the hand he offers me. He guides me to the cozy bench he was sitting on, gently pulling me down next to him before he takes my other hand.

His thumbs rub soothing circles over the tops of my trembling hands, his eyes watching me with a soft expression.

"Evie, you wanted me to show you rather than tell you. By the surprise on your face, I'm guessing you didn't realize to what lengths I would go to prove to you I made a mistake. I love you."

Second Chances

Charlie

HER BLUE EYES pierce into me, glossy with emotion, as she searches my face. Evie leans towards me a little, but she doesn't say anything for a few moments.

She pulls her hands out of mine, running her palms over her thighs as she looks around at the garden. When a tear falls down her cheek, I curse myself before brushing it away with my thumb. She leans her cheek into my hand, finally looking at me again.

"I—holy crap. This is a lot to take in. The whole gnome thing, that's so unlike you. And this reading nook, you made it—for me? I just—I don't know what to think. You told me you don't love me, but now you do, and you did all this stuff?" Her hands wave as she tries to articulate what's going on.

Before I can answer she's cupping my face between her hands, leaning in close.

"You can't do this if you don't mean it. You can't tell me you love me if you plan on pulling away in a moment of doubt. If you're not willing to talk to me through anything and put the work into this, then I want you to be honest with yourself and me."

Her eyes flick back and forth between mine, lips parting when

I grab onto her hands and hold them tightly. Pinning them behind her back, I hold them there with one hand and cup the side of her face with the other.

Leaning in, I breathe in the fresh citrusy scent of her shampoo before I crush my lips against hers. Her response is immediate, her entire body relaxing into the kiss as I deepen it. She's delectable, her sweet taste finally calming the tension I've been holding onto from the moment I left her house that day.

We melt into each other, slowing the kiss as I release her hands and she wraps her arms around my neck. Sliding my hands down her sides to her waist, I lift her onto my lap needing to feel her weight on me.

Evie pulls away, her fingers playing with my hair as we catch our breath. Chuckling, she leans forward and brushes her lips against mine once, twice, three times. "I love you, Charlie."

"I love you too, Evie. I'm so sorry I didn't recognize it right away. I'm so sorry I threw your love back in your face."

She presses the tips of her middle and forefinger against my lips. "What's done is done. This isn't something I'm going to hang onto."

She curls into me, resting her forehead on my neck. Holding her close, I shut my eyes and revel in the fact that she was able to forgive me despite everything she's gone through.

"I can't believe you built me my reading nook." Her words are muffled against my neck, I feel the smile on her face before she pulls away to look at me. "You built it at the wrong house though."

Cocking my head, I thread my fingers through her hair and lean in close. "You're not moving back into that house. You're moving in here, with me. Today."

She presses her hands into my shoulders and pushes back so we're an arm's length away from each other. My hands drop back to her hips, holding her in place.

"You can't be serious."

"I'm completely serious. I don't want to go back to the way things were, I want to move forward."

"It's too soon!"

"According to whom? Evie, not seeing you or talking to you every day has been one of the worst experiences in my entire life. I'm not scared of us anymore; I'm scared of spending a day without you because you make me live."

Standing, I hold her against me until she wraps her legs around my waist and finally relaxes her arms. Striding through the garden and up the steps to the deck, I open the sliding door to the kitchen and set her down on the new tile floor.

"This isn't a home without you in it. I don't want a part-time home, I want it to be a place we call ours, a place we share and grow our lives together. Please move in with me."

She looks around the kitchen, her eyes wide. "When? What? How did you find the time to do all of this?"

"I couldn't sleep much, so I finished my kitchen renovations and redid the master bathroom." Taking her hands, I draw her attention to me once again. "Move in with me."

Evie smirks at me, backing away and up the stairs with me in tow all the way through my bedroom and into the master bath. She gasps when she sees the changes.

"Oh my. Wow."

"I needed to make room for you." Prowling closer to her, I lift her up onto the counter and step between her legs. "Move in with me."

She hasn't said no. I can see in her eyes that she wants to say yes, but still doesn't quite trust me or herself.

Brushing my lips against hers, I try to show her how much I love her in the touch of my hands and lips. The sexiest little moans erupt from her throat as she wraps herself around me.

Pulling back, I press my forehead against hers.

"Okay. I will move in with you."

Elation flows through me as I pick her up and carry her to my bed. Laying her down, I remove her clothes as I worship every inch of her body. She whimpers as she presses her thighs together when I pull away, stripping away my clothes.

She wraps her legs around my waist as I crawl over her pulling me into her. Her lips are frantic against mine, our hands touching and stroking as we get reacquainted.

Evie's skin is smooth and soft, the sounds of her pleasure electrifying. Every part of me feels whole again now that she's in my arms, where she will fall asleep every night. Losing her taught me not to take for granted the way she makes me feel. I need to appreciate it and cultivate it.

We turn down the driveway of the inn, parking beside the steps leading up to the front doors. Tash comes out, leaning against the doorframe.

Evie turns to face me, her forehead creasing. "Do you mind waiting here for a moment?"

"Of course not." I watch as she joins Tash on the porch, their heads bent towards each other.

I can't help but notice the pinched features of Tash's face. It did not occur to me that Tash might struggle with Evie moving out. As I watch, though, Tash's expression transforms from one of stress to excitement.

That is the magic of Evie, she can take a situation which might hurt someone and put a positive spin on it. When they both look at me I know it's safe to join them.

"Don't screw this up again. I believe you remember my threat." Tash points a finger at me, narrowing her eyes before she cracks a smile.

We follow her inside, Evie's hand seeking out mine as we walk up the stairs to the room she's been staying in. It's been years since I've come here, since before Tash bought it, and I can see the amount of work that needs to be done.

Knowing Tash, she will refuse any offer of help, but I also know what she got from the town and it's not going to be enough to carry her until spring if she doesn't bring in some new business.

"Stop." Evie presses her hand into my chest, preventing me from entering her room.

"What?"

"Leave her be. She will figure this out on her own. I know that look and just stop those thoughts right now." Evie presses into me, wrapping her arms around my waist. "I love that you want to help, but she doesn't want any help."

Scrunching up my face, I grumble in submission. I know she's right.

It doesn't take much time to pack up Evie's belongings and load them into the car.

Back home, we are able to carry her things inside in one trip. Evie stands in the middle of our bedroom looking around.

Our bedroom.

Sitting down on the foot of the bed, Evie looks up at me. "I've never lived with anyone before, I'm feeling a little overwhelmed like I'm invading your space. I'm worried that once I settle in you won't like having me here all the time, that our differences will become so much more apparent because now you have to live with them."

My excitement deflates as I look at Evie's posture. Her shoulders are slumped, lines crease the skin between her brows, and there is a slight downward tilt to the corners of her lips.

I sit down next to her and pull her into my side. "You know that sparkly vampire movie you made me watch?"

Her lips quirk as she looks up at me. "Twilight?"

"Yes, it was a ridiculous movie."

"It's an awesome movie, and the books are even better, but continue."

"Well, you know after he tries to commit suicide and they're back at her house and she wakes up from a nightmare?" She full on smiles at me, but her eyes are still worried. I need to make that worry go away. "Just like Edward made an ass of himself, that's what I did. And just like Edward, I will do whatever I need to in order to demonstrate I won't make the same foolish mistake twice. This is your home now too. I am under no illusions that you will pick up any of my particular habits. There is no written agreement stating you need to do things in a particular way, I just want to eat dinner with you every evening, go to sleep next to you every night, and wake up next to you every morning. I want to build a life and a home with you."

Evie wraps her arms around me, relaxing. "Can we get another cat?"

Chuckling, I look over at Sebastian who is sleeping in a ball next to my pillow. He lifts his head before standing up and turning his back on us. "Sure, but you get to break the news to Sebastian."

Evie stands from the bed and pulls me up into her arms before finally opening her suitcase. It doesn't take her long to fill my closet and the empty drawers I cleared out for her.

Seeing her belongings mingling with mine fills me with a sense of rightness. She's not wrong, there will be times when my need for organization and her spontaneity will clash, but if there is anything I've learned since getting to know Evie is that we're both capable of making our idiosyncrasies work together.

The Cat

Evie

CHARLIE PARKS OUTSIDE of the Mistik Ridge Animal Shelter. It's a tiny building near the fire hall and police station. The entire outside of the building is a mural of animals, and as we walk inside to the reception area, the walls are covered in photos of animals and people.

Cassaundra comes out of the back, surprise flitting across her face when she sees us standing there. She quickly replaces it with a smile.

"Evie—Charlie, how nice to see you. What can I help you with?" She moves behind the desk, straightening a stack of papers.

"We're here to adopt a cat."

Charlie squeezes my hand as he smiles down at me before looking back at Cassaundra. "Evie thinks Sebastian needs a friend."

Cassaundra nods. "Okay, well, follow me and you can spend some time in the cat sanctuary to see if any are a good fit."

She leads us through a room full of large kennels. A few of

which are empty, but it breaks my heart to see the sad eyes of the dogs looking up as we pass them by. Through there we enter an empty sitting room with a couple of couches and some toys.

"Through there are our adoptable cats. You can bring them in here, one at a time, to get to know them. You will notice that in some of the kennels there are two cats, they are together because they're bonded, and they need to be adopted together." She opens the door to another room full of kennels, closing it behind us as she leaves us alone.

Charlie follows me as I circle the room peeking into each and every kennel to say hi to the cat inside. Most of them ignore me, some grind up against the bars of the kennel, but it's not until I'm circling a second time that I notice one I didn't see the first time through.

A little gray and white face peeks out from a box, disappearing again when it sees me looking at it. A white tag hangs from one of the bars of her kennel. Flipping it over I read her details.

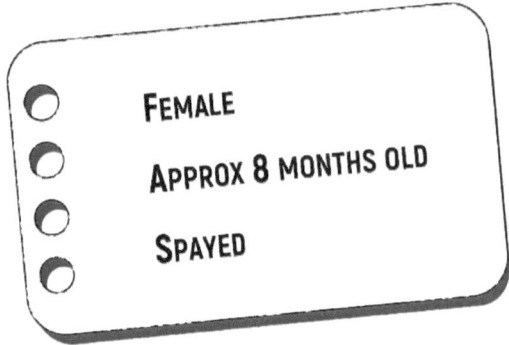

FEMALE

APPROX 8 MONTHS OLD

SPAYED

It breaks my heart that six words is all she gets.

She pops up again, this time staring at me as I watch her before hopping out of the box. She sits in front of it, cleaning her paw without moving her amber eyes from me. The tip of one ear is missing and I notice that she has three legs.

"She's the one."

"Don't you want to bring her out, sit with her for a bit?" Charlie bends, scaring her back into the box.

"No. She's the one."

He wraps his arms around me from behind, burying his face into my neck and kissing me. "Okay. I will get Cassaundra and start the paperwork."

He disappears through the doors leaving me to coax the shy kitty to me.

"What should I call you, sweet girl?"

Opening the kennel door, I rest my hand just inside. She quits bathing herself and looks at me in suspicion. It's obvious her experience with humans hasn't been the best. I have a soft spot for animals who have been cast aside, a feeling of kinship with them.

"What about Tali? How do you like that one, pretty girl?"

She stands and inches closer to me, graceful despite the fact she's missing a leg. She sits down again a couple of inches away from my hand. She lowers her head to sniff my fingers, and when she grinds her cheek into them I barely hold back a squeal of joy.

Moving slowly, I reach my other hand into the kennel and when she doesn't shy away I pick her up and cradle her to my chest.

The door swings open causing her to press in closer to me.

"Evie, Cassaundra was saying that—" He stops as he sees Tali in my arms before turning back around and walking out the door.

Tilting my head down, I whisper soothing words to her as I follow him to the reception area where he is arguing with Cassaundra.

"That cat doesn't like anyone, she won't be a good fit." Cassaundra's hands are on her hips, her back to me as she faces off with Charlie.

"I beg to differ." He points behind her to where Tali has nestled in my arms, watching them.

Cassaundra stutters, shakes her head, and hands Charlie a signed document.

"I'm waiving the adoption fee. She's been with us for six months now and no one has been able to handle her without gloves on."

She offers us a box, but I hug her close and refuse. Tali falls asleep in my arms as we drive home, and when we walk in the door she starts to purr as I settle onto the couch with her.

Charlie sits a foot away, looking at me in pure adoration. "You are incredible. Now, hopefully, she takes to the rest of us like she's taken to you."

At that moment Sebastian comes sauntering down the stairs. It's not until he's in the middle of the living room that he sees Tali. His back arches, but he moves closer. From the safety of my lap, Tali just watches him.

Neither of them make a peep as Sebastian hops onto the couch behind her and leans in to check her out. He hisses at her but then lays down right next to us.

Charlie chuckles and reaches out to scratch Tali's head. She pulls back slightly but leans into it once she realizes he's going to be nice to her.

"Looks like this is going to work." I smile at Charlie.

He looks back at me, his hazel eyes intense. "It's definitely going to work."

Pie and Sick Days

Charlie

LOOKING OUT OVER my class as they file in, I wait until all the seats are full before shutting the door.

"Good morning, I'm Mr. Greene, as you hopefully already know if you're in this classroom. On your desks is the course outline. Everything you need to know to be successful in my class is in this outline. I recommend you don't lose it."

For the next fifty minutes I go through each page of the outline. Each and every student sits up as they hear my rules. Their faces a mixture of disbelief, shock, annoyance, and the rare excitement.

"As long as you follow these guidelines, you will be successful in my class." The bell rings and the students file out in silence.

Grabbing my cell from my desk drawer, I grin at the photo Evie sent me of Sebastian and Tali cuddling. It didn't take long for them to warm up to each other.

Typing out a quick reply, I toss my phone back inside the drawer when students start filing in. It's their first day back and they're all a little wild from having the summer off. By the end of the day I will have given my spiel on how to be successful in my classroom five times.

When the final bell rings, I have a good feeling for how the year is going to go. Packing my bag, I eagerly head home to see Evie. We've been living together for almost a week now and I still feel the same excitement knowing that she's going to be there when I get home from work.

Stopping at Liliana's I order Evie's favorite pie, raspberry rhubarb.

"How are you, Charlie?" Liliana asks as she pulls a fresh pie from the display.

"It was a long day at school, Evie is home sick today and I wanted to be there to take care of her. Not that she would let me." Taking the pie, I hand Liliana a twenty and refuse the change.

Evie is asleep on the couch when I hang my keys on their hook. Setting the pie down onto the coffee table, I sit down next to her hip and brush the hair away from her face.

Her eyes flutter, a sleepy smile appearing as she looks up at me.

Kissing her softly, I rub my thumb over her cheek as I sit up and gesture to the pie. "I thought you could use some comfort food."

There is no description for the way I feel when I see the love in her eyes as she sits up and wraps her arms around me mumbling a hoarse thank you. I've taken a lot of things for granted in my life, but this feeling will never be one of them.

I'm packing up my bag to go to school when Evie comes down the stairs dressed for work.

"What are you doing?"

"What does it look like?"

"It looks like you could barely speak yesterday and slept for fourteen hours and think it's a good idea to go back to work today." Crossing my arms, I lean against the wall glaring at her.

"I'm feeling much better and don't want to miss another day." She passes me, heat radiating from her skin. I follow her into the kitchen and watch as she fills a glass with water, her entire posture defiant.

When she turns to face me, her eyebrow is arched in challenge.

"Evie, stay home. Take care of yourself. Work isn't going anywhere," I plead with her.

I glance at the clock behind her, I need to leave and she knows I won't stay to argue with her, but I risk being a little late to cup her cheeks and ask her to stay home one more time.

"I'm fine. I promise."

With a growl, I bend down and kiss her quickly before heading out the door.

When I get home early at three-thirty, I'm surprised to see that Evie's car is in the driveway. She usually doesn't get home until quarter after four.

Grabbing my bag from the passenger seat, I take the steps two at a time and unlock the front door. Evie is asleep on the couch, almost an exact image to what I came home to yesterday except today Tali is purring away on her stomach and Sebastian is tucked between her knees.

Creeping past her into the kitchen, I turn on the kettle to make her some tea and check what's cooking in the crockpot.

A warm body presses into my back, arms wrapping around my stomach. "I'm sorry I was so grumpy this morning."

"I get that you love your job, I just want you to take care of yourself."

"I know."

Turning in her arms, I pick her up and set her on the counter. She buries her face into my chest, pressing a kiss over my heart.

I hug her close. "I love you."

"I love you too."

Love and Compromise

Two Months Later

EVIE

TASH COMES AROUND the front of the house laughing when she sees Sebastian and Tali in harnesses and on leashes. They're rolling around the ground wrestling with each other until Charlie needs to untangle them.

Darcy and Guy are already here and lighting a fire in the pit.

"Can we please put the cats in the house now?" Charlie lifts them by their harnesses, grinning at me despite the exasperation in his voice.

"Yes." Linking arms with Tash, I lead her down the path now lined with all the vulgar gnomes.

"I thought you were lying when you told me about the gnomes. How did you convince Charlie to let you put them out?"

The gnomes are spaced out evenly on both sides of the path until we get to the sunken fire pit. Glancing behind me, I smile as I see Charlie come back outside from putting the cats inside the house.

Instead of telling Tash about hiding the gnomes throughout the house, yard, and any other place he frequents for a month, including convincing one of his coworkers to let me into his classroom where I hid them in and around his desk, I just shrug. "Compromise."

We join Darcy and Guy by the blazing fire, Charlie coming behind me and wrapping his arms around my waist.

Guy hands him a beer smiling at the two of us.

"There are new bets on how long the two of you will last." He smirks as Charlie rests his chin on my head.

"I heard. Someone apparently bet for us and not against us." I rub my hand over his bicep. "Anyone else is going to be disappointed."

"That was me." Tash sits down next to where her brother has settled. "So don't screw it up."

We start roasting marshmallows and playing Mad Libs. This is the first get together Charlie and I have hosted since I moved in. Mostly we've been keeping to ourselves, probably why the town is suspicious of our demise.

"How did your parents react when they found out you two are shacking up?" Darcy asks with a grin.

"Mom's exact words were 'I knew she was the perfect tenant for you.'" Charlie leans over and kisses the side of my head.

Our friends laugh, while I'm just grateful that Lorraine saw more in me than a potential renter for her son. In the past two months I've truly learned what it feels like to be loved unconditionally. Charlie and I have our ups and downs, but, at the end of the day, our differences make us stronger because we learn so much from each other.

He never fails to ensure I'm looking after myself and I make sure he never gets too caught up in his routines forgetting to enjoy himself.

All we need is to love each other and compromise with each other. At the end of the day, we're willing to put in the work.

So, when I heard that several townspeople had bet on when we would end again, I simply shrugged it off. Not everyone understands Charlie the way I do, but no one will ever understand me the way he does.

He's taught me how to trust someone other than myself. He taught me that I'm worthy and that there is someone out there who won't throw me away. Through him, I've also learned what it's like to be part of a family that wants me, for good.

Every single thing on my current list has been achieved. I guess it's time to create a new one with the love of my life.

Epilogue

EVIE

SITTING UP IN bed, I glance over at Charlie sleeping soundly. A whimper escapes as I cradle my stomach, pain ripping through my lower abdomen. I shove up from the bed and waddle to the washroom as the pain subsides.

I search for a hair tie and pile my hair into a messy bun. With a deep breath, I stroke my round belly and murmur, "Time to wake up Daddy, hey little one?"

I barely reach the edge of Charlie's side of the bed when pain rips through me again. Another small whimper escapes as I bend in half and shake Charlie awake.

"Charlie, it's time. We need to go to the hospital." My contractions are four minutes apart, I've been timing them throughout the night since I couldn't sleep anyway.

He bolts out of bed, eyes automatically scanning over me. With a wild, crazy look, he starts pacing the room. I turn on the lights, smirking as he mumbles to himself.

"We need to get the bag together. What all did they recommend putting in it? Crap, where is the book?" He swings open the door to the bedroom disappearing down the hall.

He comes back in as another contraction hits, this one seems to hurt more than the others.

"Evie, breathe." His hand is trembling on my back, his face losing color.

Once the pain subsides, I straighten back up and cup his face in between my hands. "Charlie, breathe."

He inhales, his hazel eyes locked on mine as I stroke circles on his cheeks.

"Calm down, we have a list. It's on the dresser. You packed our bag two weeks ago, remember? It's in the closet. Why don't you check off the list and get the bag? I'm going to go sit at the front door. I'll need help with my shoes." Biting my lip, I hold back a laugh as he rushes to the dresser. The wrong dresser. "Hun, it's on the other dresser."

Spinning around, he finds the paper and scans the list. His tension seems to bleed from him as he reads aloud. "Okay, first thing to do is call Dr. Aberlein."

The only outward sign that he's still freaking out is the slight tremble to his hand as he dials the on-call number for our doctor.

His deep voice fills the room as he speaks into the phone. I leave him to his list, knowing that he needs to go through it to feel in control, even though every other item has been checked off at least three times in the past two days.

Sebastian and Tali weave between my feet as I lower myself onto the bench by the front door. When twenty minutes pass and my contractions progress to just over three minutes apart, Charlie still hasn't appeared. With a sigh, I shove up to my feet again— my poor, swollen feet—and wander back to our bedroom.

Charlie is sitting on the edge of the bed, our hospital bag at his feet. His head is cradled in his hands, his breathing quick and shallow.

"Charlie?" Moving painfully slow, I finally reach him and rest my hand on his shoulder.

His eyes are worried as he looks up at me. "She's early. I'm not ready. I haven't baby proofed the house. What if she doesn't like the color we picked for her room? We need more supplies."

Chuckling, I slide my hand down his arm and pull on his wrist until he lumbers to his feet. Stepping into him, I angle my swollen belly to the side and try to wrap my arms around him. "Charlie, we don't need to baby proof for a long time. And she's not going to care about the color of her walls. Lastly, I doubt we can fit any more baby supplies in this house. She's one baby and we have enough diapers and wipes and whatever else to last us for months. Months. Now we need to leave, otherwise I'll deliver this baby on our living room floor."

That spurs Charlie into action. I'm not sure which upsets him more, the idea of our baby being born at home or the mess it would create.

Within fifteen minutes we're at the tiny Mistik Ridge Hospital.

"Stay here." He opens the car door, jumping out.

"Why?"

Without answering he shuts the door with a look. I watch in amusement as he races to the entrance doors and returns with a wheelchair.

He opens my door and helps me out.

"Seriously? I can walk to the doors."

Charlie doesn't respond, just gives me his "don't argue with me" look. Shaking my head, I lower myself into the chair and watch as he swings our two hospital bags over his shoulder, because one bag wasn't enough.

Once we're checked in, we follow a nurse into a private room. One of the joys of living in a small town is that our hospital isn't overcrowded.

Charlie and the nurse help settle me onto the bed, the nurse disappearing with a promise that Dr. Aberlein will be in shortly to evaluate my progress.

Seeing Charlie so flustered, wavering between his excessive control and losing it completely, is distracting me from the increasing pain of my contractions.

When Dr. Aberlein comes in she walks us through what to expect. "Now that you have the information, we never settled on whether or not you're getting an epidural."

Charlie and I answer at the same time. "No." "Yes."

Looking over at him, I narrow my eyes. "Who is giving birth to this baby? You or me?"

"You," he grumbles. "But…"

"No buts. This hurts like hell and I'm not even pushing yet. Studies have shown an epidural can reduce adrenaline and make the birth a calmer experience. Something that is better for both me and the baby. Yes, I did research. No, I will not consider doing this naturally."

Dr. Aberlein looks between us, a small smirk on her face as Charlie frowns, his mouth opening and closing a few times before he nods in agreement.

"Okay, I will be back with a nurse shortly." She walks out of the room, her steps brisk and focused.

Once we're alone, I reach my hand out for Charlie's. Grasping it tightly when another contraction hits. Each one hurts more than the last.

"We still haven't decided on a name." I breathe out as the pain subsides.

"I have a list of names I like, but it seems weird to pick out a name until we meet her." Charlie presses the back of my hand to his lips as we smile at each other.

"I love you."

"I love you too."

♥

Charlie

T HE TINY BABY girl in my arms is perfect. Of course she's perfect, Evie brought her into this world. Tearing my eyes away from my daughter, I meet my wife's tired gaze. "You're the most incredible person I've ever met."

She smiles up at me. "I couldn't have done it without you. Thank you for being calm. I was a little worried for a while there."

Grimacing, I feel my cheeks flush. I don't think I've ever been as flustered as I was leading to the moment the doctor told Evie to push. "I knew you needed me to be in control."

Leaning down, I gingerly place our sweet little girl into Evie's arms.

"What do you think of the name Olivia?" Evie can barely keep her eyes open, but I know she isn't ready to fall asleep quite yet. The only person that can distract me from looking at my sweet baby is Evie. Even exhausted and sweaty, she's the most beautiful woman I've ever seen.

"I love it." I watch as Evie smiles in pure happiness, her eyes fluttering closed as she finally drifts off.

I lift Olivia from Evie's arms and cradle her into me. I know my life is about to become uncontrollable. Messes are inevitable. But when I look at the tiny infant in my arms, it's all going to be worth it.

Evie wakes up after an hour, her eyes searching the room until she spots me and Olivia in the corner. "How is she?"

Her words are slurred with sleep.

"Good. She slept the whole time." I put Olivia in Evie's arms, smiling when she stretches in her sleep. "Are you ready for everyone to meet her?"

Evie nods, so I make my way to the waiting room. Despite my best efforts to keep the crowd small, the Mistik Ridge grapevine made that impossible. The hospital waiting room is full. So full, I need to search for my parents, Natasha, Everett, Guy, and Darcy.

Sighing, I give the rest of the room a tired smile. "Evie went through twelve hours of active labor. This afternoon we welcomed our baby girl, Olivia, into our family. While we really appreciate you all coming out, Evie is exhausted and, at this time, only family will be allowed to visit. Once we're home, we will organize an open house so you all can come meet her."

Everyone is pretty understanding as they congratulate me before filing out of the building. Soon just my parents and our friends remain.

"Mom and Dad, why don't you come meet your granddaughter?" Both of them look moments away from crying as they follow me into the room and see Evie holding Olivia.

"Darling, how do you feel?" Mom brushes Evie's hair back from her face.

"Like I've been torn in half, but she is worth the pain." Evie holds Olivia up so Mom can take her.

We watch as she and Dad fawn over the baby.

Dad coos at her, telling her how amazing she is. He's in better shape than ever, coming to the gym with me every day. I can tell how grateful he is that he's here and healthy as he takes his grandbaby from Mom's arms.

Over the next couple of hours everyone meets Olivia until she wakes up hungry. The nurse supervises to make sure she latches to Evie before leaving the room.

"It's true what they say. After you get pregnant, you just get used to people seeing all your bits and pieces all the time." Evie winces a bit as she shifts. I jump to her side, adjusting the pillows.

By the time we get home, we've been gone for a day and a half. The cats are crying as we walk in the door. When Olivia responds with a cry of her own, they bolt from the room.

"That's going to be interesting." Evie grins. She settles onto the couch, lifting her shirt to feed Olivia.

Instead of putting everything away, I sit down next to her and wrap my arm around her shoulder. We sit in silence as Olivia eats before falling asleep.

When I look over at Evie, I smile when I see she fell asleep too. With my free arm, I reach for the blanket and cover her as best I can. In this moment, the mess by the front door means nothing. My entire world is on the couch with me, and these minutes are fleeting. I need to appreciate them. There will always be time later on in life to keep an orderly house.

I watch my family sleep peacefully, my heart full and happier than ever.

The End

Also by Ashley Erin

Rule series
The No Asshole Rule

The No Bad Boy Rule

The No Jock Rule

The No Player Rule

All or Nothing series
All About Us

All About Hope

All About Forever

Standalones
Without Walls

Why Not Me?

Acknowledgements

Acknowledgements

Thank you to all my readers for your support. I hope you enjoyed reading Charlie and Evie's story as much as I loved writing it.

I had the support of an incredible team for this book. Thank you Dana for the incredible cover, Missy and Jessica for doing an amazing job editing, Virginia for proofreading, and Tami for making the inside as beautiful as the outside.

Thank you so much to all the bloggers and authors who helped spread the word about this story. Your support is appreciated immensely.

About the Author

Ashley Erin lives in Alberta, Canada. She hates socks and wears flip flops as soon as it's above freezing. Ashley is the mother of two beautiful daughters. Her two cats and two dogs are incredibly spoiled. When she's not writing; she's learning Korean, crocheting, painting, or spending time with people she cares about.

Ashley is a self-published author of contemporary and new adult romance. Follow her on Facebook to keep up with her current and upcoming releases.

Contact
Ashley Erin

Visit Ashley Erin's website for information on new releases

www.ashleyerinauthor.com

You can also find her on

Facebook
www.facebook.com/authorashleyerin

Twitter
@Ashley_Erin21

Instagram
@ashleyerin21

www.ingramcontent.com/pod-product-compliance
Lightning Source LLC
Chambersburg PA
CBHW021334250626
47155CB00002B/690